Origins

A JTF 13 Anthology

INTER CAELUM ET INFERNUM

13

Three Ravens Publishing
Chickamauga, GA

Credits:
Origins: A JTF Anthology was written by authors listed above and published by Three Ravens Publishing.

Origins: A JTF Anthology by: Cannon Publishing, 1st edition, Cannon Publishing 2019
Origins: A JTF Anthology by: Three Ravens Publishing, 2nd edition, Three Ravens Publishing 2020
Trade Paperback ISBN: 978-1-951768-16-4

There is a thin wall between our world and that of the Fae and, during times of war, it is easily stepped through. The passions and emotions stirred by violence and combat bleed over, and the supernatural often awakes from long slumber to meddle in mortal affairs. Then also, there are the humans who purposely force that wall down seeking glory and power.

Either way, there have always been those among us willing to meet the supernatural threat with cold steel, burning hearts, and grim determination. In modern America, they are the men and women of Joint Task Force 13, those who have proven they have the metal to confront soul-blasting otherness on the battlefield. This unit, this organization, though, has been intertwined with our country since its birth. The name changes, but they are always there, ready to answer the call. Unknown, seeking no glory, asking no reward. They hold the line…

…BETWEEN HEAVEN AND HELL

Table of Contents

Devils & Dust

J.F. Holmes

Origins

J.F. Holmes is the owner and editor of Cannon Publishing, as well as being an accomplished author in his own right. He currently has seventeen books out, including two Dragon Award finalists. His work can be found here on Amazon.

Redeye

Dan Humphreys

Dante Accardi slung his battered rucksack into the storage compartment over the business-class seat. The seats were at the ass-end of the section, jammed right up against the lavatory, but the sections to either side of the center row consisted of only two seats on each side. No chance of armrest thieves boxing him in was good enough, but on this Airbus, the section in front of the bathrooms was one of the three exit rows. He had more than enough leg room, even with his carry-on stowed behind his feet.

He rocked forward from the impact of a shoulder into his back and turned in mock annoyance. "It's a sixteen-hour flight, bro, keep your pantyhose on."

Tyson Fisher grinned as he hoisted his own pack into place. Where Dante was stocky and olive-skinned, Ty was long and lean, his curly hair bleached blond by the sun, a classic central casting surfer dude. "I love how hot and bothered you get without a chute, Super Mario."

Sliding into the window seat, Dante scratched the side of his nose with a middle finger.

His friend chortled and plopped into his own seat. "You have to admit it, dude. This is definitely worth the upgrade." He checked the stream of passengers moving down the aisle and lowered his voice. "No sweaty Iraqi taking up the armrests while he waxes poetic about his gold toilet or whatever."

Dante grunted in agreement. Their companion on the flight over had been annoying as hell, even after both men had plugged in earbuds to drown out his incessant bragging. Considering they'd all flown to Qatar in economy class, the Iraqi was probably full of shit.

A tone sounded over the plane's speakers, and one of the flight attendants made a short speech in Arabic. Dante knew enough to get by, so when the same voice shifted to English and repeated the same announcement in a cultured British accent, he already had the gist of it.

"Ladies and gentlemen, welcome aboard Qatar Airways flight 755, with non-stop service to Hartsfield-Jackson International Airport in the United States. Should you need any assistance finding your seat, seek out a member of the cabin crew, and we'll be happy to help."

Another tone sounded, and the plane fell silent, save for the usual boarding sounds—feet shuffling over the carpet, crying children, and murmured conversation. With little else to do but wait, Dante crossed his arms and watched the train of people, while Tyson whistled and drummed his fingers on his armrest.

Much like the flight they'd taken to Doha, this one held an eclectic mix of passengers. Native Qatari men in long shirts and gutra mixed with Asian and white—European, Dante supposed—businessmen in their fine suits, though most of the latter had doffed their jackets and loosened their ties in recognition of the marathon flight ahead. Most of the women wore abaya and Shayla, though a small number wore full burqa. The few Western women were modestly dressed—long skirts or slacks, high necklines, and long sleeves. Qatar was the richest country in the world, socially advanced in comparison to the rest of the Middle East—but it also had a government-enforced dress code for its own people.

That bipolar aspect to the culture, combined with the fact that he hadn't been home in six months, left Dante eager for the pilots to get the proverbial show on the road.

When Tyson had called him nine months ago with a job offer, he'd been reluctant at first. They'd met during their time in the 82nd Airborne at Fort Bragg, and the unlikely friendship they'd forged had endured well past the time both men had left the service. Managing a construction crew for his dad's company had left Dante questioning his life choices, especially during rush hour on I-95. Yeah, Khost and Karbala had well and truly sucked, but at least they'd been able to run over and shoot their way through any obstacles. Pleasant daydreams aside, Boston PD tended to frown on any such displays within their jurisdiction.

Origins

In the end, the money won out as much as the change of pace. Once Dante reacclimated to the climate, it was even a little boring. The contract required them to provide protection for a team of scientists studying a potential new oil well out in the Qatari desert. To Dante's surprise, the work mainly consisted of office work, looking over satellite photos, ground surveys, and other information well above his area of interest. Trips out to the site were few, far between, and uneventful. Although Dante welcomed the lack of action in one regard, it had made the long contract seem all that much longer.

On the bright side, their 'net connection was good enough that Dante, Tyson, and the rest of the crew had plenty of time to catch up on Netflix and polish their Madden skills.

The flight attendants gave the usual spiel accompanied by helpful videos in multiple languages, and began the process of takeoff. Tyson shifted in his seat and raised an eyebrow.

"In the event of a water landing," he whispered, "you'll be thousands of miles from land, so keep a firm hold of your seat cushion and kiss your ass goodbye."

Dante snorted a chuckle and shook his head. "That was funnier the first time." A flash of movement caught his attention, and he raised his head to see a wrinkled face peering back at them through the gap in the seats. "Sorry, sir," he said, louder. "My friend's had too many head injuries over the years, and it's affected his sense of tact."

The elderly man blinked in surprise, then chuckled. "Quite all right, lads. You Yanks do tend to love your gallows humor." He extended his hand between the seats. "Graham Hales."

Tyson and Dante shook it in turn. "Brit?" the latter asked. "You're a long way from home."

"I could say the same to you, but yes. Our children and grandchildren concocted a 60th anniversary trip for the missus and me." The old man chuckled. "I think I read too much Jules Verne to them at bedtime—they got it in their head to send us 'around the world in 80 days'."

Another face peered into the gap. "Don't let him fool you, boys. The old grouch is having the time of his life."

Tyson grinned. "That sounds like Dante, all right." He elbowed his friend in the ribs "I think we've just gotten a glimpse at your future, bro."

He forced himself to smile and added, "As I said, no sense of tact."

The plane lurched, and conversation became more difficult as the hubbub and hustle of takeoff filled the airframe with familiar noises. Some men might have simply thought of the rising whine of the turbines and the feel of acceleration as they rocketed down the runway as merely takeoff. For Dante, those sounds and sensations translated to something more primal. Home. I'm going home.

He leaned forward and tugged a battered Michael Connelly thriller out of his carry-on. He'd read the book enough times that the mystery offered no surprise, but there was something familiar and comforting about the meticulous nature of the book's detective as he worked through the evidence. It made for a perfect mental checkout for the long flight. He'd tried reading new books on flights before, and the nervous tension of an unfamiliar story had made for an uncomfortable combination with his general anxiety toward air travel. It was an idiosyncrasy his friends found humorous, but he took the ribbing with good humor.

A few hours later, he pulled himself out of the book with a yawn and opened the window shade. Dante considered the dazzling, unending blue of the ocean beneath them. We're chasing the sun, he thought, or it's chasing us. The immense distance the journey covered amplified the inherent surreality. Take off at eight in the morning and land just after four—eight hours by the hands of the clock, but double that for those inside. Any way you went about it, a hell of a long day.

He gave his paperback a considering look, shrugged, and leaned his seat back after lowering the shade. The book wasn't going anywhere, and at that moment, sleep was a far more appealing option.

He jerked awake, heart hammering, although he couldn't identify what had shattered his dream. Then he heard it, muffled under the constant drone of the plane's engines, but recognizable nonetheless—a high-pitched scream, abruptly cut off.

Dante jammed an elbow into Tyson's side. His friend cracked an eyelid momentarily and muttered in incomprehensible sleep language.

Frustrated, he hissed, "Ty. Wake the fuck up, Ranger!"

The other man jerked into an upright position. Blinking, he scanned the seats in front of them before turning to Dante. "What?"

"I heard something. It—there." The scream repeated. It lasted a bit longer this time, and the passengers who weren't asleep or wearing headphones stirred. A few looked around, trying to determine the source of the noise, but all shrugged it off and returned to what they were doing. Just a sound from a movie, he imagined them guessing, and for a moment, he wondered if he wasn't jumping to conclusions.

No, Dante decided, the scream was real. There was a visceral element to it, making the sound different enough from some special effect to raise the hair on the back of his neck. He'd heard that sort of cry before, and never in a good context.

He'd toted a tricked-out Mk11 for the last six months, and hadn't fired a shot outside the firing range the entire time. It figured things would go sideways as soon as he was unarmed. Murphy was a sadistic bastard, after all. He met Tyson's eyes, and the other man gave him a tight nod of silent assent. "Back there," he murmured.

"Yeah." Dante released his seatbelt and turned to face the opening to the economy cabin at the rear of the plane. He hooked a finger into the curtain and studied the area beyond. Three sections of three seats made up each row, separated by a pair of aisles. The section was less than a third of the length of the entire plane, but he guessed at least half the total number passengers were packed into the section. The upgrade was more than worth it.

Many of the passengers had drawn their shades, casting the entire compartment in intermittent shadow. "When in doubt, go to sleep," he whispered to himself. Particularly when the airline packed you in like a sardine. Still, the tableau before him seemed a little off. A few of the passengers at the front of the section glowed with the telltale sign of tablets or e-readers, but further back— nothing.

He frowned. Tyson stepped close to his back for his own look. "Hijacking?"

"I don't think so," Dante said. As he watched, a lowered shade close to the back of the plane cut off the sunlight and left the last few rows cloaked in shadow.

"Gentlemen, you need to return to your seats, please."

The two men turned. The flight attendant for their section was a slender, petite woman with an olive complexion and ink-black hair. If Dante hadn't been on high alert, her French accent might have merited some of the patented Accardi charm. He glanced at the name badge clipped to her blouse.

He pitched his voice low so as not to be overheard. "Giselle, is there an air marshal on the flight?" From the way her eyes widened, he guessed that wasn't the best way to open the conversation. "We're U.S. Army," he said. The half-truth was simpler and more succinct than explaining retirement and private contracting. "We heard a cry in the back." He stepped aside and gestured at the curtain. "But something's not right."

She frowned. "Only a movie, n'est ce pas?" Stepping forward, she took her own long look through the curtain. The flight attendant stepped back with a look of confusion. "That's strange."

"What is it?" Tyson said. In spite of their attempt to remain quiet, some of the passengers in their section were turning to look at the gathering. Dante noticed Graham Hales and gave what he hoped was a reassuring smile. From the old Brit's frown, he didn't think he'd pulled it off.

"The galley is dark," she explained. Dante glanced at Tyson, but the other man shrugged. He didn't get it, either. Giselle sighed. "We will dim the lights, yes, but never shut them off entirely. For safety reasons, do you understand? In case we need to see to strap in." She lifted a phone handset attached to the wall of their own galley and pressed it to her ear.

Dante glanced back through the curtain in time to see a red LED flash on the twin to the handset the flight attendant held. She stood there for a good thirty seconds before replacing the phone in its cradle.

"They should have answered," she said with a frown.

Dante didn't know how to reply. The shadows at the rear of the plane were creepy enough without the rest of the flight crew's failure to respond. Given the atmosphere, it was no surprise that the hair on the back of his neck stood on end. What he couldn't understand was why none of the densely packed people in front of him had picked up on the strangeness.

I can feel it! he wanted to shout. Why can't you? A few of the folks closer to the front glanced at the intermittent opening in the curtain with questioning eyes, but that remained the extent of their curiosity.

Giselle picked up the phone again and pushed a different button. After a moment, she said quietly, "Samira, I need your help back here, please." After she hung up, she met Dante's eyes and visibly composed herself. "Wait here, please. I'm sure it's nothing."

Tyson opened his mouth, but Dante gave him a minute shake of his head. The other man bit back his retort and shrugged.

Samira, the other flight attendant, was close enough in figure to Giselle that they could probably share a wardrobe. If that was a policy of the airline, it was great for aesthetics, but bad for security—he probably weighed as much as the two of them combined. The two conferred in hushed voices behind the back row of seats, then split up. Samira moved to the port-side aisle, while Giselle returned to where Dante and Tyson waited.

The rest of the passengers in their section had realized something was up now. Most had turned in their seats, or even got up to face the rear. The low buzz of conversation hadn't overwhelmed the background hum of the aircraft, but that wouldn't last forever. Dante considered the crowd, then raised a finger to his lips and hoped the symbol for quiet was universal enough that it would carry through. He turned back in time to see the flight attendants slip through the curtains.

Tyson tapped the bulkhead with his knuckles. "Think there are any field-expedient weapons lurking in the bathrooms?"

"You going to whack someone with a toilet seat?" Dante said mildly. "Besides, she said to wait here."

"Yeah. We both know that ain't happening."

"Boys," Graham murmured, "Take this." He stuck his arm up above his seat, proffering a black lacquered cane. The shaft was well-dented, obviously old, and as Dante took it, he raised an appreciative eyebrow. Damage aside, it had impressive heft, and as he studied the wooden shaft, he noted that the short handle was a single carved piece with the rest of the walking stick. Serious piece of craftsmanship.

"They don't make them like this anymore," he said. "Thanks."

"I've got a newer one at home—aluminium." Dante smirked at the foreign pronunciation as Graham finished, "This one is an antique—but it's got more authority if one has to deal with unsavory sorts during one's travels, what?"

"Roger that. Thanks, Graham." He turned to Tyson and murmured, "Let's go."

"What, I don't get anything?"

"I'll protect you until you get that toilet seat," Dante promised. He eased through the curtain, his friend at his back. Samira and Giselle were a half-dozen rows ahead. At first, he wondered why they hadn't advanced further, then realized that the two were pausing at each row to ask the passengers in the window seats to raise their shades. The front of economy had brightened to a significant degree, but shadow still cloaked the rear.

That shouldn't be possible. He swallowed past a dry throat and choked up on the end of the cane. He wouldn't have much room to swing, but the handle would still hit with some serious oomph. Normally he'd have been self-conscious, carrying an old man's walking stick like a baseball bat. Here and now, he was glad to have it.

Giselle looked back over her shoulder and caught sight of them. For a moment she looked as though she might say something, but something like relief flashed across her face, and she looked to the next passenger row.

A loud voice responded to the flight attendant's low request to raise the window shade. Dante's Arabic was a little rusty, but it was evident from the overall tone and cursing sprinkled throughout the rant that this guy wasn't interested. He took a step forward, intending to assist, but stopped dead in his tracks at the new sound.

Low growls filled the air in seeming response to the outburst. In the deep shadows at the back of the plane, paired clusters of red lights shone.

"Tell me those are warning lights or something," Tyson whispered.

"I think I'd be lying," Dante managed before all hell broke loose.

Figures rushed out of the shadows in a liquid mass, filling the aisles and pouring over the seats. Screams filled the air. The passengers behind Dante, already wary, had, for the most part, turned to watch the strange procession of the flight attendants and their escort. They had a front row seat to the unveiled horror. Their cries warned those who'd not yet been alerted to anything wrong, and they turned, for the most part, in time to die.

The creatures with the glowing red eyes were people. Flight attendants, men, women, even a few children. Their clothing was as varied as the rest of the passengers', but all bore grievous wounds—jagged, bloody rents in flesh gone chalk-white mottled with black. They moved in stutters and stops, a painful, broken-boned form of locomotion as unnerving as their freakish appearance.

Blood painted the bulkheads as they descended on their first row of victims. Jaws opened impossibly wide, they savaged their victims, but only momentarily—all too often, they discarded their target and pounced on the next in line even as the former bled out.

The aisles filled with panicked people, and Dante heard Tyson yelling, but he couldn't make out the words over the hubbub. He had his eyes locked on the horrific tableau before him, frozen and unable to move.

Caught up in the rush of passengers attempting to flee the sudden horde, Giselle went down, trampled as the very people she'd been trying to help left her to her fate. Rage rose in Dante and overcame the terror. He shoved his way forward, ignoring wide eyes and screaming mouths. The way cleared, and he met the flight attendant's pleading eyes. A trickle of blood descended from one nostril as she rolled onto her stomach and tried to get on her hands and knees.

"Come on!" Dante leaned over and extended a hand. She grabbed it. He pulled her to her feet, turned to run—and something tore her from his grip. He turned back in time to see a pair of ravaged Arabs tearing at her with hands and teeth. The flight attendant had enough time for a single abbreviated scream before they tore out her throat.

"Bastards!" Dante yelled. He choked up and swung the cane overhead. The handle settled into the crown of the left beast's head with a crisp crack of bone. The thing let out a pained, bat-like shriek. He pulled back for another swing, but had to step back as the monster's partner advanced with a hiss. He changed targets, swinging from left to right, and slammed the tip of the handle into its temple. The red glow faded, and the creature sagged to the floor.

Good. They can be killed—or re-killed, I guess.

Tyson screamed in his ear, "Come on!"

Dante snapped back into situational awareness, realizing that he'd left himself far enough forward to attract attention from the right side. His only saving grace was his friend, and the fact that the seats blocked the things' struggle to move across the plane. He staggered back, jerking his head to and fro as he tried to figure out their next move. The bulkheads and bathrooms placed between the two sections would bottleneck the things into the aisles, but they'd need to barricade those openings somehow.

He considered the amount of space between the leading edge of the creatures and the curtain and despaired. We aren't going to have enough time.

The horde reached the last aisle where the flight attendants had directed the passengers to open their windows and recoiled. High-pitched screams jabbed into Dante's ears, and he flinched from the sound even as he rejoiced in their lucky break. A few of the creatures reached out or stepped forward across the border between shadow and light, only to shrink back in obvious agony. Blackened skin blistered and smoked, and the entire line retreated back into the remaining darkness. The front row straightened, impassively regarding Dante and Tyson.

"Shit," Tyson breathed. "Holy fucking shit."

Dante swallowed, noticing a glob of black, tar-like matter on the end of the cane. He scrubbed it on the carpet and tried to ignore the coppery reek of blood filling the air. "Here's hoping we don't run into any storms on the way," he muttered. "Let's get out of here."

The last thing he saw before they slipped back through the curtain was Giselle, standing amidst the crowd. She regarded him with a pair of glowing red eyes.

The soft sound of crying filled the compartment as Dante and Tyson wedged the drink cart sideways between the bulkhead and the wall of the lavatory. It wasn't a perfect fit—they had to leave it at a bit of an angle—but with the wheels locked, it was steady. Even with luggage jammed in the space between either side of the cart and the seats, it was a laughable barrier, but it was what they had. They'd debated the merits of leaving the curtain in place but ended up tearing it down. It let more light into the rear of the plane and would let them see what was coming.

If any of the passengers or remaining flight attendants had a problem with them taking charge, they hadn't said anything. That was more than likely shock. Dante hoped they'd come out of it, and soon. If the things rushed their section, he and Tyson wouldn't be able to hold it alone.

Even with the survivors from economy packed into first class and business, they had plenty of room. He didn't know how many people had started out in the rear of the plane, but whatever had happened had claimed a sizeable number of them.

Dante stared into the rear of the plane and resisted the urge to start counting. How in the hell did they not notice what was happening? The creatures must have been silent as thieves at first, working their way toward the front with no one the wiser. Given their reaction to sunlight, he supposed that the sudden sunlight had provoked them into a more overt response. If not for the cry that had woken them, it was impossible to say how far they might have gotten before anyone noticed what was happening.

Samira stepped between Tyson and Dante. Her look over the drink cart didn't last long before she turned away, pale. "The pilot and copilot aren't answering my calls."

"Lovely," Tyson said. "They're not—they're still human, right?"

"I believe so," she said. "I think one of them must have stuck his head out, seen the panic, and returned to the cockpit. They've secured the door. I can hear them in there, but they ignore me even when I knock."

Dante shrugged. "Smart. Selfish, but smart."

Samira looked over the survivors. "Can we get away from…here?" She pointedly refused to look into the darkness.

Dante hesitated. He wanted to keep an eye on things, but the sun did seem to be keeping them at bay for the moment. "Sure," he said. Refugees from the rear had taken his and Tyson's seats. He moved up and leaned against the seat in front of Graham. As the adrenaline rush left, his arms and legs started to shake with fatigue.

He offered the cane back, but the old man shook his head. "Hang on to it. God willing, I'll use it to walk out of here when the time comes."

"All right," Dante said. We need to go through the plane, see what other makeshift weapons we can dig up. If it comes to it, maybe we can hold the aisles with two or three people on each. He made a quick assessment of the passengers and decided that might be a tough order to fill. Most of those capable of meeting his eyes looked shaky as hell, while others curled themselves up under blankets or coats as though hiding from the menace aft.

"I asked before, but I didn't get an answer—is there an air marshal on board?"

"He was in the back," Samira said. "I don't see him here, and he'd surely have helped out."

"Great," Tyson said. "There's a gun in coach, we just need to figure out which one of the monsters has it."

Dante snorted. "Not like he'd have enough ammo. I was hoping for another,"—he almost said 'body', didn't like the connotation, and changed gears to— "set of hands."

The passenger who'd claimed Tyson's seat leaned forward and interjected, "What good are hands against those things? They eat people and turn others into beasts like them—they are ekiminu, what you Americans call zombies." The slender Arab wore a crisp white dress shirt, gray slacks, and a matching tie. Fine droplets of blood stained his shirt in a narrow track on either side of the tie, where his missing jacket hadn't shielded him from arterial spray.

Tyson's laugh rode the edge of hysteria. "Zombies don't have red eyes or hide from sunlight, dude. Those things are vampires."

"I'm not a dude—my name is Hassan."

"All right, Hassan. Trust me on this. I'm American, vampires and zombies are kind of our thing."

"Can we bloody well focus on the problem at hand?" Graham snapped. "Half the plane is full of monsters, and you're debating what to call them. Who gives a damn?"

"Graham's right," Dante agreed. "Whatever the fuck they are, how the hell did they get on the plane?" he demanded. "I'm pretty sure you can't walk a zombie past security."

Tyson shrugged. "Why does it matter?"

"If there's a patient zero, that's probably better for us than it would be if there's a virus in the water supply or something."

"That's not a happy thought," Graham said.

Samira closed her eyes and shuddered. "If they timed it right, they wouldn't have to hide it from security. It started in the back of the plane—if I had to guess, it was up in the crew rest compartment. The access stairs are at the rear of the plane. One of the economy class attendants opens the door, and it begins."

"That's good," Dante said. He let out a breath he hadn't realized he'd been holding. "You have to be bitten to be infected, or whatever it is." He didn't know of any sort of infection that made eyes glow red or created impenetrable shadow, but he didn't mention it. The surviving passengers were already teetering on the edge of panic. He didn't want to shove them all the way over.

The impromptu committee fell into silence until Graham turned to Dante and said, "So, what do we do? What's our plan?"

He stared at the older man, wishing someone better qualified was around to take the lead, then shrugged. You go to war with the army you have. "We keep all the shades up and stay away from the openings. We're scheduled to land in Atlanta when the sun's still up, so we get off the plane from up here and let the police or military handle things."

"And pray," Hassan said. "Pray that we don't fly into cloud cover or a storm."

"That, too," Dante agreed.

Getting a planeload of half-panicked passengers into some semblance of order was the next closest thing to herding cats. On the bright side, Samira and the rest of the flight attendants were well-versed in that sort of thing.

The first-class passengers didn't have the benefit of the personal experience of those in the other sections. They raised most of the resultant fuss when told they were being reorganized to put women and children close to the front. One in particular, a hawk-faced businessman named Omar, flat-out refused to move. He sat in his seat, belt fastened and arms crossed, until Dante and Tyson manhandled him out of place and frog-marched him down the aisle to get a long look at what they were up against.

Things settled down after that.

Origins

The flight attendants broke into the snacks and drinks and tried to convey a sense of normalcy. Maybe the passengers fell for it, but Dante could read the tension in their eyes and posture. The sun was keeping them safe for the moment, but there were any number of things that could change that.

In the end, it wasn't all that different from life. Whether by a car accident, stroke, IED, or vampire-zombie, death came when you least expected it more often than not.

Dante took one last look at the horde to ensure they hadn't advanced, then turned away. "Give me a couple of hours," he said to Tyson, "then rack out yourself." He handed the cane over. "We're going to need more than a walking stick. Get with Samira, we need to go through the plane and find anything we can use for weapons. If nothing else, it'll give you guys something to do instead of standing around."

"Hurry up and wait." His friend grinned.

"Shit never changes, does it?"

"Not even a little bit."

His was a half-sleep, semi-aware the whole time of where he was and what he was doing. His dreams consisted of odd surrealities, the soundtrack provided by the low conversations and background noise around him.

He jerked awake when Tyson touched his shoulder.

"All clear," the other man whispered. "Suckers don't even blink."

Dante wasn't awake enough to do anything other than grunt. He accepted the cane and assessed the blockade. Everything seemed as he'd left it, though the handful of people standing guard had switched up a bit. Omar and a pair of other men he didn't know warily eyed the port opening, while Hassan and Renard, one of the first-class flight attendants, had his side covered.

"They've got coffee in the front," Tyson pointed. "I'm out."

His options were a dainty ceramic mug or one of the flimsy plastic cups used for soda, so he chugged his first cup and refilled the mug for the walk back to his post. He nodded to the two strangers and said, "Dante."

The first guy held onto an umbrella stroller banded with luggage straps and seatbelt extenders with the same fervency a drowning man might clutch a life preserver. Dante was dubious as to how effective it might be if they needed to fight, but if nothing else, it should work to keep one of the things at arm's length until someone else could come along and assist. Stroller guy took a deep breath, visibly composed himself, and responded in a British accent, "Ajay."

Origins

The other man gave a half-shrug and a simple, "Khalil." The Arab was shorter than Dante and plainly clothed, but his shoulders and arms were thick with muscle. Oil worker, Dante guessed. Khalil looked like he'd be good in a fight, and he was glad to have him.

Omar had mellowed since being forcibly introduced to the problem in the rear of the plane, but that didn't keep him from assuming an imperious air as he scoffed, "He doesn't speak English. I'll have to translate if you need him to do anything."

Dante gave the other man a long look before he said, "I bet his English is about as good as my Arabic. Not my first rodeo, champ. We'll make do." He and Tyson couldn't instruct the guy in advanced physics, but you couldn't serve for long in the sandbox without picking up enough to get by.

If his remark had chastened the hawk-faced man, he couldn't tell. Omar turned to look into the darkness aft. The small fire extinguisher he cradled didn't have the reach of Ajay's stroller, but it would hit a hell of a lot harder with enough force behind it.

Ajay followed Dante's eyes and shuddered. "My mother often told me that men were the only real monsters in the world." He chuckled. "Usually after I did something to displease her."

Dante grinned. "Not very subtle, was she?"

"She was a professor of sociology. I often wondered if I wasn't of more interest as an experiment than an actual child."

"Yeah, well, one way or another, we need to keep her promise, Ajay."

"You think we can make it out of here alive?" Ajay hefted the stroller. "You don't have to tell me how ridiculous this looks."

With a half-shrug, he replied, "Survival's not our first priority."

Shocked, Omar interjected, "What in the world do you mean by that?"

"As fast as this spread through coach, what happens if one of these things gets into a major city? Maybe they have to hide from the sunlight, but we're talking exponential infection growth if they have the night to roam and spread." He looked from Ajay to Omar. "Our number one priority is keeping this thing contained. The best result for us is the plane landing and the authorities putting it under quarantine after we get off."

"And the others?"

"Worst case, ATC has us orbit while they figure out what the hell to do. Depending on how long that takes, the sun could go down. Maybe there's a quarantine then, and maybe not, but that ends badly for us."

Ajay cocked his head to one side. "I don't know that I regard that as the worst case, sir. To me, that would be those things rushing us right here and now." The three of them looked into the shadows. A brief moment of panic flashed across Khalil's face, and he turned and muttered something in Arabic—wondering what they were looking at, Dante guessed.

Omar sighed and bit off a terse reply. The other man frowned and nodded.

Dante grinned wolfishly at Ajay. "Nah. If we can't make it out of here alive, that's our next best option. If they make a push and we can't hold them off, I figure we retreat, then try like hell to bust into the cockpit and lawn dart this bitch into the ocean."

Ajay raised a single eyebrow, but Omar was less circumspect—the Arab laughed. "An American hijacking a Qatari aircraft and killing hundreds. Ironic, wouldn't you say?"

"Well, half of those hundreds are already dead," Dante pointed out, "and weighed against the possible deaths of tens or hundreds of thousands?" He shrugged. "Yeah, I'll make that call."

"Time will tell," the hawk-faced man grunted. "All will be as Allah wills it."

"I hope red-eyed, man-eating monsters aren't in his plan," Ajay murmured.

Hours passed. The creatures remained in place. Dante worked his way through another half-dozen cups of coffee and engaged in small talk with the rest of those who'd volunteered to stand watch. Not long after Tyson woke, the plane's deck shifted slightly under their feet.

"Here we go," Dante breathed. He slid between the back row of seats and the bulkhead and leaned over to peer out the window. The green smudge on the horizon remained too far away to discern any detail, but everything about it screamed "home".

The pitch of the engines increased, and the plane banked to the left. His first instinct wasn't to worry about the unsecured passengers, but rather how the shift in vector would impact the sunlight coming into the plane. Even as he turned to look into the back, the aircraft leveled out.

A shaky voice sounded over the speakers, "Ladies and gentlemen, air traffic control has diverted us to an alternate airfield. We will be landing shortly. Please fasten your seatbelts and ensure your tray tables and seat backs are in their full upright positions." As though struck by the incongruity of that oh-so-common statement with their situation, the voice hiccoughed laughter before cutting off the speakers.

"We've got company," Tyson murmured. Dante looked up in time to see his friend nod out the window. Leaning over, he caught the distinctive silhouette of an F-16 riding herd on their starboard wing.

"The professionals are on the case," he muttered. "We're landing damn close to the coast. Savannah, maybe?"

"Hunter," Tyson said, nodding. "Plenty of long runways. We're about to get a warm welcome from the 3rd Infantry Division, my man."

"I'll take it."

The deck shifted under their feet. He'd made more landings than he could count, but this was the first one he'd done standing up. Without a parachute, at least. Dante leaned against a seat and braced his legs. Glancing at the other watchers, he indicated the crowd in the rear of the plane. "Stay sharp, guys. This might be an opportunity for them to try something." If the sudden angle of the deck was of any discomfort to the creatures, he couldn't tell. Cloaked in shadow, all he could make out were vague silhouettes and glowing eyes.

Samira moved down the aisle with practiced ease, pausing periodically to touch a shoulder or speak a calming word. When she reached Dante, she brought her lips close to his ear and whispered, "Some of the passengers are worried about the change. Where are we landing?"

Dante thought about keeping his voice low, but if there was an edge of panic running through the lane, transparency here would be the better way to nip it in the bud. "It looks like Hunter Army Airfield, near Savannah. From a security standpoint, it's a much better option than

Atlanta. They can direct us to an open area and contain the situation without worrying about those things getting loose in a civilian building."

She held eye contact for an extended moment before nodding. "All right."

"Here we go!" Tyson crowed. Buildings flashed beneath them, small at first, then swelling larger as they approached the ground. It felt fast, but landings always did, didn't they? The process of take-off was laborious and strained in comparison, the duel against gravity accompanied by the thunder of engines and the pressure on your chest. Landing was controlled chaos, a terminal fall balanced on the edge of wing lift and stall speed.

Tires kissed tarmac, jostling the passengers. There were cries from the front—from those sitting on the floor, Dante assumed—but he forced himself to keep his eyes on the rear section. There was an odd rippling effect of bouncing red eyes as the things shifted in time to the vibrations of the plane, but other than that, they remained still. The engines thundered as the pilots reversed thrust to slow the craft.

Any landing you could walk away from, after all—but would they be able to walk away from this one? Red and blue lights drew his attention to the window, and while the view outside wasn't entirely a surprise, it wasn't one that brought comfort, either.

A pair of MP Humvees with strobing light bars rode fore and aft of a no-kidding Bradley Fighting Vehicle.

Origins

The muzzle of the 25mm cannon in its turret pointed near enough in Dante's direction for him to make out the open bore.

Institutional rivalries aside, he trusted the guys in the Brad to hold fire until they absolutely had no other option. The aircrew locked in the cockpit was another story entirely. "Drive straight, boys," he muttered.

Whether at his urging or the direction of some unseen air traffic controller, the trip down the runway was uneventful. When the engines cut out, silence reigned, save for the bark of tires on the tarmac outside. Other vehicles appeared around the perimeter, parking and forming up, as best as Dante could tell, around the entire aircraft. The line mainly consisted of Humvees, with more Brads to stiffen the formation. Between the Brownings, Mk 19s, and the heavier hardware mounted on the APCs, there was enough firepower to turn the Airbus into very fine debris.

In another lifetime that might have brought Dante some comfort, but not when he and the rest of the passengers were about to be on the receiving end.

A figure stepped out of one of the Humvees and brought a megaphone to his mouth. The thickness of the cabin walls muted the volume, but his words were understandable.

"Do not attempt to leave the plane!" the MP shouted. "We will fire upon anyone doing so. Remain calm until we can begin an orderly process of evacuation."

Dante bit back a curse as the rest of the passengers reacted. Their reaction to the announcement was the opposite of the intention, for obvious reasons. Wails, cries, and angry shouts filled the air. As though roused by the caterwauling, the things in the back stirred. He turned and stared into the shadows, knuckles white on the shaft of Graham's cane. Ignorant of the reaction they'd caused, the passengers continued shouting, and after a moment the things settled back into their motionless wait.

"Shut up!" Tyson yelled. The volume dropped, if only as the rest of the passengers turned to see what was going on, but it began to ramp back up.

"Quiet!" Dante roared. Samira and the rest of the flight attendants rushed forward, shushing those old enough to listen. Many of the children sniffled and sobbed, but that wasn't so piercing to him as the high-pitched shrieking had been. Quieter, he continued, "You're piquing the interest of those things in the back. We need to stay quiet."

The message passed forward, and after a few moments, the plane fell silent. With a sigh, Dante took another look out the window at the line of soldiers and resisted the urge to start screaming in frustration himself.

"How long till the sun goes down?" Tyson wondered.

Dante checked his watch. "An hour, maybe?"

Staring out the closest window, his friend muttered under his breath. "They've got to be bluffing. No way they open fire on a bunch of civilians going down an emergency slide. This is nuts."

"Dude, there are zombies on the damn plane. Of course it's nuts." He shook his head. "And they will absolutely fire. No way they risk this thing getting out of quarantine. The whole country is fucked if they don't keep containment. A few hundred passengers are an acceptable loss." Dante's prior sentiment tasted like ashes in his mouth—they'd made it, damn it! They'd landed, they should be huddled up in a hangar somewhere while the active duty guys figured out the best way to take care of the menace aft.

"Gory, gory what a hell of a way to die." Tyson's normal nonchalance had turned to exhaustion, morale crushed by the realization that they'd traded potential death in the air for inevitable death on the ground, the dwindling moments of their lives measured by the fading light of the sun.

Gritting his teeth, Dante stared out the window and tried to think of another way out of their predicament. Get your fingers out of your asses, boys. You've got survivors in here if you'll do something about it. Movement at the rear of the formation caught his eye, and he pressed his nose to the glass with a frown. "Ty, look at this."

An unmarked cargo truck had pulled up behind the ring of armored vehicles and Humvees. Heavily armed men in tactical gear unloaded from the back, formed up, and jogged toward the front. That in and of itself wasn't so strange. The fact that the camouflage pattern they wore clashed with the ACUs worn by the Army personnel around them was odd, though. "Marpat?" Tyson guessed.

"They've got enough Brads to turn this plane into Swiss cheese," Dante muttered. "Why bring in a squad of Marines?"

"What did you say?" Omar blurted. Dante and Tyson turned to see the businessman scrambling across the aisle toward them.

Ty gave him a look, but Dante just shrugged and jerked a thumb over one shoulder, pointing out the window. "The Marines have landed. See for yourself."

The Arab shoved his way between them and pressed his face against the window. He considered the unfolding tableau, then cursed in a low, harsh-pitched voice. The words tickled something in Dante's eardrums, and he found himself twisting his neck in an involuntary cringe.

Tyson wiggled a pinky in one of his ears as though seeking an elusive drop of water. "Dude, what was that? It wasn't Arabic, was it?"

Omar turned to face them and straightened. "That was a tongue unfit for Western mouths, fool. It is the language of creation, you uncultured monkey!" He waved a hand, and an invisible fist slammed into Dante's chest, carrying him and Tyson to the opposite side of the plane. An armrest slammed painfully into the small of his back, and he'd have cried out if the punch hadn't blasted the air from his chest.

"Damnable American cowboys," Omar spat. He kicked Dante in the stomach. "Talk about crashing my plane, will you? Disrupt my plans?" He braced his hands on his hips and stood over the two men with an imperious air. "The problem, gentlemen, is that while my minions don't like the sunlight, their fear of it is not what's kept them back." He smiled, but the otherwise cheery expression didn't touch the cool cobalt of his eyes. "I am."

Dante's fingers scrabbled across the carpet, seeking out the reassuring weight of Graham's cane. The hot, salty taste of blood filled his mouth. His body ached from the three rapid-fire blows he'd taken, but he'd be damned if he'd go out lying on his back. He found the cane. "You talk too much," he rasped, then swung.

There wasn't much mustard behind the swing, but the handle sank into Omar's bicep and elicited a yelp at the same moment Tyson slammed a heel into the Arab's opposite knee. The yelp deepened into a howl of pain, punctuated by the crisp celery crack of ripping cartilage. He ain't gonna walk that off.

Dante pushed himself to his feet as Omar staggered back. He spat a glob of mucus and blood and brought the cane back around for another swing. "You got at least one thing wrong, dickhead. We're Rangers, not cowboys."

"Attend me!" Omar shrieked, and a chorus of growls rose from the rear of the plane. Hassan and Ajay had watched the sudden conflict in stunned silence, but the explosion of activity from coach elicited cries of dismay.

The Brit's scream was loudest. "They're coming!"

Tyson's voice turned uncharacteristically serious. Dante couldn't help his smirk. When surfer bro turned mean, it was on like Donkey Kong. "Handle it. We've got Omar."

In spite of his pained tone, the Arab didn't sound all that impressed. "Oh, have you now?"

Dante glanced at his friend and nodded slightly.

As Omar raised his hands to attack, Tyson pulled the pin on his own fire extinguisher, spraying the Arab's face with a dense blast of white powder. The other man coughed. Rather than swiping at them with another invisible fist, he brought his hands involuntarily to his eyes. Dante rushed forward, holding the cane out with both hands. He clotheslined the Arab in the throat with the shaft, shoving the bigger man up against the bulkhead. In a flash, he realized that he'd carried the fight in front of his own seat. The corner of his abandoned paperback stuck out of the storage pocket, but that wasn't what drew his attention.

He had Omar pinned against the emergency exit door. "Ty!"

Dante kept one hand on the cane, pinning the struggling wizard, or whatever the hell he was, and reached down for the lower release handle. The single word and his action were more than enough to signal his intent, and Ty joined him. The other man pulled the upper handle down, and—

He was falling free on top of Omar, who remained on top of the door. The shift lifted the pressure off the Arab's neck, and he narrowed bloodshot eyes as he raked his fingers at Dante's face. They hit the ground before the other man could strike, the impact blasting the air from Dante's chest as he sandwiched the other man between himself and the chunk of the aircraft.

He rolled to one side, sucking in desperately greedy gulps of air. He'd lost the cane in the fall, and he fumbled for it even as Omar hopped to his feet with a screech. Dante's hope that the knee injury might slow the maniac down crushed, he frantically slid himself across the tarmac on his back, using his elbows and heels for leverage.

Dante's adrenaline rush blurred the shout over the loudspeaker into an indecipherable mess. If Omar heard it, he didn't react—his eyes locked onto Dante, and he staggered toward him, face contorted into a bestial snarl.

The first bullet didn't stop his course, but it jerked his shoulder to one side. Dante didn't know if it was the pain or the impact that finally drew the Arab's attention to the troops surrounding them. His eyes widened in shock, and he raised his hands in a familiar gesture. The air turned suddenly electric, and all the hair on Dante's body stood on end. Whatever was coming, it felt a hell of a lot worse than the invisible fists the madman had thrown around inside the airplane.

Staccato thumps pounded Dante's body, and he howled in victory as a burst of tracers transfixed Omar and tore him limb from literal limb. Evil wizard versus one of the long-enduring fruits of John Moses Browning's genius?

Browning won.

All was silent, and Dante realized that even included the plane. He raised his head. Tyson stood in the exit row opening, eyes wide.

"They stopped," his friend shouted. "They all just quit fighting and hit the floor. They're dead, again."

All was still for a moment, and then Ajay called out, "Can we get off the plane now?"

Humorless Marines ushered Dante and Tyson into the small room as soon as they contained the rest of the survivors in an empty hangar. He'd been carrying the responsibility for the civilians for so long that he almost refused to go in until he knew the people would be taken care of, but Dante told himself to relax. The little voice in the back of his head continued to point out that a world of monsters and magicians was something totally new.

In spite of that, he felt secure in the knowledge that the troops would take care of the shell-shocked passengers and flight crew.

They shoved Dante and Tyson into a small room, about ten by ten. Four chairs and a rectangular metal table bolted to the concrete floor under a single, flickering light fixture were the extent of the décor.

With a shrug, Tyson pulled a chair out and sat facing the door. A pair of water bottles, dripping condensation, sat neatly in the center of the table. While his friend cracked the bottle and downed half the contents in a single swallow, Dante sagged into his own chair and tried not to wince. He wasn't thirsty, but he could have done with a couple dozen ibuprofen and maybe a beer. His entire body ached, and he couldn't remember the last time he'd been so sore. Iraq, probably.

They sat and stared at the walls until, perturbed by the silence, Dante said, "How far did they get into the plane?"

Tyson pushed the cap of his water bottle around on the table for a moment before answering, "That hole you left made for one hell of a big picture window. The sunlight didn't burn them up." His friend sounded almost disappointed. "It slowed them down, though, made them stumble around like they were drunk. All the passengers crushed forward while we held the line. Everyone else made it."

Dante grunted, then smirked. "I told you they were zombies."

Metal scraped on metal as a lone figure pushed the heavy door open and strolled into the room. The Marine was a tall, powerfully built black man. The bare skin of his scalp gleamed under the intense glow of the overhead lights, and the creases in his fatigues could double for knife blades. Dante was Airborne to the core, but even he knew what crossed rifles under three rockers meant. The lizard-looking thing with wings on the unit patch was less recognizable, but he went with it. "Gunnery Sergeant," he said with a nod.

The new arrival smiled. "I hate to break it to you, but they weren't zombies, either, Sergeant Accardi. Based on the lore, the most fitting term is barrow-wight. A particularly nasty form of undead raised and controlled by a necromancer." The Marine slid a printed copy of what looked to be a painting across the table. The paper might have been new, but something about the clothing the figure represented in the art wore told Dante it was old. Artistic license aside, it was quite evident that Omar was the subject of the painting. "Nazr bin Omari, on the occasion of his visit to the Tang Dynasty of China, circa 645 AD. This guy's your basic mystical cockroach—he's got more lives than Toonces the Driving Cat. One-time acolyte of Abdul Alhazred, until he went his own way because his mentor was too kind-hearted for his taste." The gunny's voice turned thoughtful. "On the bright side, barrow-wights are only contagious as long as their creator's still around. Otherwise, the entire plane would still be in quarantine."

Dante thought back to the mess on the tarmac. "You're shitting us, right?" He was about to say the entire premise was impossible, then remembered the red-eyed creatures and Omar's invisible fists.

"You guys turned the asshole into Hamburger Helper," Tyson pointed out.

"Off the top of my head, that's at least the fourth time on this continent in the last century," the gunnery sergeant said with a shrug. "Dude's been around since before Mohammed, and he's got a real mad on for the world. Letting a horde of undead loose in a major metropolitan city is right up his alley."

Dante blinked a couple of times before he found his voice. "You're serious."

The Marine laughed. "Son, you've never met anyone more serious. Gunnery Sergeant Aloysius Blakely, Joint Task Force 13, USMC."

"What's that, some kind of specialized recon unit? We've rolled with those boys before," Tyson said. He took another drink of water, but Dante could tell that his friend was rattled.

"I saw that," Blakely said. "Recon's tough, don't get me wrong, but they've got it easy. The things they fight are usually human." He slid a phone out of a pocket and flipped through it. "I've got to say, you two have pretty impressive records. Contractors, though? Don't you think that's kind of beneath you?"

Dante sensed the test and pushed down his initial instinct to react defensively. "The money's great. Chow's good. The commute's a bear, don't get me wrong. But the 95 through Boston ain't much of a peach, either."

Blakely's eyes bored into his own. To his credit, Dante had just spent the last twelve hours staring at red-eyed monsters and fighting, if the gunny wasn't full of shit, an immortal wizard with nothing more than a freaking stick. He kept eye contact and didn't blink.

He didn't know if the gunnery sergeant had gotten what he was looking for, but the other man's expression softened. One corner of his mouth drew up in an amused smirk. "Not going to lie to you guys. The pay's okay, but you aren't going to get rich on it. Chow and the commute depend on the day. But…" He let the word hang, and when Tyson leaned in with his elbows on the table, Dante knew that his friend felt the same way he did. "We hold the line."

"Which line?" Dante murmured.

"The only one that matters. Inter Caelum et Infernum. The line between Heaven and Hell."

He caught Tyson's look out of the corner of his eye, but Dante didn't turn away from the gunnery sergeant. In the end, what else could he say? He'd seen the line up there on the plane, keeping ordinary men, women, and children safe from things of darkness. To step away now was unfathomable. "We're in."

Daniel Humphreys is the author of the Z-Day series of post-apocalyptic sci-fi thrillers and the Paxton Locke urban fantasy series. His first novel, "A Place Outside the Wild", was a 2017 Dragon Award finalist for Best Apocalyptic novel. He is a frequent contributor to Cannon Publishing, and his work can be found here on Amazon.

Origins

Revolution

Lucas Marcum

The following events were compiled from the personal letters and diaries of Major Sean Tillerson, commander of the 4th Pennsylvania Rifles, from his time on campaign with the Continental Army during the American War of Independence. The papers were discovered amongst a trunk of his personal effects some two hundred years after his death. The following was composed by his great-great granddaughter, Major Sally Tillerson-Hensly, United States Marine Corps, and published in 2017 by the Joint Staff Support Directorate, Joint Task Force 13, United States Marine Corps.

Origins

Chapter One

"A Summons"

November 20th, 1777

My dearest Abigail,

I should have written you before now, but with the Army on the march and our expectations of wintering in New Jersey, I have not had time to put pen to paper. Our fortunes have soured of late, and we find ourselves encamped some twenty miles north of Philadelphia, near the Schuylkill River in a small hamlet known as Valley Forge. We have settled into winter quarters to await the remainder of the Army.

The men, while brave beyond compare, are in a dreadful state. It would rend your tender heart to see them so. Poorly clothed, afflicted by all manner of ills and pestilences, and sorely in need of shoes, this Army somehow holds on. I fear that it may not last, should the enlistments expire before some measure of victory in our great struggle is attained, even though the dreary news is as unceasing as a funeral drumbeat. It is with a heavy heart that I must tell you that despite a valiant defense, Fort Mifflin and Fort Mercer have fallen, leaving the mighty Delaware undefended and the riverway open for the British to reinforce the garrison in Philadelphia.

This is grave news, and the men's morale has suffered most terribly at this grim happenstance. Indeed, it is almost Christmas, and their state and prospect of facing the bitter winds of winter and defeat near the holidays may be too much for many to bear. Indeed, even my previously stout spirit has felt the toll of the defeats, and I long to see you and our boys and to…

Pausing, I stopped to listen to the wind howling outside my meager shelter. The banging of loose sideboards made for a constant racket, and the cold that penetrated through the cracks in the small shack was a shock every time I reached outside my blankets. Reaching for my quill once more, I heard the banging again, and realized it was someone knocking on the door. Wrapping my blanket tight, I stood and moved to the door, and opened it, pushing against the wind.

In the dim firelight I could see the burly figures of two men, hats and scarves low, obscuring their faces. Both wore swords indicating that they were officers, and they were shivering in the bitter cold.

"Gentlemen. Army business, I presume. Please, step inside." I stepped back to make way for the bundled men. They stepped inside and crowded near the small fire pit, seeming to hunger for its warmth.

The bigger of the two men pulled his scarf down and removed his hat. "Captain Tillerson, sir."

Recognizing the man as one of the general's aides, I replied, "Colonel Fitzgerald. To what do I owe the honor? I can hardly presume this is a social call." I gestured toward the door. "Not on such a night."

Colonel Fitzgerald shook his head grimly. "No, sir, I fear not. I bring both news and orders." He traded a look with the man next to him, and then continued, "May I introduce Lieutenant Jonathan Turley of the Continental Marine Infantry. Lieutenant Turley, this is Captain Sean Tillerson of the Fourth Pennsylvania Rifles."

Having uncovered a youthful face ruddy from the cold, the man offered a hand, which I accepted. He spoke in a pleasant baritone, "Your reputation precedes you, Captain. It is a pleasure."

"The pleasure is mine, Lieutenant." With a wry grin, I added, "You'll not find much shipboard action here, sir."

The young man grinned back. "Shipboard or not, as long as we get our hands on those bloody redcoats, my men and I are happy." His smile faltered. "I fear that the British are the least of our worries for the time being. Sir?" He looked at Colonel Fitzgerald, and respectfully lapsed into silence.

Colonel Fitzgerald nodded, and said, "Indeed. Captain, your men can track, can they not? We already know they are fearsome shots, with those peculiar muskets of yours." He gestured to the long rifle hung carefully on the wall, its finely engraved walnut stock shining faintly in the flickering firelight.

With a nod, I replied, "Aye. They can. Most of them are frontiersmen from Pennsylvania and skilled in woodcraft." With a slight shrug, I added, "Those that are left, anyhap."

"Aye. Your men suffered fearsomely at Germantown." He eyed me steadily, and continued, "Suffered more than most, but you held the line. May have bought the entire Army time to retreat."

"So they say, Colonel. It does the dead no good."

There was a moment of silence broken only by the wind howling outside before the other officer replied, somberly, "Indeed." The burly colonel turned back to the fire for a moment, then he spoke without turning, "Sean. The general needs you and your men for a special task." He turned back around and regarded me for a moment, then continued, "There's something out there." He gestured at the flimsy wall of the hut. "Something dangerous."

Tilting my head and trying to conceal my surprise at the usually formal officer's use of my given name, I replied, "Hessians?"

The man shook his head slowly. "No. Worse."

Glancing doubtfully at the Marine officer, I said, "We are a bit far inland for Indians, but perhaps with the war, they grow bold…"

The big man sighed, glanced at the younger officer, then replied, "Captain, I'll be frank. You and me, we're both from the old country. We know the legends and have heard tales of things that are…perhaps not legend."

He nodded at the Marine, who began to say in a serious tone, "This evening, the southern watch post on the Germantown Pike was scheduled to be relieved as usual by the oncoming sentries. When they got to the post, the sentries were gone."

"Deserted," I replied calmly. It was common enough these days.

"So we thought. But in their post was a great deal of blood and the signs of a struggle."

I pondered this for a moment, then spoke, thinking out loud, "Perhaps it is Indians. Seems out of season and far apace from their territory, but I suppose…"

Colonel Fitzgerald replied, "Their weapons lay where they fell. One of the muskets was discharged, the other not. No warrior I know of would leave a weapon behind."

"Wolves, then. It's not unheard of."

The big officer scowled. "Perhaps. There was a distinct trail leading to the deep woods to the south. No wolf tracks. No footprints. Just…marks in the snow of someone being dragged."

He stared at me, daring me to come to the conclusion I was avoiding. After a moment of tense eye contact, I broke it off and sighed. "I didn't think they'd come this far into civilization.

"Perhaps they didn't. Perhaps they did. Perhaps these are from here, or maybe this is something else. Regardless, here they are, and here they must be dealt with."

Looking down, I considered for a moment, then replied, "I don't know if I have enough men."

Colonel Fitzgerald gestured at Lieutenant Turley, "The lieutenant has a squad of equipped, well-trained and disease-free Marine infantry."

I turned to examine the young man's ruddy, honest face. After a moment, I said "Lieutenant, do you know what you're about to get into?"

"No, sir. But I have eight Marines under arms, and plenty of shot and powder. We'll make do. Just put us on the trail. There's little in these woods that well-disciplined musketry can't solve."

After a moment regarding the earnest young man, I held out a hand. "Welcome to the Fourth Pennsylvania Rifles."

The young man returned the shake and replied, "The way I see it, Captain, is you and your riflemen are joining the Marine Infantry." He grinned.

Colonel Fitzgerald spoke, "Very well. Captain Tillerson, you have your men. You meet the general at dawn. He wishes to speak to you personally."

With a firm nod, I replied, "We shall be there, sir."

Origins

Chapter Two

"To the Hunt"

November 21, 1777

My dearest Abigail,

I have been summoned to the headquarters of our Commander in Chief, the Honorable General Washington. While the nature of the summons yet is a mystery, I fear very much that it entails having to face those whom I faced those many years ago while defending the frontier. I pray to the almighty above that it is not so, but I have prepared as if the worst is true.

I pray that you do not worry for my safety. I will be well protected, for we have attached a complement of Continental Marines. They are a rough, sordid sort of men, foul of mouth and manners, but of the utmost bravery in battle, and indeed, almost chivalrous on the field of conflict. I pray that you are warm and comfortable through this bitter winter and know that I love you and the boys and you are constantly in my thoughts and prayers.

Your eternally loving Husband, Sean.

The next day broke clear and cold. Opening the small door to my hut, I ducked outside. The bitter cold caused my breath to catch in my throat, and I paused to pull my scarf tight, and my hat low on my head. The quiet of the predawn camp made the scene of pitiful huts, occasional soldiers, and followers bundled against the cold seem serene. The camp was covered in a thick layer of fresh ice, and the smoke from the hundreds of fires left a haze in the air. A touch of the biting wind from the night before had the flags fluttering. The splashes of unit colors stood out, marking divisions and regiments, and occasionally the bright red, white, and blue of the new flag of our combined effort. Despite the magnificence of it, I knew that the suffering of the soldiers underlying the scene was immense and tinted with quiet desperation.

"Captain Tillerson, sir." Looking to the left, I saw a young soldier trying to stand at attention despite his violent shivering. With a nod, I responded.

"Soldier. You are my escort, I presume?"

The young man replied through his chattering teeth, "Yes, sir. I'm to take you to General Washington straight away."

"Very well. Lead on." The young man courteously fell in beside me, and we began the trek across the camp. After several minutes of walking and silently watching the camp beginning to come to life around us, we happened by a parade field. A company of soldiers stood in the middle of it in formation, with rifles shouldered and bayonets fixed. They stood stock still as a massive man in an unfamiliar field uniform roamed back and forth in front of them, screaming in a foreign language. Despite not being able to understand the language, I recognized profanity when I heard it. Despite our pressing engagement, I found myself enthralled, and paused momentarily to watch.

After the man had screamed nonstop for several minutes, barely seeming to stop to draw breath, a stocky sergeant standing nearby spoke in a thickly accented voice.

"Ze general is displeased with your performance. Return to the starting position, and we begin again."

The formation, previously as still as statues, suddenly came to life as the soldiers began removing their bayonets from their muskets and returning them to their scabbards. My escort spoke as he eyed the men on the parade field.

"Baron Von Steuben is a hard man, but even after these short few weeks, the difference is visible. That's the Sixth and Seventh Pennsylvania. They were in a bad spot after Germantown."

Absently, I replied, "I know. I am a Pennsylvania man myself." I continued watching the bayonet drill as the men methodically went through the steps.

The young man didn't reply. After a moment, he said carefully, "Sir, we must not keep the general waiting."

Origins

With a nod and a last look at the drilling soldiers, I turned. "Indeed. Lead the way, soldier." The young man silently turned and lead the way, heading towards a nearby hill. Near the top of the hill, a sturdy, two-story stone building stood, smoke issuing from its chimney, and two burly guards with muskets outside the door. As we approached the door, the two men came to attention. The man on the left spoke.

"Captain Tillerson. The general has been expecting you." He reached over and opened the door. Nodding my thanks to my young escort and the guard, I stepped inside, immensely grateful for the relief from the bitter cold. A nearby servant stood waiting to take my coat and hat, which I handed over gratefully. Another waiting servant stepped forward and gestured for me to follow, which I did. Moments later we were in front of a door.

The servant knocked, then opened the door, and stepped inside, and as I followed, announced in a formal tone, "Captain Sean Tillerson of the Fourth Pennsylvania Rifles."

I stepped in, took three smart steps, came to attention, and saluted. In the room stood three men. Two were leaning over a large table with a map, with small markers on it. The third, a tall man with broad shoulders and sandy brown hair pulled neatly back at the nape of his neck, stood by the roaring fire, his hands clasped behind him. His identity was unmistakable. The two at the table looked up at me as I entered. I recognized Colonel Fitzgerald from our meeting the previous night.

He straightened up, stepped toward me, and spoke formally, "Captain Tillerson. May I present the Honorable General Washington, and my colleague, Colonel Hamilton."

I nodded courteously, and replied, "Good morning to you both, sirs. It is a pleasure to meet you, despite the circumstances."

The general gravely returned the salute and gestured to the sideboard, where several fine china cups were laid out. "A pleasure, Captain. Are you well? May I offer you coffee? I'm afraid we are a bit short of tea at the moment."

His tone had a hint of humor in it at the last statement, and I could not help but smile as I replied, "I am well, sir. I understand we are pressed for time."

He nodded and responded, "Indeed we are. However, I would be remiss if I did not offer my commendations on for your men's performance at Germantown. Your Pennsylvania men and their fortitude in covering the retreat may have saved this Army."

Gravely, I replied, "Thank you, General, although it is of little enough comfort to their wives."

"Indeed. Please send them my condolences on their tragic loss and thank them for their sacrifice to our young nation." I nodded graciously at the kind words. He regarded me intently for a moment, then spoke abruptly, "To business. Alexander?"

The red-headed young man at the map table moved to another table with a smaller map and beckoned me toward it. Curious, I stepped up and regarded the map. It appeared to be a map of the area of Germantown, and had the markings left from the battle, with unit markers positioned as it had ended. The map also had a finely detailed examination of the areas surrounding our encampment.

Colonel Hamilton spoke, his voice pleasant and even, "Captain, we have summoned you here to assist us with a problem, as Colonel Fitzgerald mentioned when you were summoned." He placed a finger on the map. "We appear to be losing sentries." He paused, carefully measuring his words. "Or, perhaps more precisely, something is taking our sentries." His slender finger tapped the map, then moved to several places in sequence. "Here, here and here. Twelve men over the last four days, all on southern sentry line."

He tapped the map on the thick wooded area that lay between our encampment and the pike that lead to Germantown.

Tilting my head, I regarded the map for a moment, then said thoughtfully, "You believe it's in those woods."

Hamilton nodded. "Indeed. The pattern suggests that whatever it is, is in this area, as the attacks seem to center there." He tapped an area with a small red circle around it.

Still regarding the map, I nodded silently and folded my arms.

Suddenly General Washington spoke in his powerful baritone, "Captain, I cannot emphasize enough how crucial it is that you find and eliminate whatever it is that is taking my troops." I looked up from the map at the general. He had stepped to the map table, and his face was stern. He continued, "The morale of this Army is precarious. Disease, desertion, and the recent misfortune at Germantown have all made the preservation of the spirits of the men of the utmost importance. If word were to get out that men were disappearing again..." He fell silent, his face hard.

I considered this for a moment, then asked, "Again? Has this happened before?"

The two aides traded a look, then Fitzgerald spoke carefully, "We have had...misfortunes for a year now, usually after major engagements. At first we attributed it to other things. Wolves. Indians. Desertion, brigands, or madness." He paused and then looked at General Washington, who silently nodded. Fitzgerald continued, "After several months of these trickling losses, we started seeing patterns. Whatever this was, it was following the Army on campaign. From Massachusetts, to Delaware, now through Pennsylvania."

Origins

General Washington spoke abruptly, "Captain, I served in the west in the wars against the French. I heard the rumors of you and your scouts, and the…price you extracted for the massacre at Fort William Henry."

I looked down momentarily, then back up at the general, and replied, "I know the rumors, General. Suffice it to say that things were not as they appeared out there."

Washington regarded me for a moment, then nodded. "I suspected as much. They seldom are." He turned to Hamilton and spoke in a commanding tone, "Ensure that the captain has men, horses, and shot, and link him up with the men we discussed. He'll leave as soon as his men are assembled."

Hamilton nodded and turned to a nearby writing desk. General Washington turned back to me and spoke grimly, "Ride hard and fast, Captain. Go into those woods, find and remove the threat to this Army. Most importantly, report back. I must know what threat we face if we are to maintain this Army and win this war."

I came to attention and saluted. "By your command, General." He gravely returned the salute, and I turned and left the room.

An hour later, having broken my fast with boiled beef and bread, I retrieved my horse from the general's excellent stables and made my way to the southern parade ground to meet my new men. Lost in thought, I scarcely noticed the camp and its multitude of miseries around me until I was at the appointed meeting place. As I drew near, I noted a small group of men, their shoulders hunched against the cold, standing near a small fire attempting to warm themselves. They wore varied uniforms concealed under heavy winter blankets. Upon seeing me, they fell into a formation of two lines and stood to attention. I recognized the young lieutenant of Marines from the night before and returned his crisp salute.

He spoke crisply, "Captain Tillerson, sir. The men are present and assembled."

Spying familiar faces in the ranks, I dismounted my horse and made my way to the men. Moving up to the first rank, I ordered, "Rest easy, soldiers."

The men relaxed, and I spoke to the big man with hard, flinty eyes in a battered tan uniform coat with stained red facings. On his shoulder rested the distinctive long rifle of the Pennsylvania regiments. "Sergeant Armistead. Good to have you."

The big sergeant nodded and responded in a thick Scottish accent, "Happy to help, sir." He nodded to his left at the two men next to him. "Brought Haskins and Lewis, sir."

Nodding, I asked, "How are the rest of the men?"

The big sergeant shook his head and responded, "Able passed of the flux last night. Johnstone and Blackman caught the fevers, and Murphy's finger turned to gangrene. He's in hospital. Perhaps they'll save th' arm. Perhaps not."

"Damn." I shook my head and regarded the three men, then remarked, "So we are the last of the mighty Fourth. What a sad lot we are, indeed."

The big sergeant nodded and gave a crooked smile. "Sad we may be, we aren't finished yet, sir." He looked sideways. "Right, lads?"

Haskins and Lewis smiled grimly and nodded in acknowledgement. I turned to Lieutenant Turley and asked, "How are the men for arms, Lieutenant?"

The young officer replied, "Sir, your riflemen have double loads of shot and powder, and a freshly issued saber each from the armory. My Marines have muskets with bayonets, and a cutlass and pistol each." He gave an amused look at the green-coated Marines standing in the ranks and added, "And like as not, they've extra weaponry and other devices of mischief secreted upon their personages as well, sir."

Amused, I replied, "They may well need them, should we encounter a British patrol. How are we for horses and consumables?"

The man gestured to a line of horses tethered nearby and replied, "Fresh mounts from the general himself's stables, and three days of hardtack and jerky."

"Very good. You have the maps?"

The Marine patted the case at his side and replied, "Indeed, and your sergeant has a copy as well."

Impressed with the young officer's efficiency, I replied, "Very good. Your eight men plus my riflemen bring us to thirteen." I paused and noted wryly, "Not a number known for luck." With a twist of a grin, I added, "Fortunately, we don't believe in luck. Do we, Sergeant Armistead?"

The big man rumbled in reply, "We make our own, sir." He patted the long, sheathed knife slung on his right hip.

Lieutenant Turley grinned, motioned to the horses, and said, "If there's nothing else, shall we proceed, sir?"

"Indeed we shall, Lieutenant. Move the men out." I turned and prepared to mount my horse. Settling into the familiar comfort of my campaign saddle, I waited as the soldiers mounted and formed into a column. Sergeant Armistead lead off, with me and Lieutenant Turley bringing up the rear. After a brief glance at the sky, I noted that the pure blue was now scudded with low-hanging grey clouds, and the sky to the south loomed with dark, tall clouds, as if hiding something dark underneath them.

Turley noticing my look to the sky and, mistaking my expression, said in a matter-of-fact tone, "Those speak to more snow, sir. We'd best hurry before we lose the trail."

"Indeed." I clucked at my horse and gently tapped his sides to set him to motion. As we headed south, we passed a wood and earthen palisade, which I couldn't help but notice was being methodically reinforced with additional wooden stakes being added, and the walls were being heightened by grim looking soldiers. They didn't sing or joke as they worked, merely toiled, and occasionally glanced at the woods to the south of the encampment. Turley gave me a questioning look, to which I responded with only a slight shrug.

A half hour of gentle riding later, we came to a fork in the small road guarded by several nervous looking sentries. The road cut through the forest, which had grown thicker around us.

As I drew forward, I caught one of the sentries saying to Sergeant Armistead, "…on the left, Sergeant. The other road will take you to Germantown Pike." The young, pimpled sentry shifted nervously. "The other sentry post is about a mile down there." He paused and added, "Was down there at any rate." He looked up at the grizzled noncommissioned officer and asked, "What's out there, Sergeant? Are we safe here?"

Armistead cracked a rare smile and spoke almost gently, "You're fine, lad. It's wolves drawn by the slaughter, like as not. You and the lads wait here. We'll be back in a shake."

The big sergeant turned his horse and motioned the next men in line to begin down the road, which rapidly narrowed as it vanished into the snowy undergrowth. The treetops, while barren of leaves, remained thick and entangled overhead, making it feel like a tunnel into the forest. The gloom of the now steady overcast made the day dark, and the road even darker.

As the soldiers rode cautiously down the road, the sergeant spoke to Lieutenant Turley and me, "Sir. These woods aren't right." He gestured around him at the gloom of the dense forest. "I don't know what might be out there, but I've told the men to stay aware, and we'll dismount and proceed on foot once we locate the old sentry post."

Nodding my head in agreement, I replied, "Very good, Sergeant." The burly man nodded and hurried his horse forward. With a last glance at the now solid grey sky, I nudged my horse forward into the seeming perpetual gloom of the forest. As we passed into the thick undergrowth, the forest seemed to contract, becoming denser and darker. The thick coating of snow absorbed sound, so the only noise we could hear was the crunching of hooves, the clinking of the harnesses, and the occasional neigh and snort from the horses. The men, previously talking amongst themselves cheerily, had grown silent, and I saw more than one of the veteran campaigners subtly clearing the handle of his saber for instant usage.

I must confess that even I, the veteran of many skirmishes and battles in the woods, found the silence disquieting. I found myself touching my saber handle occasionally as if rubbing a talisman to ward off evil.

Lieutenant Turley whispered to me, "Captain. It is unnaturally still, is it not?"

Putting on a brave front, I replied, "Perhaps; perhaps not. I read in the almanac that scientists think the pressure of a storm on the creatures of the air sends them into a stupor and quiets the animals of the ground." I gestured at the silent woods around us. "That is why we are not hearing any birds nor seeing any manner of small animals. 'Tis nothing but the approach of a storm."

The young officer nodded, but his eyes kept scanning out, seeking anything that might be lurking in the gloom of the trees or amongst the snowbanks. We continued our ride in silence for nearly half an hour, the going made difficult by the narrowing trail and low hanging brushes.

Presently there came a harsh whisper from the front of the column. Knowing that this meant we had arrived, I swung down from my horse, tossed the reins to the Marine in front of me, and walked quickly to the front of the column. Sergeant Armistead was standing, his hands on his hips, staring into the forest. Haskins was kneeling, studying the trampled snow intently.

Looking up at my approach, the soldier spoke, "The area's a mess, sir. I can see the blood, but the boots of the officers who came to investigate has obscured anything else of value."

Staring at the very large, dark brown stain in the snow, I replied, "Can you make out what direction they went?"

The man silently indicated the direction the big sergeant was staring in, down a narrow path the width of a single man. In the snow were partially obscured boot prints, and what looked like someone dragging their heels. I stepped up next to the sergeant and spoke quietly, "Thoughts, Thomas?"

The big man shook his head, then took off his tricorn and rubbed his close-cropped hair. He then firmly placed the hat back on and motioned to Haskins and Lewis. "Us riflemen first, sir, to the sides of the trail, quiet. The Marines will follow a ways back and come Johnny-on-the-spot if there's trouble."

He turned to Lieutenant Turley. "Tisn't meant to give offense to your Marines, sir. We're just more practiced in moving in these woods."

The young man replied calmly, "None taken. We'll move up the trail slowly, and if we hear trouble, we will make haste to assist. Blow the whistle if you need us, and we'll come in like the devil himself was pursuing." He turned to organize the Marines into a movement order, and I could hear him detailing two of them to stand fast and guard the horses.

While the Marines prepared, Armistead turned to me and spoke in a low voice, "I'd not ordinarily ask you, sir, to be in the line, but we are desperately short of men of woodcraft. If you'll take Haskins and the right side, I'll go with Lewis on the left."

I nodded and without a word returned to my horse and retrieved my rifle. Stripping off the canvas cover from the flint, I ensured it was primed and ready to fire. Seeing my other Pennsylvania men doing the same, I nodded to Sergeant Armistead. At his return nod, I stepped off into the woods, noting that a light snow was falling.

As I moved amongst the snow-covered trees, a deep silence fell over the entire area. I knew I was but a dozen feet from the Marines and the horses, but I could not hear a thing. I glanced at Haskins. He held up a finger to his lips, then tapped his ear, then pointed at me and motioned forward. I nodded silently and continued moving into the woods.

Moving as silently as possible, I made my way through the brush. The terrain began to get rough, and more than once I stepped into deep snow that concealed an irregularity in the ground and had to carefully catch myself. Momentarily, I found myself climbing a small ridge. Crouching, trying to stay hidden from I knew not what, I crested the ridge and regarded the small valley below.

To my great surprise, I could see the distinctive scarlet of a British soldier's coat moving below us. I dropped to my belly in the snow and worked my way forward. I could hear the minute sounds of Haskins close behind. We inched our way forward, taking great care not to wet the locks of our rifles, and made it to a large boulder that happened to have a clear view of the small gulch below. Bringing my rifle up, I took aim at the scarlet shape and watched intently.

After a moment I could see that the man was stumbling, and his face was pale. He wore no hat, and his brown hair, once neatly pulled back, was in disarray. He did not appear to have a musket, but had a sword belted to his waist. He occasionally turned his head from left to right as if seeking his way in the snow and moved with a stagger.

Behind me, Haskins whispered, "Think he's lost, sir? He looks deathly ill."

I replied in the same low tone, "Looks like he may be. Separated from his party in these damnable woods, no doubt. We should get him and find out where the main body is. We've been expecting an attack for weeks now." I thought for a moment, then cupped my hands and made a soft bird call, similar to the mourning doves near my boyhood home. Three short coos, and a longer one; a signal to my longtime sergeant, concealed in the woods nearby.

After a moment, a return call came. Two short coos. Sergeant Armistead would remain hidden and watch.

Without taking my eyes off of the stumbling officer below, I spoke, "You stay here, Haskins. I need your rifle trained on him as well, just in case this is some trickery."

Haskins nodded silently and raised his rifle, blinked once, and became deathly still. In a company known for excellent riflemen, Haskins was once of the best, and deadly accurate to over two hundred yards. More than one British officer had been sent to an early grave by the big farmer from Lancaster.

I stood up and with my rifle held low, but ready, I made my way down the slope. Stopping at the bottom perhaps thirty feet from the Englishman, I held up a hand and spoke.

"Hail, sir."

The man stopped, turned, and stared at me, but did not seem surprised, nor try to get away from my sudden appearance. His eyes seemed strange; all black, with no white visible. For a moment he stood stock still, slightly tilting his head at me.

I spoke again, gently, not liking the look of the man, "Sir, you look ill. We shall take you to the Continental Camp, where you will be fed and cared for and paroled back to your Army in due course."

The man took a staggering step toward me, then stopped again. He opened his mouth but remained silent.

Unnerved and attempting to cover it with boldness, I called out again, "Sir! Do you not speak English? Are you wounded or…"

With a terrifying shriek, the man suddenly lurched into a sprint and rapidly charged at me. I began to raise my rifle, but realizing I would not make it in time, dropped it and reached for my saber. The man raced at me, the horrible shrieking echoing through the silence of the forest, his hands outstretched. As I drew my saber, I knew this, too, would be too late.

Suddenly there was a tremendous crash from behind me, and the man staggered and fell to one knee. A small hole appeared in the coat over his breast. He looked down at it for a moment, and then to my abject horror, rose again. Two more crashes came in rapid succession, and the thing that resembled a man stumbled again and fell. I wrenched my saber out of its scabbard, now hearing my men rushing down the hill behind me. The man, the thing in front of me, rose again and began the shambling sprint at me once more. My saber bare, I stepped back and spun away as he lunged at me, striking one of the man's arms as he went by, and then kicking him hard in the back. It sprawled onto its face in the snow, and then rolled over and tried to rise, but was slow to do so due to the terrible wound I had inflicted on the wretched thing's arm.

Taking advantage of this moment, I thrust forward with my saber and pierced it in the side, feeling the blade bite deep into the chest, a surely mortal wound in any man. The thing screamed and hissed and tried to climb again to its feet. I drew back my saber for a second strike and thrust it directly through the beast's heart. Its black eyes fixed on me, the thing grabbed the blade and pulled it further into its chest, drawing me closer to its grip and open jaws. I tugged on the handle of my saber, feeling how tightly it was held, but I refused to let go. A split second later there was a flash of steel, and the head of the monster that looked like a man fell backwards from its body into the snow. The grip on my sword loosened, and I was able to jerk it back and out of the body. The headless corpse stood for a moment, then collapsed into the snow, falling onto its chest. Sergeant Armistead stood behind it, blade bare. He stared down at the severed head, which still stared and worked its jaw rhythmically.

Seeing that it no longer posed a threat, I shakily lowered my sword and spoke, attempting humor, "Well timed, Sergeant. Next time a bit faster would be lovely."

Armistead, Haskins, Lewis, and I stood over the body and stared. After a moment Haskins spoke, "What manner of unholy thing is this? I shot him right in the heart. The captain stabbed him thrice. Is this sorcery?"

Lewis, usually quiet, suddenly spoke, "I know this man." All of us turned to look at Lewis in astonishment. He indicated the head, still silently working its mouth,

"Aye. I know him. This is General Andrew, a brigadier with the Fourth Regiment of Foot. Fact of the matter is, I killed him at Germantown." He stared down at the man's face and fell silent.

I looked up at the snow-covered gully and the trees looming above us. As I looked, I saw an astonishing sight. A man stood on a boulder about fifty yards down the gulch, clad in stylish clothing, all colored the deepest of black. He stood silently, watching us. He was of indeterminate age, and didn't move. I spoke to my compatriots.

"I think, lads, that the gentleman over yonder is likely knowledgeable about the fate of our brigadier here." Suddenly furious, I pointed at him with my saber and spoke, "We need him alive."

I had scarce taken a step when the man moved. He merely raised a hand, his palm facing up. Near my feet a snowbank suddenly started to move, then sat up. The pale flesh and black eyes of another man became visible, this one wearing the tattered remains of a dark blue uniform coat. He struggled to his feet, showing the worn uniform of a Continental soldier. Beyond him, several other piles of snow were moving as well.

Over my left shoulder, I could hear Sergeant Armistead hiss, "Behind us, sir."

Setting my feet in a firm stance, I spoke loudly, "Make ready your blades, gentlemen. There will be no quarter here."

Origins

The thing in front of me screamed and charged. I sidestepped again and struck with my sword, then blocked a hand clawing at my face from my left. From then on it was a confusing melee, slashing and shouting. I ducked, blocked, and struck with whatever was readily available. My gloved free fist, the pommel of my saber, the flat edge of my blade. Time seemed to stand still as we fought for our lives. Indistinctly I could hear the short, sharp blasts of a whistle, blowing over and over.

Somewhere in the back of my mind I thanked God above that my sergeant was as cool and reliable as ever and was blasting on his signal whistle for help. Dispatching the creature in front of me with a short, sharp stab to the eye, I whirled in time to see Armistead burying his hunting knife into a creature's chest. It screamed furiously in his face and lunged at him. Slashing at the back of the beast's knees, I managed to wound it, allowing the big sergeant enough time to jerk his knife out and plunge it into the side of the beast's head. As it fell on the ground, I spun again, only to see three more of the figures in tattered uniforms. I could hear the men behind me breathing heavily as they dispatched the last of the creatures with their knives and tomahawks.

In the distance the man in black stood, watching us calmly. More of the snowbanks began to stir, and more dead men stood. I raised my blade cautiously and spoke without removing my eyes from the figures now approaching us, "Armistead, check to the rear. We cannot win this fight."

"Behind again, sir. More this time." The man's gruff voice was calm.

I took a breath and commanded, "Cut through them. I will hold these in front." The snow was falling heavier now, and a slight wind made the flakes whip and dance. I raised my sword to the ready position just as the ghouls began to shriek and charge. I could hear faint shouting from behind me, then the familiar roar of musketry. Two of the figures dropped immediately, one with a hole in its head. It did not rise, but the other, struck in the chest, did.

A loud voice, which I recognized as Lieutenant Turley, bellowed, "Second rank: FIRE!" There came another roar, and more impacts on the creatures, slowing their charge. I ducked the outstretched arms of the first and slashed at the second when I heard another command bellowed from above us.

"Marines! CHARGE!" There then came a fearful yelling, and out of the corner of my eye I saw the fearsome and beautiful sight of the Marines—led by Lieutenant Turley, brandishing a bare saber—tilting down the hill, their bayonets fixed, coattails flying. In moments they were amongst us, plunging their bayonets into the creatures, which screamed with rage. A flash from my right caught my attention, and I threw myself back as a creature lunged at me, teeth bared. Stumbling and falling onto my back in the snow, I threw up my free arm to protect my face from the outstretched fingers. Suddenly the creature screamed and clutched at its chest, which sprouted a length of shining steel driven by the burly arms of a Marine sergeant.

Rolling out from under the beast, I scrambled to my feet and turned. The Marine was cursing horribly, trying to free his rifle from creature. With another burst of profanity, he dropped the rifle, reached into his coat, and drew a pistol, cocked it, and fired into the creature's face from a distance of mere inches. The ball tore through the creature's disfigured face, and the powder set what remained of its ruined visage alight. The remains slumped to the ground, twitching in a horrifying manner, and its head smouldering.

The Marine dropped the pistol and jerked the bayonet out of the body. Reaching out to me, he hauled me to my feet. Seeing no more beasts nearby, I turned just in time to see a creature leap onto a Marine who was struggling with another. It knocked him down and was tearing into his neck with its teeth as he screamed. Two other Marines rushed up to defend their compatriot. One grabbed the beast's hair and coat and pulled it bodily off, while the other used what appeared to be a small, spiked cudgel to strike it repeatedly in the head. The thing fell quickly under the blows.

Looking up, I could see the man in the distance, staring. The falling snow had picked up, but I could still make his features out. His face had a dark, twisted expression on it, an expression of demonic fury. I could see him starting to raise his hand again. Spying my long rifle in the snow nearby, where I had dropped it before the first thing had attacked, I snatched it up, cocked it, and took careful aim. With a brief prayer to the Almighty above that the powder was not wet from the snow, I squeezed the trigger. With a spray of sparks and a flash, I could see the man jerk as my bullet struck him. He looked down, touched his side, then looked up with a shocked face. The expression of shock suddenly turned to pure fury. He pointed at me and screamed something deep and guttural in no language I knew. The words made my blood freeze and chilled me unlike anything I'd ever encountered. There was a gust of windy snow temporarily obscuring the man, and when it passed, he was gone. I stared for a moment over the barrel of my rifle and was startled to feel a hand on me. Jerking away, I turned, rising my rifle to strike, then staying my hand as I saw the familiar face of my comrade, Lieutenant Turley.

He gently guided my hand down and said in a shaky voice, "I think that's the last of them, sir." He looked in the direction the man had vanished, and added, "I don't know who that was, but I believe we should leave this place."

Nodding, I lowered my rifle and turned. The Marines were prodding the bodies nearby, ensuring that the dead men were truly dead.

Spying Armistead kneeling over a body, I called to him, "Sergeant, tend to the men."

The big soldier stood and gestured down, and replied softly, "Lewis, sir."

I moved over to the body on the ground. The man's eyes stared sightlessly into the snow-filled sky, his throat a bloody ruin. His blonde hair had already begun to collect tiny flakes of snow. I removed my handkerchief and gently draped it over the wound. I knelt, removed my tricorn and rested a hand on his chest, bowed my head, and prayed silently for his wife. Armistead and Haskins stood silently nearby. The Marines gathered respectfully a few steps back.

After a moment I stood and replaced my hat, and spoke somberly, "And now the Mighty Fourth are but three." Turning to Turley, I spoke, "Your men? I saw one fall."

The young officer pulled his eyes from the body on the ground and replied, "No injuries, sir."

Puzzled, I looked around at the Marines. One of them shrugged and held up a stiff leather ring, which appeared worn and tattered. I peered at it, and then realized that the collar the Marines habitually wore had absorbed the teeth of the creature, saving him from the fate poor Lewis had suffered.

Turley spoke, breaking the stunned silence, "Marines, reload and prepare to move. Riflemen, to the flanks." His voice was clear and confident. He turned to me and spoke in a low voice, "Sir, we must report to General Washington. I know not what we have found, but he needs to know."

Nodding my head, I replied, "I agree." Looking into the whirling snow again, I strained my eyes for the mysterious man.

Seeing where I was looking, Turley asked, "Sir, was that the devil?"

I shook my head firmly, "No. I hit him, and if we can hit him, we can kill him."

Turley seemed to consider this for a moment, then replied in a practical tone, "Well, we'd best get started then, sir."

With a last hard look into the snowstorm, I replied, "I couldn't agree more, Lieutenant. Let's go." We turned and began the slow, cold walk back to our mounts.

Origins

Chapter Three

"A Plea for Assistance"

November 22, 1777

My Dearest Abigail,

I write this letter in haste, as Gen. Washington has dispatched myself and several men to Philadelphia. While it is most unusual for men under arms to travel toward enemy territories, we travel under a flag of truce and carry a letter to the British commander, General Howe. After the events in the woods of several days previous, the details with which I will not trouble you, I am relieved to be moving out of the camp and into the city for some time. While I have not been to the great city of Philadelphia for some years, I do look forward to it, and seeing how that great city is withstanding the loathsome presence of the British and her soldiery. I shall make every effort to obtain some lace and other sundries, as I know it has been scarce back home, and shall send as much as I may reasonably obtain.

Origins

Alas, I must bid adieu, as I hear my lieutenants approaching. My deepest affections to the boys, and my eternal love to you.

Your loving Husband, Sean.

The early morning sun shone bright and cold, as I stepped out of the stone building that served as the Army headquarters. The wind was whipping, and all around the encampment, soldiers and followers scurried to keep out of the bitter bite of the wind. I made my way through the mud and snow to the stables, from whence we were to set off. Making my way inside, the warm, horse-scented darkness of the stable was a relief after the brilliant cold of the day outside. Seeing a lamp on a barrel nearby lighting a group of men, I made my way over and nodded.

One of the Marines, the burly sergeant by the name of Nelson, nodded amiably. "Sir. What says the general, then?" I recognized him as the man who had saved me from the creature the day before.

Removing my hat and loosening my scarf, I replied, "We ride today."

One of the other Marines nodded, as he'd expected this, and replied, "Figures, then. Heard from me mates that there's another set 'o sentries gone missin'. We going huntin' again, then?"

Lieutenant Turley's voice cut through the gloom, "As you were, Marines. Get the captain a cup."

A shape stepped out of the darkness and handed me a tin cup. "Here, sir. To warm yer belly." I gratefully took a sip, expecting coffee, and was startled to find it full of rum. After a surprised cough, I managed to down the rest of it in several bold swallows. There were several chuckles from the darkness as I did so.

I wiped my mouth, looked around the dim area at the faint faces, and spoke, "Here's the meat of it, lads. The general's sending us to Philadelphia."

There was a beat of silence, then a low voice growled from the darkness, "Th' city's crawlin' with bloody redcoats, and he's sending us into it?"

I held up a hand and replied calmly, "Let me finish. We're going in under a flag of truce to take a message to General Howe. What we saw threatens all decent men, and despite our differences with the English, we share common bonds and a common fate."

The burly sergeant looked at the Marines on either side of him before responding, "Sir...me and the lads. I don't know if ye wanta be taking us with ye." He gestured at a nearby man with a terribly scarred face. "Jenkins there was an East India Guard and left in ill repute." He pointed at two moustached men sitting nearby, cleaning their muskets quietly. "Johannes and Heinrich there were previously involuntary soldiers for England, and didn't leave the proper way, if you get my meaning." He pointed at another man. "Svenson there got his farm burned for giving water to a Patriot." His finger swept to another. "They think Linden there is a bloody pirate, and I'm wanted fer knocking a young English officer's head against a rail a few years back in a misunderstandin'."

He jerked his thumb at three other Marines in the darkness tending to the horses. "Those three were bailed outta' th' Walnut Street Jail fer drunkenness and aggressions against nature."

My curiosity piqued, I could not help but ask, "What sort of crimes against nature?"

The young man shyly replied, "I partook heavily of strong drink and struck an Englishman's horse with a fist in anger."

Suppressing a smile, I replied, "I see." Looking around for a moment, I stated in a clear voice, "Whatever your crimes against the Crown, they are not my concern. I concern myself with loyalty to these United Colonies, and to each other. We travel under a letter of protection from General Washington and will not be molested by the British."

There was another moment of silence as the men considered this, then the big sergeant spoke, "All right then. If we got your word, sir. What after we visit his lordship?"

With a smile, I replied, "Officially, all we are to do is to enter the city, speak with Lord Howe, and deliver General Washington's message."

With a crooked smile, Sergeant Nelson replied, "And unofficially?"

"Unofficially, our cause still has friends in the city. They may have information for us. We're to make contact and find out what we can." With a glance at Lieutenant Turley, I added, "With the exception of your officer, I believe you men all have practice evading British agents. That skill may come in handy quite soon."

The men nodded as they considered this, then a voice from the darkness asked, "Sir, what were those things?"

Handing the cup back to the Marine nearest me, I shook my head. "I do not know. Not for certain." I hesitated, considering what to tell them, then made a decision. "Lads, I'll not keep secrets from you. These things...I've encountered them before. Sit down." The men knelt or sat around me. I sat on a nearby barrel, undid my top coat button, and began to tell the tale. "Some twenty years ago, during the war with France and her Native allies, I was serving as a young militia officer. It was toward the end of the war, and we'd been tasked to relieve a detachment of beleaguered regulars up in New York, at Fort William Henry." I looked down at the ground, reliving the terrible memories of those days. After a moment, I started speaking again, "We'd been on the trail some three weeks, and were about a day's march from the fort when we found them."

In the dark someone stated in an accented voice, "The massacre."

With a nod, I agree wearily, "Aye. The massacre. We found the garrison where they'd fallen. The regulars tried to fight, to defend the families, but…they'd been slaughtered to the last man, woman, and child. We told people it was Indians, but…" I hesitated, then sighed and continued, "It wasn't. They hadn't been scalped, nor did their bodies bear wounds of weapons." I looked at the men, their eyes glinting in the dim lantern light. "They'd been torn apart with teeth and claws." Feeling my fury and horror from the sights long in my past, I continued, my voice firm, "We tracked them. After all, we were scouts and trackers—the best in the colonies. We were the famous Pennsylvania Riflemen! Two days later, we caught up to them."

The barn was silent, save the dim noises coming in from outside and the occasional breathy exhalation of the horses. After a moment, a voice asked, "What happened then, sir?"

"What happened then was that we found out that not everything in this world is explained by Man or God's laws. The creatures that had torn the garrison apart were no longer human, although they looked it. They had pale skin and black eyes and shrieked as they came at us." I looked down again, then said, "In our fury, we fell upon them with sword and tomahawk. Not a one was left intact, and we left their corpses in the forest as a warning." Now looking around the dim barn, I made eye contact with the hard-faced men around me, and said, "If this is what I think it is, we have bigger problems than the English, gentlemen."

Several hours later we rode in silence down the pike toward the city. The snow-covered countryside was deserted, with few people in sight. Occasional farmhouses dotted the gentle rolling hills, with the smoke from their chimneys noticeable in our nostrils. Ahead of us hung the haze of the city of Philadelphia, the smoke from the hundreds of stoves and furnaces making a column into the sky marking the great city's place in the world. The wind whipped, snapping our cloaks and cutting through our thin clothes. I pulled my overcoat tighter, grateful for the leather and wool lining Abigail had sewn into it back in the summer when I was last home. It had seemed overmuch at the time, but the winter had been colder and wetter than expected, and the coat had served me well.

"Captain," Lieutenant Turley's voice cut into my musings and I looked up. The young man moved his horse up next to me and nodded in the distance. The burly sergeant rode next to him. Sweeping my eyes up, I could see a rough wooden palisade, with the distinctive dark red coats of the British regulars atop it. A short way past the barricade stood a small cottage. A curl of smoke rose from the chimney.

I looked at Turley and nodded. "Time, Lieutenant."

The young man nodded briskly and spoke to the Marine sergeant, "Parley flag, Sergeant Armistead." The burly man reached behind him and produced a square of white linen. After a moment of work, he'd attached it to the barrel of his musket, then resting the butt of the weapon on his knee, nodded at Lieutenant Turley.

Turley turned back to me and said simply, "Ready, sir." I nudged my horse forward and advanced slowly toward the fortification.

As we moved toward the palisade, the soldier on the platform lowered his musket at us and called out clearly, "Halt! Identify yourselves!"

With a glance at the Marine lieutenant at my side, I commented jovially, "Well. Now we see if the arrangements came through!" I raised my voice and called out, "Captain Tillerson, Fourth Pennsylvania Rifles. We come as a special envoy of General Washington!"

The young soldier regarded us for a moment, then turned and said something to someone out of sight. He then turned back to face us, raised the musket so the barrel was aimed at the sky, and called again, "If you'll hold fast for a moment, sir."

I raised a hand to acknowledge the soldier and spoke aside to Lieutenant Turley, "Until we speak to General

Howe, I'd like to keep the men with us. The less time the British get to speak to them, the better, for several reasons."

Turley nodded thoughtfully, and replied, "I tend to agree, sir. That said, most of the men were mustered into the Marines here. They have contacts throughout the city. If the British grant us free run of the city, we can get a lot of information quickly."

I considered this, then replied, "Perhaps. Until we get a feel for what the nature of this task is, I'd prefer to keep the men close. For their protection, seeing as they're wanted by the Crown." I glanced at the young man again and asked, "May I ask how you came about such a crew of unsavory characters?"

With a shrug, the young man replied, "After we were authorized to begin recruiting by the War and Ordnance Board, Major Nicholas went looking for men who could fight and shoot." He grinned sheepishly. "He wasn't so particular about the other aspects of the men's lives. He said that if they 'stayed true to the colonies and maintained discipline while in ranks', they'd be treated as free men." Turning in his saddle to check on the ranks of mounted men a dozen paces behind us, he continued, "What he got were these men. Tough, disciplined, and ferocious, but most with a checkered past. All excellent marksmen, and experienced soldiers and sailors." He turned back forward and smiled faintly. "After the raid on Nassau, they were tested severely by British fire." He fell silent, then continued, "Now, after that little skirmish in the woods against…whatever those things were, I have no doubt of their skill or steadfastness in battle." With a serious look at me, he added, "There's few enough men in this world that would have kept their nerve, let alone engaged those unholy beasts at close quarters."

I nodded thoughtfully, watching two soldiers exit the cottage ahead of us. One came sprinting toward the palisade. The other mounted a horse and kicked his heels, taking the horse to a gallop, headed south toward the city. The young runner disappeared behind the palisade.

There was a moment of silence, then the man on the rampart called, "Captain Tillerson. You may advance, sir. The captain would like a word. You men may move to the cottage."

I raised my hand in acknowledgement and, clucking at my horse, moved forward, followed by Lieutenant Turley. Sergeant Nelson wheeled his horse around and could be heard giving orders to the men.

Passing the wooden palisade under the watchful eyes of the youthful soldiers, we saw waiting for us a young man in the brilliant red coat of an officer. Dismounting, I made my way over to the man. He was slender, fine of feature, and serious of expression, with his uniform immaculate and well-tailored; clearly a gentleman.

Stopping in front of the man, I removed my riding glove and saluted. "Sir. Captain Sean Tillerson, Fourth Pennsylvania Rifles, on special assignment from the Continental Army."

The young man gravely saluted in return and replied in a polite tone, "Sir. Captain John André of the 26th Foot. I'm General Howe's aide de camp. We've been expecting you, sir." He gestured toward the road. "I'd offer you tea, but we have orders from General Howe to proceed with utmost speed to Philadelphia. Events are occurring that we need to bring you up to date on."

I nodded and replaced my glove. "Very well, sir. Let us make haste."

The young man nodded and, turning to the horse that a soldier had brought up while we spoke, swung deftly up onto it. He motioned courteously to me, and tapping my horse forward, we started at a fast walk through the fields and woods ahead. Two British soldiers rode ahead of our little band, and another two behind.

Captain André gestured at the men apologetically. "I apologize for the lack of respect, sir. We have caught many men attempting to sneak into the city during our time here. Some of them rebels, some of them spies, some of them merely common criminals; all to a man bent on mischief. The general thought it best we escort you in so as to expedite your progress."

I nodded and responded, "A prudent precaution, Captain. No offense is taken." After a few moments of riding in silence, I queried, "May I ask if you are aware of the nature of our parley?"

The young man shook his head grimly. "I do not know the exact nature, as General Howe did not see fit to share his correspondence with me. I only know your specific task, after which you will meet with the general." He fell silent for a moment, then added, "It is my belief that the man in black and the…creatures…you encountered in the forest are the reason." I raised an eyebrow and regarded the young officer. He gave a sly look, then said with a smile, "We are neither blind nor stupid, despite the actions of some of the officers in this Army."

With a chuckle, I responded, "Oh, I'm aware, as is General Washington. That said, given the nature of how secret this was inside our own Army, I fear that we shall have to do some investigating upon our return."

Captain André replied, "Oh, there's no need. There's no secret source. General Washington and General Howe have been corresponding on the matter for some weeks. Your little encounter in the woods proved that these…'attacks'…are more than random. The man you saw has also been seen here in the city."

Astonished, I looked at the man, then asked, "Inside the city? But how did he cross the lines?"

With a tilt of his head André responded, "One question of many." He hesitated for a moment, then asked, "Tell me, sir. How are your men for arms?"

Still astonished at the knowledge that the man in the woods was known to both sides, I replied, "Enough. We have a three-day supply with ample shot and powder. Rifles for my men, muskets for the Marines, and blades and pistols aplenty."

"And your men? Battle tested?" He turned in his saddle to regard the Marines and the two remaining riflemen riding some twenty feet behind us.

"Aye. My Pennsylvania men have been on campaign since the beginning, and the Marines were at Nassau and Princeton." I added after a moment, "And that encounter in the woods." Ahead of us I could see the large column of smoke from the hundreds of fires in Philadelphia reaching into the crystal blue winter sky.

Gravely André replied, "Very good, sir. It may well be that we march to a fight. The Light Company of the Coldstream Guards have a warehouse on the docks surrounded."

Lieutenant Turley, having ridden up during the conversation, asked, "Pardon me for asking sir, but what will eight Marines and a few riflemen do where the mighty Coldstream Guards have failed?"

André glanced at the young lieutenant and replied in a friendly, paternal tone, "They are good men, Lieutenant, but the Scotsmen are deeply religious. Their blood turned to water after they'd lost the first seven men to the beasts. The rest fled, convinced they faced the demons of hell." The young Englishman shook his head sadly.

"Brave men who'd faced the worst the cannonades and musketry the French could throw at them, without flinching or breaking, turned tail and fled." He looked back at the Marine officer and added in a firm tone, "They're holding the perimeter, but cannot be counted on to enter again."

"Surely you have other men…"

André shrugged. "We do, but we'd prefer this be kept quiet. There are also…complicating factors. Factors that require discretion."

Raising an eyebrow, I asked, "Such as?"

The man looked at me for a long moment, then sighed and replied, "The warehouse the beasts are roaming in contains, amongst other things, two hundred and fifty barrels of gunpowder destined for New York." I could see the shock on Lieutenant Turley's face as this fact registered.

With a frown, I responded, "Well. That does complicate things, doesn't it?"

André replied, "It does, indeed." We fell into silence as we approached the city.

Chapter Four

"Gunpowder, Torches and Steel"

My dearest Abigail,

Someday, I will tell you the tale of these cursed events. I can't bring myself to tell you now for fear you will think me mad and my words nonsensical. I scarce believe it myself, and in the days since, I find myself questioning whether we saw what we saw, or if it was a terrible nightmare. I see the visions of the dead when I sleep. When I do wake, I find myself questioning my sanity, but then I see the eyes of the men alongside me, and know that if it be madness I suffer, I am not suffering alone. I see their haunted looks and know that they saw the madness and terror I witnessed in that warehouse, and the surreal events that followed. Nothing in these two long years of war has shaken me so. I know that, while we oppose the British, we now know there are far greater evils in this world. I must go now; I am being summoned. Give my best to the boys. I miss you all more than I can put into words…

As we made our way through Philadelphia, I couldn't help but notice the state of the citizens. They appeared thin and sullen. Most stared at our small column with dull eyes. Some eyed us with hard looks and a few jeers. Others merely regarded us coolly, as if assessing us as a threat. The streets were busy with people going about their business. Here and there could be seen the red coats of the British soldiers, their watchful eyes constantly scanning the crowds.

I spoke softly aside to the young British officer, "The citizenry seem disaffected. Has it been hard for them?" I watched two young boys make a rude gesture at us, then vanish into an alley. I added, "They seem angry at us."

Captain André nodded, eyeing the crowd cautiously. "Aye, it has. The citizens suffered greatly during the siege. The local monies are inflated; goods are scarce, and prices are high. Even the Loyalists who remain chafe under our soldiers patrolling the streets."

An anonymous male voice in the crowd cried out, "Go back to the woods, you savages!" Another voice yelled, "Oi! Where's your fur hats, you Royalist wags?" There was a brief cheer of support and a murmur of angry agreement from the throng of people.

I looked at André, who shrugged and replied, "The green coats make them think you're Queen's Rangers, like as not. We should not disabuse them of the notion. It may give you respite from the Loyalists."

With a dry tone, I replied, "And from the Patriots?"

With a wry smile, André replied, "There aren't many left in the city, but we'll try to get you out before they get word to their more…how shall I put this? Their more radical members."

Thinking about this, it suddenly came to me. "Ah. The Sons of Liberty."

"Precisely so, sir. They're mostly known to target loyal Englishmen, but aren't discriminating. If they suspect you're Queen's Rangers…" The young man shrugged and fell silent.

Cautiously watching the sullen crowd as we rode, I thought about this. After a moment, I asked, "I wasn't aware the Sons had a presence here. Have they been a problem?"

Shaking his head grimly, André replied, "Not as much now as in the early days. More than a few were tarred and feathered by Loyalist mobs or thrown in the Market Street Jail by the Tories as the rebel government fled. Others I have…located and arrested. It was a tumultuous several weeks before the city was calm. It took better than a regiment of regulars to regain order. Most of the Sons either fled with the government or went deep underground." He glanced at me and smiled humorlessly. "We're telling the people we have rebel spies pinned inside the warehouse. It's a convenient excuse to hold until we get the ruthless men of the 'Queen's Rangers' here to capture the 'rebel saboteurs'." I nodded, silently agreeing with the ruse. It seemed wise.

We turned a corner and came into view of the State House, with its distinctive red brick exterior marred by guards posted at each door. The distinctive red, white, and blue crosses of the Union Jack waved from the bell tower. I watched in silence as we rode. I could hear Lieutenant Turley muttering something inaudible under his breath.

André, seeing my gaze, spoke in a harder voice than before, "It's used now as a hospital for your countrymen. Each time we send a foraging party into the countryside, we take fire. They hide behind fences, rocks, and trees. Each turn in the road conceals another sharpshooter, and each stand of brush another line of concealed militia, ready to volley fire onto our men and flee. Those we capture we keep here, which many feel is far too good for them." He added as an afterthought, "We send the healthy to the prison ships, as is fitting of traitors to the Crown." He indicated the State House and added in a reproachful tone, "Civilized men would capitulate when their capital falls. Civilized men would also stand and fight."

Gently I rebuked the young officer, "Now, sir, that is an unfair accusation. We stand and fight. We fought at Bunker Hill, as well as Germantown and Brandywine. We stand when we must."

With a slight nod of his head, André replied, "Indeed they were, sir. I don't need to tell you how those turned out. Surely you can see the folly of this foolish war?"

Gravely I replied, "Were we afforded the rights and protections of every other Englishmen, I would agree.

But we are not, and the king has refused to listen to our grievances." I shook my head and indicated ahead of us. "There will be time for discussion of politics later, I assure you. This is our destination, I assume."

Ahead of us I could see a company of burly soldiers surrounding a stout brick building. Every third man was turned inward, facing the stout warehouse. All had muskets shouldered, with bayonets fixed. Outside the line of soldiers an angry crowd stood, hurling insults and snowballs at the soldiers, who stoically accepted the abuse.

Seeing our approach, the soldiers lowered their muskets and, using the tips of their bayonets, forced the angry crowd back to allow our small column through. Moving to the wall of the warehouse, I dismounted. Turning around, I saw two red-coated officers waiting. Upon seeing my companion, they saluted.

Dismounting, Captain André removed his glove and returned the salute, then turned to me. "Sir, may I present Captain MacCloud of the Third Company of the Coldstream Guards, and Lieutenant William Pitcairn of the Second Royal Marines."

Shaking the men's hands in turn, I replied, "Gentlemen. Captain Sean Tillerson, Fourth Pennsylvania Rifles. My lieutenant is Jonathan Turley of the Continental Marines." I hesitated for a moment, then closely regarding the Royal Marine, I asked, "Tell me, sir. Are you Major John Pitcairn's son?"

The young man nodded gravely. "I am, sir."

"Your father was a good man. It grieved us greatly when we learned he had fallen at Bunker Hill." I offered a hand again to the young man. "Please accept the deepest condolences on behalf of myself and the Pennsylvania Regiments."

The young Marine accepted my hand with a firm grip and replied curtly, "I thank you, sir."

The captain next to him spoke, his voice thick with the accent of his homeland in the Scottish Highlands, "Sir. Allow me to bring you up to date on the situation."

I nodded, took off my tricorn, and rubbed my head. I glanced at the sky, noting that it had clouded over again, the crystal blue winter sky now sleet grey and darkening fast. The wind was starting to pick up, biting through our clothing.

The Scotsman began to speak, in a firm, matter-of-fact tone, "Yesterday eve, a couple of the lads on patrol noticed some strange activity at this warehouse. Given the nature of the contents, and the risk of rebel sabotage, we'd been keeping a close watch on it." He gestured at the main door, a sturdy construction of oak and iron. I couldn't help but notice that it was barred from the outside, and the bars were chained together. All the high windows were boarded up and sturdily locked. I frowned at this and turned my attention back to the officer. He continued, "Our private soldiers reported seeing strange goings on. Green lights and screaming, and a wagon being loaded by unknown persons." The man scowled, and continued, "One of the soldiers ran for their corporal, and the other stayed to watch. When the corporal returned, the private soldier was gone, as was the wagon and the men loading it. The corporal took his man to investigate, believing that there was thieving in progress. They entered and were attacked." He glanced uneasily at the building. "The private soldier was knocked down and dragged screaming into the darkness. The corporal managed to make his way to the door, where he summoned help."

Lieutenant Pitcairn spoke, picking up the story where the Army officer had stopped, "I was detailed to respond to any sabotage or Rebel activities inside the city. We came flying with a dozen men." He glared at the building as if daring the bricks themselves to defy him, and continued, "Less than a dozen steps inside, we were attacked by…something. They looked like men but weren't. Their flesh was cold, and their eyes black as the pits of hell."

He looked back at me with hard eyes, and I felt a chill in my spine. I slowly nodded. "Aye. We know the creatures of which you speak."

I looked at Lieutenant Turley, who said somberly, "We encountered similar creatures ourselves, and also lost men."

Captain McCloud replied flatly, "We lost seven in a matter of seconds. Nearly the entire patrol, gone. The survivors pulled back, and we secured the entrance and called Lord Howe for assistance. By a twist of fate, here you are, less than a day later."

With a sidelong look at Captain André, I commented, "Perhaps not by fate. It seems our commanders are prepared for this." The young man nodded his head thoughtfully but said nothing.

Lieutenant Pitcairn spoke, the deep anger again coming through in his voice, "Very good, sir. Shall we proceed?"

"Indeed we shall, Lieutenant." I turned to the Marines and the two remaining riflemen. "Sergeant Armistead."

The big man turned and replied, "Yes, sir?"

"Prepare the men for action. Close quarters, no long firearms."

"Yes, sir." The sergeant turned to the Marines and began to issue orders in his customary coarse language. Satisfied that the Marines were preparing, I turned back to Lieutenant Pitcairn, who was loosing his saber in its scabbard.

I raised an eyebrow, and said, "Lieutenant, given the loss of your men, no one will fault you if sit this one out."

"And let a group of Rebel soldiers into a warehouse full of powder and war supplies? I think not, sir. We have our orders." The man paused, then added, "Additionally, I have a disagreement with these…things…that killed my men." He turned and, reaching over to a nearby horse, retrieved a finely made dagger. He unsheathed it, checked the blade, placed it back into the scabbard, and said firmly, "I'm coming in with you."

I nodded and replied, "I thank you, sir. Another blade will be much appreciated." I hesitated, then added, "We found, through misfortune, that the only way to stop the creatures is with a shot or blade to the head." I grimaced, remembering the feel of my blade entering the creature's chest and hearing its howls as it tried to pull me in closer to its teeth. I looked at the young man and stated firmly, "Keep that dagger close to hand, Lieutenant."

The young Marine nodded. I then turned to check on my men. They had stacked their muskets and drawn other weapons from their clothing. One bore a short club with iron spikes protruding from it. Another man had a series of forged iron rings that covered his knuckles, with short, sharp pieces of metal protruding like claws. The two Hessians each carried a saber, and a short, wicked-looking sword in their other hand. The remainder of the men were all variously armed with other brutish objects intended to be used in close quarters. Tomahawks, machetes, and frontier knives all supplemented the cutlasses each Marine carried. Sergeant Armistead had organized them into three groups: two groups of three men, one group of two. Every third man held a small, heavily shielded iron lantern.

The big sergeant spoke in his deep voice, "We'll move in groups. No men alone, and we watch each other's backs. Captain, you'll take this group." He gestured to the two Hessians and the quiet lad who'd been arrested for hitting an Englishman's horse. Armistead continued, quickly setting Lieutenant Turley with the second group, and himself into the third. Lieutenant Pitcairn watched silently, then came and stood by my side and asked simply, "Where shall you have me, sir?"

I considered this for a moment, then spoke to Sergeant Armistead, "Armistead, I'll have the lieutenant with you. He's a battle tested Marine, and his father…"

Armistead nodded, waving me to silence, "Aye. I knew his father. A good man, he was." He gestured to the small group. "We'd be honored, sir."

With a wordless nod, the British officer moved to the small group and unsheathed his sword. With a rapid glance at the men to satisfy myself they were ready, I checked the cock on the pistol tucked into my belt, then drew my saber.

Captain André gestured at the guards near the door, and the men began to work the chains off the massive door bars.

As they did, André said to me in a low tone, "Use utmost caution, sir. Finding the man in black is of the highest importance. He is the key to all of this." He paused and added, "If you find it impossible to take him alive, removing him as a threat will suffice." He gestured to the soldiers standing guard nearby. "I shall await your return, Captain."

I nodded to the man and turned to the massive doors, which were swinging open. Beyond them, the inky blackness of the warehouse waited. I hefted my saber and said firmly, "Follow me." Without hesitation, I strode into the darkness.

As I advanced, I could see there was no light but what was filtering in from outside the warehouse, from behind us and from the cracks in the boarded windows high above. Stacks of crates, boxes, and various other items shrouded in the darkness stretched toward the ceiling, leaving us in a narrow pathway. There was no sound, aside from our bootheels tapping on the worn floorboards. Another dozen paces in, and we came to a junction. The path stretched into the darkness off to our left and right.

From behind me I could hear Lieutenant Pitcairn whisper, "Careful, Captain. This is where they attacked us." I reached back and, taking a lantern from the nearest man, I swung the dim beam straight ahead. It revealed a very normal appearing pathway leading into the darkness among the various items. I then carefully moved the light to the left and right passages, then back to the front. Something caught my eye, and I knelt to examine the floor. In front of my boots was a large, dark stain, and the boards were very deeply scored, as if struck repeatedly by a sword or an axe.

I looked back up, right into the black eyes and pale face of one of the dead men. It shrieked and lunged at me, and then things began to happen very quickly. I swung the lantern at the beast, its heavy iron case cracking into the side of the thing's head. I could hear the sickening crunch as the jawbone broke, and it stumbled. This gave me time to deftly slide back and adjust my footing, and with a short, sharp thrust with my saber, I speared the beast through its left eye. It fell to its knees, then onto its face, twitching. Raising the light, I rapidly swung it in front of me, scanning for more. Hearing a commotion behind me, I whirled. As I did, I saw shadowy shapes leaping off the tops of the stacks of crates, shrieking as they fell onto the men below.

The next few moments were a confused, terrifying melee. The flashing of blades, the screams of the beasts, the wildly flickering lights of the stout iron lanterns, the hoarse shouting of the men, and the horrible, meaty noises of weapons striking flesh. The fighting was up close, savage, and in what felt like seconds, over. Silence once again descended on the warehouse.

I lowered my blade, raised the lamp, and called out in a steadier voice than I felt, "Lads, sound off."

In the dim, dancing light, the men called out, and Sergeant Armistead's voice came from the rear, "Two gone, sir. Haskins and Linden." I moved the line of men back. Haskin's body was wrapped around one of the beasts. Its teeth were wet with his lifeblood, and his arms were wrapped around it, his frontier knife dug deeply into the base of the creature's skull. I pulled the beast off of him and knelt and gently closed his eyes.

Lieutenant Pitcairn's voice came from next to me. His tone was somber. "Did you know him well?"

I nodded and replied distantly, "Aye. He mustered into the company in seventy-five with me. His farm adjoins mine. His wife makes a cherry cobbler that is talked about all the way to Lancastertown." I paused and added, "Her name is Sarah, and his boys are Jonathan, George, and William." I wiped my face with the back of my glove and stood, regarding the still body for a moment, then turned to the two lieutenants. Their faces were drawn and tense. As I started to speak, I realized I could see them both clearly. Perplexed, I stopped and looked around. I noticed a sickly green light coming from deeper in the warehouse.

Narrowing my eyes and pointing with my sword tip, I declared, "I don't know what that is, but it's claimed two of my men, and several from both of you. It's time to finish this. Gentlemen, if you will follow me." I turned and started firmly into the green-lit gloom.

As I advanced, the green light grew brighter, and I began to notice that the air was thick and it was hard to draw breath. It smelled of death and rotten things, mixed with the cloying, sickly-sweet smell of burned flesh. I coughed and paused to draw my scarf over my lower face. Satisfied that I could breathe, albeit with difficulty, I continued my advance. Taking several more steps, I could now see clearly. I turned a last corner and saw him. The man in black stood in front of a pile of something that looked…like human bodies. I stared, transfixed in horror, noticing that the pile of body parts contained heads, and they were moaning. Their eyes were opening and closing, and their jaws working. There were other parts, too, hands and feet, arms and legs, all moving slightly as if trying to escape. In horror, I jerked my eyes back to the man, who stood and smiled at me. The smile was cold and contained a deep darkness that, even if I were to live a thousand years, I'd not want to see again.

After a moment the thing spoke, its words liquid and flowing together. It felt like it was insinuating itself into my mind, and I was powerless to do anything, "Captain…we meet again." I could feel my sword start to sag, and my willpower starting to drain. I took a step forward, although I didn't wish to. "Yes…come closer…my old friend…" The hypnotic voice slithered into my ears and into my mind, and I found myself obeying again.

In my left ear I heard a voice as if from a thousand miles away, "Captain Tillerson! Sir!" Another voice shouted, "What are you doing, sir!" I took another step, transfixed, my sword tip dragging on the ground.

A third voice that sounded familiar, speaking in a loud voice. "Bugger this." There was a clicking, then the same voice again, "I'll see ye in hell, ye unholy bastard." There was a click, a brilliant flash, and then the body of the man in black twisted, and a large hole appeared on his left chest. I jerked as if shaken awake and snapped my head to the left. Sergeant Armistead stood beside me, lowering a smoking pistol and reaching for another from his waistcoat.

Regaining my wits, I reached to my waist and pulled my own pistol, thrusting it at the man in black's face. As I did, I saw a momentary look of terror on the creature's face. I pulled the trigger. Another flash, and the ball tore into the man's jaw, dropping him to the floor near the pile of flesh.

I could hear Armistead bellowing behind me, "Get him, lads!" The Marines surged past me with their weaponry in hand and surrounded the man in black, beating, stabbing, and hacking. After a few moments of savage strikes, the men began to step back, their chests heaving. Shoving a man aside, I looked at their handiwork. The man in black lay on the ground, a bloody mess. His head was stove in, a bloody unrecognizable ruin, one of his arms was severed, and his fine black garments were sticky with a dark, thick blood. The mountain of flesh quivered and moaned, and I looked up. Swallowing my horror, I realized the mountain was a large chair…no, a throne, comprised of living flesh. The moaning and screaming was getting louder, and the sourceless green light was starting to flicker.

Gasping to catch my breath, I glanced around. Nearby, I saw some of the kegs of powder. One was tipped on its side, the powder bags within spilling out. A shout drew my attention to the man on the floor again. As we watched in horror, the severed arm slowly started to pull itself toward the bruised and battered body. The crushed skull also began to push out, slowly reforming itself.

I could hear Lieutenant Turley shouting in my ear over the now deafening screams of the flesh-covered throne, "Sir, we have to get out of here!"

I nodded and gestured to the door. The light was now flashing, and the screaming overwhelmed our hearing. The Marines were moving past, heading for the exit. I could see the men flickering past me in snapshots of green light as the flashes illuminated them. I could see a burly figure in the flashes doing something; it was Sergeant Armistead. He had leaned over the now twitching body of the man in black on the floor and was shaking something over it, then turned and started to run. He grabbed my arm and bodily hauled me along. The walls flickered past as the green light flashes came faster and faster. A few seconds of sprinting later, and suddenly the door was ahead of us. From the dark to our rear came a blood-curdling, floor-shaking roar. Several shrieks like those of the dead men came from the dark to our sides. Armistead's grip on my arm grew tighter, and we flew toward the entrance and burst into the daylight.

Staggering, I tried to get my bearings, when someone shouted, "Marines! DOWN!!" I promptly threw myself onto my face in the freezing cold muck. I had never been so grateful for the disgusting, manure-filled frozen slush of a city street in my entire life. I lifted my head and saw the magnificent and terrible sight of three ranks of the Coldstream Guards formed up in a firing line.

The Scottish captain sang out, "First rank...FIRE!" There was a roar of musketry, a blast of white smoke, and the zipping of musket balls over my head. From behind us there was a chorus of terrible shrieking. The barrel-chested captain drew another breath. "Second rank...FIRE!" There was another roar of muskets and the zip of shot. I rolled onto my back and saw a dozen of the black-eyed creatures that looked like men at the door stagger as the musket balls rocked their bodies. As they staggered back, there was another bone-shaking roar from deep inside the building.

To my left I could hear Armistead snapping, "Lantern. Lantern! Now!" I looked over at him just as he took the iron chimney off one of our lanterns and carefully touched it to the ground. The bright sparks of burning gunpowder began to spit, and then moved away from us in a rapid line, following the trail of powder on the ground toward the door. I could see the empty, discarded powder bag on the ground nearby. The sergeant had left a trail of powder behind us as we fled.

The creatures had struggled to their feet and were screaming again. The Coldstream officer took a breath and bellowed, "Third rank...FIRE!" Again the roar of muskets came. The bright spot of burning powder disappeared into the black of the tunnel.

I paused a moment in shock, then I realized what was about to happen. I leapt to my feet and screamed, "Get back! The powder! THE POWDER!" I sprinted down the street, my head down and arms pumping. I could hear the ranks breaking behind me as the soldiers joined me and the Marines in our flight. Spying a watering trough, I dove behind it and covered my head. A few seconds later there was a peculiar feeling. It was not unlike the time my brother Benjamin had hit me in the head with a tree branch. I was spinning, then I tumbled, and ended up upside down in something soft and very cold, with my ears ringing. After a moment I struggled to roll over and spit out a mouthful of snow. Hearing another tooth-rattling explosion, I turned to see what was happening. The warehouse was engulfed in flames, with fire shooting out of the roof. The explosions of the powder barrels were throwing objects skyward, and there was ash and various bits of blasted and scorched equipment raining down. I could distantly hear the ringing of bells as the fire brigades were summoned.

Dazed, I sat up and looked around me. In the streets nearby were dozens of men. The red of the Coldstream Guards, the dark green of the Marines, mixed with civilian clothes here and there, all sitting up and looking stunned.

Suddenly there was another roar from the inferno, and then a green streak shot skyward from the fireball, arcing up toward the Delaware riverfront and out of sight.

I yelled, my words incomprehensible even to myself, and pointed. Nearby, a man caked in mud who vaguely resembled Lieutenant Turley yelled something back. Seeing the faint green smoke trail disappear, I collapsed back into the mud, exhausted. After a moment, the tremendous ringing in my ears had faded and, hearing someone move next to me, I raised my head. Standing above me I saw Lieutenant Pitcairn, his once pristine scarlet coat covered in mud and soot. He sat down, dazed. After a moment, he spoke, his words thick and slurred, "Did we get it?"

Closing my eyes, I replied wearily, "I don't think so, but I think we taught it a hard lesson."

"Shit," the young man observed. I couldn't help but laugh. After a moment, he asked, "What do we do now?" I struggled to a sitting position and watched the Philadelphia Fire Brigade starting to form a bucket chain to prevent the roaring flames from spreading.

I responded honestly, "I have no idea. I do think I need to talk to General Howe, though." After a moment, I added, "Washington, too, if Howe doesn't throw us in jail for blowing up his warehouse." The young lieutenant didn't respond, merely watched the scene unfolding in front of us in silence.

Origins

Chapter Five

"Under a Scarlet Flag"

My dearest Abigail,

My time in Philadelphia is drawing to a close. I am to be assigned to a particular unit with a particular task that I am not at liberty to discuss. We will no longer take part in the active fighting, which I know will be of great relief to you. While I regret that I am no longer able to join my countrymen on the field of battle, what I am doing is of great importance. Indeed, the safety and security of our fledgling nation depends upon it. I have enclosed some lace and some spices that I acquired from a young gentleman here in Philadelphia by the name of John André. He is a good man, even if he wears scarlet. He has invited us to dine with him after the war, regardless of the outcome. He is a fine fellow, and much admired here in the city.

I am due to depart with my men from Philadelphia within the day. We will be returning to Valley Forge and rejoining the Army, at least temporarily. I pray that you will forgive my words of the last letter. When I wrote, I was most distressed about the events I had witnessed. Someday, perhaps I shall tell you of them.

In the meantime, I intend to ask Gen. Washington for a month's leave to come home and see you and the boys before starting off on my next task, which may take me away for many months…

With an icy look, Lord General Howe began to speak in a hard, unforgiving tone, "One hundred thousand sovereigns. That's the total value of what was in that warehouse, Captain. Cannon. Spare rigging. Powder. Field tentage. Thirteen hundred brand new muskets, all of it destined for the Northern Force." He glared at me, his anger palpable. "I do hope you are aware that I shall ask General Washington and your precious 'Continental Congress' to assist us in recouping the cost." He held the glare for a moment before sighing, then shaking his head and continuing, "If I hadn't seen it myself, I wouldn't have believed it, and if I didn't have multiple eyewitness reports from loyal men, I'd have you hung as a saboteur." He looked at me with his piercing eyes and continued, "That being said, General Washington and I have been in communication. He suggests that, for the duration of the war, we work together to seek out and neutralize these unholy threats to our civilization." He looked down at his desk, picked up a piece of paper, and scowled at it.

After a moment of silence, I asked, "Am I to be tried?"

With a sour look, Lord Howe replied, "On the contrary. You're to be promoted to major and placed in command of a provisional unit. It will be a special detachment of men, selected from each side, to hunt down and eradicate these unholy threats."

I breathed a sigh of relief. When I had been summoned before Lord Howe, I had feared the worst. After a moment of considering his statement, I replied, "May I make a suggestion? Make the teams of Marines, both Royal and Continental. They're a hardy sort of man; rough, but reliable in battle. Less prone to panic than regiments of the line, and comfortable in close quarters combat." I hesitated, then added, "I'd offer my frontiersmen, but it seems I'm the last left from my brigade." Lord Howe's icy look softened at this. After a brief pause, I added, "I'd also request that young Captain André to be part of the team. He is an exceedingly bright young man. I see a lot of potential in him." I fell silent.

General Howe looked up from the paper at this statement and regarded me for a moment, then spoke thoughtfully, "A good suggestion, Captain, given the nature of this force." He set the paper down and added, "As for Captain André, I agree as to his potential, but request denied. I have other plans for him. Lieutenant Pitcairn will be available for you, though."

He put the pen back in the inkwell and stood. He turned and took several steps to the window, and stood with his hands clasped behind his back, regarding the busy street below and the docks in the distance. He was quiet for a moment, then said in a thoughtful tone, "We'll need something to identify this new unit. It will need to be distinctive. Something that will be readily recognizable, by officers on both sides, through the chaos of battle."

He turned back to where I sat and regarded me for a moment, then declared, "I believe I have just the thing." He motioned to the young soldier sitting quietly at the desk near the door. "Orderly, go to my private study. On the wall is the flag my brother brought back from the Orient. Go get it." The young man snapped to attention, then hurriedly scurried out the door.

The general regarded me again for a moment, then said in a hard voice, "It must be understood, Captain, that any misuse of this emblem as a tool of subterfuge will be considered a grievous offense to the Crown."

I nodded courteously and replied, "Of course, sir. I will make it clear to General Washington."

With a dark look at me, the general replied, "I'm not concerned about Washington. As misguided as he is in his politics, he is a man of honor." His dark look continued and he added, "I was referring to you."

Tilting my head, I replied, "General, I must protest. I have acquitted myself with nothing but the most honorable of actions, both in our dealings here in Philadelphia, and on the field of battle."

With a frown, the regal officer replied, "You have, but I know your reputation from the Wars against the French. You have a reputation for trickery."

With a wry smile I replied, "Against the French, sir, that is the only way to fight. Treachery, at least, is a language they understand."

With a grunt, he nodded. "On that, at least, we agree. Nonetheless, no trickery with this heraldry, or you will assuredly hang by the neck until you are dead."

"I would expect nothing less, sir. You have my word of honor, as an officer and a gentleman, that this symbol will be respected and used only in times of utmost need."

There came a rapping at the door. With an icy look at me, the general spoke loudly, "Enter!"

The young soldier, his face red from exertion, entered the room with a folded piece of red cloth in his arms. He moved toward the large table at the side of the room. As he did, General Howe gestured for him to spread it out.

Curious, I stood and moved closer to the table for a better view. As the orderly spread it out on the table, the beauty of the flag struck me. Comprised of a fine material that appeared to be silk, it was a deep scarlet in color. In the middle of the field of scarlet was a hand-stitched dragon that appeared to be of Chinese origin. The thread shone as brightly as true gold, and the scarlet was the purest color I had ever seen.

Seeing my awed expression, General Howe stated, "I received this from my brother Thomas upon his return from his first trip to the Orient." He gestured at the dragon in the middle. "He got it from a deposed Chinese warlord, who claimed to be the descendant of a clan of demon fighters since the early ages of China." With a dry note in his voice, he added, "At the time I received this flag, it seemed a fanciful story, made up by savages. Now it seems strangely appropriate, and somehow fitting, that this flag fly once again in pursuit of the unnatural."

Staring at the scarlet and gold emblem, I replied slowly, "Indeed it does, sir...indeed it does."

Three days later I arrived at the tavern that served as General Washington's headquarters. Presenting myself inside, I reflected on the events of the past week. So lost in thought was I that the orderly had to touch my shoulder to gain my attention. I stood and said to the man, "My apologies, Private."

"If you'll follow me, sir." The young man quickly showed me to the same room where I'd met the general before. Stepping inside, I came to attention, saluted, and reported, "Sir. Captain Sean Tillerson of the Fourth Pennsylvania Rifles."

The general, sitting behind his desk, rose as I entered. Another man sitting in front of the general's desk also rose. A tall man myself, I was startled to see how massive the man was, broad of shoulder and belly, and with a pleasant face. A third man stood by the window his hands clasped behind his back.

General Washington extended a hand, indicating I should sit, and said, "Major Tillerson, this is Colonel Knox, one of our leading artillerists. Colonel, this is the Pennsylvania man I was speaking of earlier." Washington gestured to the man standing by the window. He had a youthful, honest face, and wore the uniform of a dragoon. Washington added, "This is Major Benjamin Tallmadge. He's my chief of Intelligence." The young man nodded in a courteous manner.

Colonel Knox reached for my hand, enveloped it in his massive grip, shook it with a crushing strength, and said politely, "The general was telling me all about how your men held the line at Germantown, sir. Very well done."

"Thank you, Colonel." I took my seat and added, "We took fearsome losses, I'm afraid."

At this, General Washington replied, "Indeed, your men suffered, and those who remained suffered more in the trials that followed. That's why we're here, to that end." He gestured at Knox and continued, "Colonel Knox is one of my most trusted advisors. He'll be tasked with the provisioning and oversight of this new force. He reports directly to me." Washington gestured at the Intelligence officer standing at the window. "Major Talmadge will collect intelligence and provide your targets."

Origins

The tall general sat down, as did Colonel Knox. Washington then steepled his fingers and regarded me over them for a long moment. After a time during which the only sound was the ticking of the clock, he spoke, "I'll not ask if the explosion in the warehouse was accidental. You said it was, and I'll take you at your word."

Knox laughed heartily. "A jolly good show, that, accident or not! Our sources in the city said the fire spread to a nearby third-rate ship of the line and damaged two frigates. The HMS Somerset is apparently out of the fight for months for a refit!"

With a stern look at Knox, Washington continued, "Captain, you say that you believe the…creature…escaped? Why do you believe this?"

I thought for a moment, then replied, "I don't know for sure. I strongly suspect, and I fear it did." I then relayed how I had seen the fiend healing, and the peculiar streak of smoke shooting out of the fireball.

When I had finished my tale, Washington and Knox exchanged a glance, then Washington said gravely, "Well done, Major. I fear we have another task for you." He looked at the young Intelligence officer by the window.

The young man cleared his throat and began to speak in a polite, cultured tone, "Sirs. It has recently been reported that our troops up north near Fort Ticonderoga have been reporting strange events in Lake Champlain.

Apparently something is attacking our patrol boats. We've lost three this past month."

With a half-smile, I replied, "Not, I assume, our friends in red?"

With a serious expression, Talmadge responded, "No, sir. Apparently these attacks consist of something crawling out of the lake and over the gunnel of the patrol boats and slaughtering the crews, or dragging them screaming into the icy waters of the lake." He added distastefully, "Apparently they are described as eyes, teeth, tentacles and claws, and with a shriek like something from Dante's Inferno."

I nodded thoughtfully and replied, "It'd be unfortunate for them if they tried that on a patrol boat filled with Marines with loaded muskets and cutlasses at the ready."

"Precisely so, sir." The young man picked up a leather-bound packet of papers, stepped forward, and handed them to me. "Your orders, maps, and local support teams." He gestured at Colonel Knox. "The colonel has notified all commands to be on the lookout for your heraldry."

"When do I leave?" I asked, fearing I knew the answer.

Washington replied, "As soon as your men are reprovisioned." He looked down at his desk for a moment, then said, "It will be necessary to have your men travel by way of Trenton, where you will meet with your British counterparts. From there you travel north under the scarlet flag." He paused, then said in a somber voice, "I wish you luck and pray for the strength of the Almighty to guide your path and protect you." He stood and said in a firm tone, "God protect you, Major Tillerson."

I stood, returned the salute, and replied, "God and the United States Marine Infantry, sir." I turned and exited into the ever-present bite of the winter wind.

Epilogue

Major Sean Tillerson went on to lead a combined force of Royal and Continental Marines for the duration of the American Revolution. While he never again fired a shot in anger at the English, he and his team were responsible for the location and elimination of multiple supernatural threats throughout the war. Sadly, the records of this unit have long since been lost, with the bulk of the official documentation being destroyed when the Library of Congress was burned by the British in 1814. The detachment of Marines he led would eventually evolve into the Joint Task Force for Supernatural Defense we know as JTF 13. Major Tillerson retired after the war and moved back to rural Pennsylvania to his estate, where his family lives to this day. He died of advanced age in 1826, and is buried in the Mount Pleasant Presbyterian Church Cemetery, Mount Pleasant, Pennsylvania.

Lieutenant William Turley stayed in the Marines and was one of the first United States Marine Corps officers to lead Marines on foreign soil when they landed in Tripoli in 1806. He was killed in action in 1816 against the British at the Battle of Bladensburg, leading the Marines in the desperate rearguard defense of

Origins

Washington DC. He is interred in his family cemetery in Boston, Mass.

Sergeant Jonathan Armistead took his discharge after the war and returned to Lancastertown, Pennsylvania, where he was lost to history.

Lieutenant William Pitcairn continued his service to the Crown and served a long and distinguished career in the Royal Marines, reaching the rank of lieutenant colonel. He eventually returned to England and served an additional twenty years as a Member of Parliament. While in Parliament, he was instrumental in creating the Royal Marine Special Force, which eventually became known as 13 Marine Commando—the Crown's equivalent to Joint Task Force 13. He was knighted by Queen Victoria as a Knight of the Order of St. Michael and St. George in 1850. He died of advanced age in 1853, and is buried on his family estate on the Isle of Shelley, England.

Major John André was promoted to chief of Intelligence for the Royal Army in the Colonies. He was caught behind the American lines on a mission to retrieve the American traitor Benedict Arnold, and after a short trial, was hung as a spy by the Continental Army on October 2, 1780. He is interred in Westminster Abbey as a Hero of the Realm. He was 30 years old.

Origins

Lucas Marcum is a Neurological Critical Care Nurse Practitioner in a busy Pennsylvania trauma center and an officer in the US Army Reserve. He is the author of the best selling "Valkyrie" novel, about a medevac unit saving lives in a brutal 23rd century conflict. His work can be found here on Amazon.

Run Through the Jungle

L.A. Behm II

You ain't going to believe this, but…

Officially we were at Khe Sanh Combat Base collecting local intel on the NVA operating in the no go zone of the DMZ. Unofficially, Colonel Conrad had sent my company up here because there were rumors of strange things—well, stranger than normal—in the jungle. Naturally, you can't walk up to the commanding officer of 1/1 Marines and say, 'Sir, heard there were some monsters running through the jungle. We're here to help!' so I was laying in the VIP bunker reading Hell in a Very Small Place before turning in when Master Guns Huggins came around the grenade wall.

"Major, the OP out on Hill 558 has got a 'weird one'," Master Guns said, shaking his head at my choice of reading material.

"Weird, how?"

"Local came running into the OP just before dusk, covered in blood and babbling. Lucky for him he was also waving one of those Chieu Hoi safe conduct leaflets; otherwise, the boys up at 558 probably would have greased him. The LT in charge of the OP doesn't have the force to go outside the wire and investigate, so he kicked things upstairs."

"Dusk was a couple hours ago, Master Guns," I replied, tucking Fall's book into my rucksack.

"Yes, sir. Bit of a problem with translation—they medevac'd the guy who's supposed to be translating at 558 out of here this morning with a case of the shits," Huggins replied, handing me my flak jacket from where it was hanging over the back of a chair. "Took time for things to work through the intel guys with 3/26 H&S."

"And you found out…"

"I was waiting to use the radio to make a call, sir. I went through basic with the master sergeant in charge of 3/26's intel unit. It wasn't Lieutenant von Rhor's fault, Major."

"I'll take your word for it, Master Guns. I take it you offered the services of the amazing Nguyen Brothers to the lieutenant?"

The Nguyens were a pair of Kit Carson Scouts attached to my company. Unlike most of my boys, who had volunteered for MAC-V (SU-13) without seeing anything, the Nguyens had seen 'things' before defecting to the South. Huynh told me after they became my translators that watching a political officer get his head bitten off by a snake eating cow had been amusing, but it was also a sign they needed to head south.

"Yes, sir."

"We going to him, or are they bringing him to us?" I said, grabbing my Ithaca shotgun.

"Resupply convoy rolled out to the OP's two hours ago, sir," Huggins said, glancing at his watch. "They should be back in the wire with the prisoner in ten minutes. Which gives us enough time to get to the H&S intel shack."

I dropped my steel pot on my head at a jaunty angle. "Lay on, Macduff."

* * * * *

Calling the bunker where 3/26 had their intel operation a shack was an insult to shacks everywhere. At least it wasn't the rainy season. Someone had attempted to raise the level of the floor in the bunker with pallets and plywood. Since the engineers had built the bunker by the book, that meant anyone over about five eight had to walk hunched over. Even with all that, it was out of the elements, and a relatively quiet place to question someone.

By my government issue Timex, it took eleven minutes to walk from the VIP hooch to the intel shack. The Nguyen brothers were inside, waiting to start questioning the local.

"Major Miller?" a voice called from the darkness.

"Yes?"

"Over here, sir."

I followed the voice to the bunker. Leaning against the sandbags was a skinny kid in salty boots and threadbare utilities.

"Lieutenant von Rhor, sir. I run the intel section here. Sorry it took so long to notify you about the situation, sir."

"No problem, Lieutenant. We found out about it, and that's all that really matters."

"Yes, sir. Prisoner should be here from the motor pool at any minute. They were delayed by enemy action," von Rhor said, pulling a pack of Marlboros from his helmet and offering me one.

I took one, lighting it, and waited for the guest of honor to arrive.

"Oh, Lieutenant, one more thing."

"Sir?"

"Anything you hear is top secret."

"Yes, sir," von Rhor replied with a gulp.

I hate sounding like a bad movie, but most days there isn't a better option. Odds were that an NVA patrol had slaughtered the village for reasons only known to their political officer, but better safe than sorry was MAC-V (SU-13)'s unofficial motto. Last time I checked, the official one is still classified. Sad thing was, von Rhor probably handled Top Secret information every day. I'd just made things special in his mind, and therefore more memorable. However, rules is rules. Not that anyone would believe him if he talked, but I'd hate to see his career go down the hole because he'd told the wrong 'No shit there I was' story in the wrong bar.

I'd smoked that cigarette and offered von Rhor one of my Camel non-filters before the local came up, walking between two Marines from Motor-T and looking like he was going to lose control of his bowels at any minute. I took him from the Marines and escorted him into the bunker.

He started babbling as soon as he saw the Nguyens. The Nguyens had a routine for situations like this—Huynh, the older brother, would start talking to the local, trying languages until he hit on one they had in common. Minh would come stand next to me and offer a running translation. It took a while for Huynh to find a language in common. Huynh took the babbling local over and ensconced him in a chair while they were trying to find a common language. After about ten minutes of back and forth, Minh started a running translation.

"He's from a village about twenty klicks north of here," Minh said.

"That's just this side of the DMZ," Master Guns supplied.

Huynh and the villager talked, and the team corpsman moved over and started checking over the local—after Huynh explained that Doc wasn't going to steal his soul or work any magic on him. The villager still gave Doc the hairy eyeball while trying to explain to Huynh what happened.

Origins

Huynh came over and conferred with Minh, and then they both went over and spoke with the villager.

"Major," Huynh said, coming to where I stood, "you gotta understand, this guy's a farmer by day and running supplies to the VC and intel to the NVA by night."

"Figured that."

"He's also got less education than a Tokay gecko, so what he's feeding us might be a line of shit." Huynh shrugged.

"Right."

"So anyway, he's one of the Nung who moved south when the French left in 1954. They settled here by the DMZ, probably so they could inform for the North. Problem is, the tribe that was here wasn't real happy to be displaced, and the Nung village reported the usual atrocities, including cannibalism."

I looked at Huynh. "Really?"

"Yes, sir," he replied, looking over his shoulder at the local. "The original tribe probably didn't really eat the commie bastards, but you know how those stories get around. So about 1960 or so, the Provincial Governor got the right level of bribe, or finally got tired of the complaints, and decided to clear out the 'bastards with the filed teeth', and sent in an expedition. The expedition moved through all the villages out in the jungle north of Khe Sanh, ate all the rice, and molested all the women…."

"We've heard that one before."

Huynh grinned. "Yes, sir, we have. But he also says the expedition drove off the cannibals and left them in peace for a while."

"Uh huh. I'm betting the NVA drove off the 'cannibals'," I replied, pulling out a smoke and offering Huynh one.

We lit up before he continued.

"Yes, sir. Probably elements of the NVA 304th Division, from what he's let slip," Huynh said, taking a deep drag from his cigarette. "But that leads us to today."

I took out a notebook. Before we did anything, I'd have to radio Saigon for permission, and notes would be important.

"What happened?"

"Charlie here"—Huynh hooked a thumb at the villager—"claims he was out in the jungle hunting. He was probably burying a weapons cache or supplies for units moving down the Ho Chi Minh Trail." Huynh paused and delicately removed a piece of tobacco from his tongue. "From the way most of these villages operate, he may have been trying to figure out how to get a better price for his wife. Anyway, he says he heard gunfire from the direction of the village. His first thought was the Americans were there killing everyone, so he hid."

"Much as I hate to say it, it's a sensible approach."

"He did let slip that the gunfire didn't sound American. He says it was more grouped single shots than the usual American burst fire."

"Interesting."

"Yes, sir. Discounting the usual North Vietnamese propaganda, Charlie here says the gunfire died down and he was able to sneak back into the village." Huynh raised a foot and butted out the smoke on the sole of his boot before continuing, "This is where it gets weird, sir."

"Okay."

The villager interrupted Huynh. Huynh replied.

"He keeps saying we might be able to save them if we get there now, sir," Huynh said with a Gallic shrug.

"Save them from what?"

"The cannibals are back from the dead, Major."

It took about an hour to get permission to roll out the gate—I got Colonel Conrad on the radio down in Saigon, and he cut orders so 1/1 would let us go wandering through the jungle. Command started producing Tiffany cufflinks anytime anyone mentioned going anywhere near the DMZ or Laos—even though the NVA had thirty thousand troops in the area, making 'Demilitarized' a bad joke, and Northern Laos might as well be Western North Viet Nam. We'd driven north until the road petered out, leaving Second Platoon with the trucks, while First and Third had mounted shanks mare for a lovely nighttime walk through the jungle. Charlie, with

wondering how I was going to convince the
to let us follow the zombies north into the DMZ.
n brought the radio over as a flamethrower
l to life.

Jackal is on the horn for you," he said, handing
handset.

al, Hammer. Send it."

n't picked my call sign. The colonel did that
lly.

t's the situation?" Colonel Conrad had never lost
wl he'd learned growing up in the middle of
e, South Carolina, before his appointment to the
Academy. I could hear the beat of rotors behind
e.

inite Code Grey, Jackal. I'm bringing back
s for analysis and disposing of the remainder per
d operating procedure."

er that, Hammer. I'll be at your location in three
copy?"

y, Jackal. We should be back on site in five." It'd
ly be closer to four, but it never hurt to give
lf a bit more time when moving through the

e end, it was closer to six—Charlie decided he
didn't want to go into a prison camp in the south,
made a break for it, and a Marine shot him for his
es. We humped him back out to the road, and then

Huynh translating, led us to his village—it was a small
place, no more than a few hooches with some straggling
fields losing a fight against the encroaching jungle a
couple of clicks south of the DMZ. Just the kind of place
Victor Charlie and Uncle Ho liked—right near the
Laotian border, and close enough to the Ho Chi Minh
Trail that the villagers did a brisk business with units
passing down the trail.

Somewhere I could hear music playing. A few
unhealthy-looking chickens scratched at the dirt or tried
to catch the flies that rose in clouds from the drying pools
of blood. The sonorous droning of the flies almost
drowned out the music; this was going to be a bad one.

"Notice anything, Major?"

"Master Guns, I've got all the major signs of
something going down—blood and a lot of spent brass,
mostly from the MAS-36s the ARVN fobbed off on the
local militia," I replied, digging through a pile of brass.
"Although this is interesting."

'This' was a handful of cartridges, bright green with
verdigris.

"Let me see one," Master Guns Huggins said, holding
out a hand.

I tossed one of the cartridges over.

"Been abused," he said, turning the cartridge over in
his hand. "Primer never fired."

I checked the primers on the rest of the ammo—every round had the telltale dent of a firing pin strike into a bad primer.

"I think its Japanese ammo sir," Huggins said, tossing the round back.

"I think it's been buried in the damn jungle for twenty years if that's the case," I replied, dropping the rounds.

"Major? We found a cache over here," Private Lilly called from a hooch. "There's a couple of bodies."

"On the way," I shot back, rising from a crouch. "Master Guns?"

"Yes, sir," he replied, leading the way to where Lilly stood.

From one of the thatch roofed hooches I heard the new AFN DJ, Pat something, give the traditional morning greeting, "Good Morning, Vietnam!"

"They're getting AFN all the way up here?"

"Probably picking up the repeater over at Khe Sanh. We haven't found the radio yet, Major, it's in one of the hooches we haven't searched yet," Master Guns replied, working a hand under his chicken vest.

One of the bodies was a half-naked kid, not more than about ten. Whatever had killed him had ripped his throat out, nearly decapitating him. The other one was…interesting. Not in a good way.

To begin with, it was still twitching. The eyes tracked me as I walked over and squatted down in front of the skull, which was about three feet from the torso.

"Master Guns! Get on the blo Grey," I said, looking at the secon

"Roger."

The second body was in pieces black and shiny with varnish. Altho moving, there was enough to tell it time before someone had put it to pieces. The rusted machete sticking bit of a macabre touch, in my opini

Huynh brought Charlie over. Cha kid to the body and started babbling

"Major, he says that that," Hu dismembered body, "is one of the de

"Zombie," I replied.

"Yes, sir. Charlie also sa these…zombies make the survivors bodies and carry them to the north."

I sighed. I hate paperwork, and the to require a lot of paperwork.

"Major, Saigon replies 'Roger' and next communication," Master Guns s

I fished through the pockets on the to a set of dog tags, with Japanese ch before rising and looking at the villag

"Master Guns, you know the c samples of everything, serial num weapons, batch numbers off the am thing, pile the bodies in a hooch, and Zi

drove back to the combat base, where the colonel was waiting.

He'd pulled out all the bells and whistles—somewhere he'd acquired a pair of mobile command posts that fit under the CH-54 Tarhe, and the aircraft and flight crews to move them. Engineers were crawling all over both command posts, sandbagging them in place between the runway and taxiway, and the Tarhes with escort were clawing back into the air when we rolled through the gate.

"Master Guns, get with the platoon leaders and tell them to be ready to roll north again in twenty four hours," I said, taking the bag of special samples and photos—the usual stuff, letters from home, copies of Uncle Ho's writings, serial numbers off of weapons—Lt. Fox, third platoon leader, would turn over to the intel shop here. I turned to Lilly, who was driving the Jeep. "Let's go."

We drove to the flight line, where we stopped and checked the Jeep for loose objects that might fall off on the flight line, and then drove down the taxiway to the colonel's impromptu command post.

Master Gunnery Sergeant Lee, who'd been with the colonel since Conrad was a lieutenant and Lee a PFC driver, was waiting outside one of the command posts, the butt of a thick, black cigar firmly anchored in the corner of his mouth.

He removed the cigar and examined it before speaking.

"Major. Five hours, huh? Huggins must not be keeping as close an eye on you these days."

"Not his fault, Master Guns. Prisoner decided that being eaten by a tiger in the jungle was preferable to spending the next year in a cage."

Master Guns tossed the cigar butt and took another cigar out of his utilities.

"Got a light, sir?"

I handed him the Zippo I carried.

"Still carrying this thing, sir?" Lee asked, looking at the 82nd Airborne patch on the lighter before lighting his cigar.

"It kept dad alive when he fought trolls in Europe," I replied when he handed it back. "It works for me."

"There's some sort of blasphemy there, a Marine depending on luck from the Airborne," Lee replied. "Colonel should be ready for you, sir."

Lee opened the door into the command building. I ducked through the hatch, and Lee followed, closing the door behind him.

"Major, good to see you," Colonel Conrad drawled from the far end of the CP. This pod was a briefing room—a long table and all the needs of modern briefing, including film projectors.

"Colonel. Sorry for the delay. Our source decided to run off," I replied with a shrug.

"You called Code Grey?"

"Yes, sir," I said, setting the sample bag down on the conference table. I pulled a smaller bag out and set it on the table, where the hand inside crawled out.

"Colonel, it's been a while since we did field work, but I'd say that's affirmative on it being a Code Grey," Lee said with a chuckle.

"That the only one you found?" Conrad said, ignoring Lee.

"Yes, sir. There was a kid there; something ripped his throat out. We consigned him to the fire just to be on the safe side."

The hand continued to crawl toward the edge of the table. Lee pinned it in place with a KA-BAR.

"No such thing as zombies, Major," Colonel Conrad said. "Outside Haiti, anyway."

"What would you call a reanimated Japanese soldier, then?" I asked, tossing the dog tags on the tabletop.

"Daemon-possessed and animated, Major," came a voice from the entry hatch.

"Ah, Father Trahn. Your timing is perfect, as usual," Conrad said.

Standing in the hatch was a small figure wearing the old Marine camouflage trousers with a black priest's shirt and collar on top.

"Major Miller, Father Trahn, formerly of the South Vietnamese Marines," Colonel Conrad said. "Father Trahn, Major Miller."

"Father Trahn."

Trahn waved a hand at the introduction, walking around the table to where the hand writhed, trying to get loose from the knife pinning it like a butterfly to the table. He pulled a prayer book out and paged through it, finally settling on a page and reading from it. The hand shivered and smoke poured from it briefly. As Trahn finished the prayer, the hand curled in final rictus, then the desiccated meat of it dissolved in a puff of dust, the bones rattling on the tabletop.

"Yes. Daemonic possession is indicated," Father Trahn said.

"You know this how?" I asked.

"Major, Captain Trahn is in charge of a specialist unit in the ARVN," Conrad said.

Specialist units in the ARVN ran the gamut from very good to places for wealthy scions of the better families of South Vietnam to hide from actual combat service because they were off 'training' in the States.

"You'll like these guys, Major," Master Guns Lee said. "Tho san ma."

"Ghost Hunters?" I asked. I'm crap with languages, but there's some things you pick up.

"Yes, sir," Trahn replied. "Colonel Conrad suggested I form the unit as a counterpoint to yours. We can go some places that Americans cannot."

If the colonel had suggested Trahn form the unit, he was a Number One hard charger.

"Great. Daemons. What's the SOP on daemons, Colonel?" I asked.

"Fire destroys the host body," Father Trahn said. "However, we need to do something about the necromancer who is raising the daemons to infest the hosts."

"What about the daemons if the host is destroyed? Doesn't that release them?"

"Yes, Major, with the destruction of the host, they don't have a tie to this plane of existence. Besides, most daemons at that level are minor imps—mischief-makers at best. Once released from a human host, they don't have the power to do more than sour milk or fish sauce here," Trahn said with a smile.

"And if the host lives?"

"Major, the daemons we're discussing aren't strong enough to possess a living person. It's why the necromancer has been using dead bodies."

"Lee, grab that map we were working on last night and spread it on the table, would you?" Conrad said, dropping a pile of folders on the table. "Father Trahn, I think your suggestion was correct."

"That does not make me happy, Colonel Conrad," Trahn said.

"I'm not pleased with it, myself," Conrad replied, moving folders to hold the edges of the map Lee unrolled across the table down.

"Grab a cup of coffee, Major, this is going to take a bit," Conrad said, taking a seat. He did something to the map.

"Yours is the third confirmed attack on villages thought to be helping the North, Major," Lee said, handing me a bottle of Coke. It was even cold.

"That's why you sent me up here, right?" I asked.

"Yes. That, the four unconfirmed attacks, plus some intel filtering out from up North of unkillable cannibals attacking NVA safe zones in the DMZ," Conrad replied.

"Yes, sir."

"The attacks line up on the plantation, Colonel," Father Trahn said, handing me a folder.

In the folder was a photo of a man in his fifties—greying, with round glasses.

"That, Major, is Dr. Jean Baird," Conrad said. "We believe he is behind the recent attacks."

"Which has what to do with MAC-V (SU-13), Colonel? You just said all the attacks have been against NVA targets or those supporting the NVA. Last time I checked, our writ doesn't run to protecting the enemy." I lit a cigarette.

"Normally I'd say you're correct," Conrad began, drinking from a coffee mug without a handle. "However, one Army patrol went missing near one of the villages in Laos, so they're not selective about who they're fighting."

"So they're enemies based on one attack?"

"They're enemies based on not being selective in who they attack. The Laotian village that was attacked wasn't giving aid to the NVA," Master Guns said.

"Roger," I replied. "Where?"

"You're going to love this," Conrad said, sliding the map over.

It took me a minute to read the map—the confirmed attacks were marked red, the possible attacks in blue, and the probable attacks in green. All the lines converged on one spot. Problem was, the spot was in the 'No Go' zone of Laos. Sure, the Air Force could bomb the ever-living crap out of the nearby Ho Chi Minh trail, but if we set one foot in the area, it was court martial time.

"How certain are you that this is the place?" I asked.

"Historical data on this type of possession shows the imps will follow orders, but they don't understand the concept of leaving a false trail. Their lines of approach and retreat are as straight as the terrain allows," Father Trahn said. "We can count on it being the location."

"We?"

"Father Trahn will be accompanying you into the DMZ, Major," Conrad said in a voice that brooked no challenge.

"Yes, sir."

"As soon as the sun comes up, there are a pair of reconnaissance birds out of Tan Son Nhat flying north of the border and taking pictures of the entire area. They're also shooting photos of the staging areas for the Ho Chi

Minh trail, so we have to wait for the film to be developed," Conrad said. "From that, we can develop your plan of attack."

"What is the target, Colonel?"

"It was a rubber plantation back when the French ran things. Which was one of the reasons Dr. Baird was on our list. It belonged to his family—he lost it after the negotiations to end the war were concluded," Trahn said.

"You seem to know more about Mr. Baird than is in the file, Father," I said.

"He and I served in the French Indochinese Forces together, Major," Trahn said. "However, since he was half French and I was pure Viet, there were some differences in how we were treated."

I'd run across similar sentiments from other Vietnamese I'd run across in the last couple of years. Under the French, the French half-breeds were lower on the totem pole than the actual French, but higher than the Vietnamese.

We spent the next three hours planning the operation based on fifteen-year-old photos and ancient French Maps—we'd firm things up when the F-4s got back and their photos were developed. We'd be walking in, but we picked areas for landing zones for dust-off flights and for extraction. We also planned the mission loadout—heavy on food and ammo. I let the company sleep. They'd need the rest.

Two days later, we offloaded the trucks at the end of Route Nine. Colonel Conrad had convinced 1/1 and 3/26 to loan us the personnel to drive the trucks and pull security for the convoy on the way.

"I don't expect to hear anything from you until you're extracting," Conrad said, shaking my hand.

"Ok, dad," I replied with a grin.

"Your father would kick my ass if anything happened to you," Conrad replied.

"True," I answered, watching my company troop past. "I wouldn't want to piss the old bastard off, myself."

Third Platoon had point, followed by Second, then my massive Headquarters team, and First Platoon on drag. I waited until the last private from second went past and into the jungle before leading the members of Headquarters into the jungle.

Three days of marching, and all I could smell was the jungle—rot and death. Word came back down the line that LT Anderson of First Platoon could see the main buildings of the plantation, and just as the recon photos had shown, someone or something was living there.

"Master Guns, halt in place, bring in the platoon leaders for one last meeting," I said.

Runners went out to bring in the platoon leaders. Just as they arrived, the afternoon rainstorm started.

"Lieutenant Fox, Lieutenant Anderson, Staff Sergeant Davis, we're in position," I said over the sound of water beating on the leaves around us. "Any questions?"

The plan was stone axe simple—First and Third Platoons would cross through the remnants of the rubber trees, while I led Second into the buildings to check for papers and to find Dr. Baird. We'd try to free any survivors, but Father Trahn had warned us not to expect any.

"What do you want us to do with any survivors, sir?" Lieutenant Fox asked as if on cue.

"Any prisoners are to be gathered here," I pointed to an area west of the plantation where we'd be cutting a landing zone for evacuation when the mission was complete. "Remember what Father Trahn said about any 'survivors'. Treat them as hostile until he's had a chance to exorcise them."

"But, sir," Fox started.

"Lieutenant, I get that you want to rescue any civilians who have been caught up in this mess. However, our job is primarily to put an end to the threat Dr. Baird poses. Compassion is a good thing, son. Getting Marines killed because of it isn't."

"Yes, sir."

Fox was damn good at the paperwork portion of the job. I'd have a chat with his fire team leaders when the mission was over, and depending on what they had to say, make a decision about moving him out of the field and into Headquarters, where he could push paper to his heart's content.

"Get your platoons in place, gentlemen, and I'll see you on the other side," I said,

I was going in with Second, not because I didn't trust Staff Sergeant Davis to run his platoon in combat, but because I could count on him to do his job, leaving me free to run the overall battle and intelligence gathering portions of the show.

It took twenty minutes to get in place. I sat with Wilson, listening to the radio for First and Third to break squelch, indicating they were in position. One click.

"First is in place," Master Guns said sotto voce.

"Now we wait on Third," Wilson said.

Instead of the three clicks we were expecting, there was a burst of rifle fire from where Third was supposed to be, followed by the deeper roar of an M-60 cutting loose.

"Well, fuck. Wilson, send, 'GO!' Davis, take the building. Headquarters, you're on me. Master Guns, let's go see what the hell Fox ran into," I spat out, rising to my feet and moving toward Fox and Third platoon.

Over the chatter of M-16s and the deeper roar of the Pig, I heard the rapid clatter of AK-47s.

"No way, sir," Master Guns said. He'd had the same thought I'd had—we'd walked for three days through a part of Laos crawling with the NVA without seeing the NVA, only to have Third platoon blunder into them while moving into position for the final assault.

The gods of war can be capricious.

"Wilson, get Fox on the radio; tell him we're coming in."

"Sir, Lieutenant Fox requests you hold position. The enemy is breaking contact in our direction. He wants you to hit them on and push them back toward Third's position."

It was the textbook answer, and if we weren't concerned with stopping a necromancer from converting living, breathing human beings into soulless soldiers for his own personal war, I'd have agreed in a heartbeat. The NVA didn't give me the option of replying to Fox's request, however—the first soldier came around a rubber tree and ran into Master Guns Huggins, knocking them both off their feet.

"Light them up!"

It was a short, sharp firefight. Master Guns knifed the guy on top of him, while the rest of my fire team, augmented by Trahn's Ghost Hunters and Fox's platoon, killed the remainder.

"Any wounded?"

"No, sir," Master Guns replied as I looked at the blood spattering him. "This is from the guy I killed. He didn't even resist."

"Major, I'd suggest removing the heads of the bodies," Captain Trahn said.

"Why?" Master Guns asked.

"No head, the body can't be reused as a carrier for a daemon. If we don't find Dr. Baird, we don't want to leave him fresh corpses."

"That makes sense, sir."

"Yeah, it does. Spread the word," I said, taking a musette bag from Fox.

"I'll let my platoon know, sir," Fox said.

In the bag was the usual ash and trash intel sources—wallets, a couple of books of Uncle Ho's poetry, letters from home, and several unusually folded bits of paper.

"Major, may I?" Trahn asked, reaching for one of the bits of, for lack of a better term, origami.

"Sure," I replied, extending my hand.

He took the paper and said a quick prayer under his breath before carefully unfolding it.

"Yes, we've seen these before," he said, handing me the slip of paper.

"I can see it's in Vietnamese, and that's about it."

"It's an Eastern Orthodox prayer of protection," Trahn replied. "We have been finding it on NVA soldiers in areas where there is reported supernatural activity."

"So the Communists are issuing prayers?" I asked, folding and slipping the scrap of paper into a plastic bag to go in my intel report from this mission.

"Yes, sir. Ho and some of his generals are a bit more pragmatic than people want to believe. It also seems that if it keeps the soldiers calm, they're willing to use it."

"That makes sense," I replied, adding the letters and wallets to the bag. "Let's go see if they've found anything at the house."

The rubber trees had lost that 'kept' look. Several looked like they'd tangled with something big, which had broken them off about three feet above ground level.

"Elephant," he replied, stroking the stubble on his chin. "Or artillery."

"We pulled the records for the last year. Nothing's fired on these coordinates, including Air America."

"You asked, I answered." Huggins shrugged. "Probably an elephant."

"I hate not knowing shit like this," I said, walking down the line of damaged trees.

"What's the worst thing that could happen, sir?" Master Guns was striding along beside me. "We all get eaten by the boogey man and shat out?"

"You are not helping, Master Guns."

We finally exited the plantation forest and crossed the overgrown road to the main house and buildings where raw latex had been process for shipping to the World. There was a beaten path through the elephant grass from the trees to one of the outbuildings, complete with one footprint in the dust of the road.

"No way, sir," Master Guns said, laying his M16 down next to the footprint and taking a photo. The footprint was longer than the rifle.

"Boogey man hypothesis looking more realistic, Master Guns?"

"No offense to Captain Trahn, Major, but have you ever seen a Viet or Laotian with a size forty-eight boot?"

"I think we know what broke the trees," Captain Trahn said.

"Yeah, a Laotian giant," Master Guns said, recovering his rifle.

"No such thing," I replied, walking across the weed-strewn gravel to the front door of the house.

One panel of the door hung drunkenly from the frame; the other was ajar. Leaves, water-swollen books, and bits of broken plaster covered the entryway floor. Small things skittered in the ruins. Private White was waiting in the main room.

"Staff Sarn't's this way," White said, leading us through the house.

Davis was waiting in what had probably been the cook's room off the kitchen. Someone had cleaned the room, unlike the rest of the house. There was a rusting, iron framed bed with a new mattress and sheets, a table with a broken leg, and a desk.

"Someone with contacts on the black market has been here, sir," Davis said, pointing to a stack of C-rations in the corner.

"Any papers?"

"A diary, sir, but it's encrypted," Davis said, handing over a pair of leather-bound books. I flipped through the pages—except for the dates in the French style, nothing was readable.

"Well, whoever wrote this has neat handwriting, at least," I said, handing one of the books over to Captain Trahn.

"This is Doctor Baird's handwriting," Trahn replied. "Other than that, yes, we'll have to hand it over to crypto to figure it out. If they can find a key."

"We also found some notes in…French, I think," Davis said, handing over a three-ring binder.

I passed it straight to Trahn. French wasn't on my list of languages.

"Creole, I think," Trahn said, flipping through the pages. "Probably Haitian. Looks like a series of potions for preserving a human body for daemonic possession."

"You can read that?" I asked, looking over his shoulder.

"There are differences in Haitian French and Vietnamese French, but there are structural similarities," Trahn shrugged, handing me the notebook. "I also spent a few years in Haiti after the seminary."

"I wasn't aware the Church offered travel opportunities, Father."

"Much like the Marine Corps, Major, the Church offers travel to exotic locations, where you can meet interesting people. The only difference being the Church officially frowns on killing them after you meet them."

"You photograph this?" I asked Davis, adding the notebook to my ruck.

"Yes, sir," he replied as Corporal Cragen stuck his head in the door.

"Sir, we found something in the processing shed," Cragen said when I saw him.

"Lay on," I replied.

The processing sheds lay between the 'big' house and the laborer's quarters—most of those were in ruins. I could smell formaldehyde and rot before entering the shed. Inside there were tables covered in dried blood and vats. The formaldehyde stench rose from the vats.

"Sir, I've seen some weird shit since I joined you, but what we found in those vats…it's disgusting."

I walked to the first vat and looked in. There was a body floating just under the surface of the formaldehyde.

"Makes sense," I said. "Preserve the bodies until you can add a motivator. I take it you found the spell circle in the other shed?"

"Yes sir, more or less. The third one, though, that's the weird one."

"Weird how?"

"Sir, you ever seen the movie Frankenstein?"

"Yes. I even read the book."

"Well, imagine that, only worse," Cragen said before leading us out of the shed.

Cragen was correct. The third shed looked like someone had taken the Tesla coils and other pseudo-scientific equipment after viewing the movie Frankenstein and then tossed in kabalistic markings and all the chemicals they could find. There were also molds for the various body parts—bones and organs in industrial sizes.

There was a partial skeleton laid out on a giant-sized prep table—all the bones of the lower body were on the table, along with the spinal column. Someone had manufactured the bones—you could see the smaller bones that made the larger ones.

"Corporal Cragen, you're correct. This is officially some weird shit," I said, looking at the silver wires that joined the bones together.

"This is nothin', Major," Cragen said, pointing to the vats at the end of the shed. "Those are full of bits—muscles segregated by type, organs, and a big old bucket of brains."

I turned to Trahn.

"You suspected this?" I said.

"Yes, Major, based on the notes in Haitian Creole. This is what you do when you want to bring a larger, more powerful daemon to life," Trahn said. "The necromancer constructs a body that's capable of holding what he brings to this plane."

"That would explain the footprints outside," Master Guns said. "What do you do with undead giants?"

"Anything you want," Trahn said, deadpan.

"Cragen, photograph everything and get the explosives rigged. We need to get out of here before Baird gets back with his pet giants."

"Yes, sir."

There was a gabble on the radio. Wilson tilted his head, putting an ear to the handset. He slipped it from his shoulder strap.

"Hold one. Major," Wilson started, "there's movement over by the LZ."

"Cragen, you got this?" A nod. "Right, let's go see what's going on over there."

"On the way," Wilson said into the handset before clipping it back to his shoulder strap.

I'd picked the LZ based on the aerial photographs of the site. Back in the 1800s, they'd probably used the clearing to do preventive checks and maintenance on the elephants they used for heavy lifting power. It'd looked clear in the photos, so we were going to do some landscaping by high explosives to clear enough area for the Sea Knights to extract everyone. The firefight started before we got there—automatic weapons fire, answered by semi-auto and bolt action rifles, along with limited automatic weapons fire.

The weird part was watching incoming tracers float past. A green ball would drift lazily toward me, and then snap past as if it was late for a flight home.

"Jesus sir, that's a Jap Type 99 machine gun," Huggins said, crouching behind a tree. "Got shot with one in Korea. I still have nightmares about the sound."

The Type 99 fell silent following the CRUMP of a 40mm grenade exploding in the jungle around the clearing. Ahead, I could see Lt. Anderson; he turned and waved me forward. I dashed and dove for cover as a desultory firing started from the other side of the clearing.

"Sorry, sir, thought we'd cleared them all out," Anderson said. "We're taking a lot of fire, but no one has been hit yet."

Three grenades going off in rapid succession punctuated his statement. A Marine ran past, humping ammo to comrades on the other side of the clearing—I could hear the grenades in his cargo pockets clicking as they bumped together, and said a quick prayer that the Marine hadn't broken both legs off the cotter pin holding the spoon down, otherwise, things could get messy.

"Looks like Doctor Baird got back," Captain Trahn said as a line of walking corpses rose from the far side of the clearing.

There was a ragged "Banzai!" and the corpses broke into a shuffling charge.

"Damn, Major," Master Guns said, dropping down next to me and putting a three-round burst into the head of the corpse waving a broken wooden stick—probably the remains of a flagstaff. "At least they're not playing bugles."

"Thank god for small miracles," I replied. Master Guns and I had been together a long time—since the Frozen Chosen. I'd mustanged up after we got back to the states. Master Guns had said to hell with that and stayed enlisted. He liked to joke that I was an idiot and needed someone to watch over me, so once I'd finished Officer Training school, he'd followed me to various scenic vacation locations around the world.

"Either way," I said, looking at Lt. Anderson and borrowing his M-79.

Anderson mouthed 'high explosive' before continuing to direct his battle.

"Either way, sir?"

"Either way, we've still got to kill all these bastards before we can get out of here," I replied, firing the bloop gun.

It kicked my shoulder, and I knew the shot was going to land just where I'd wanted it to—just in front of the corpse with a sword. The grenade went off, scything the corpse and the two closest to him down. They continued to crawl forward.

"Headshots, Major," Master Guns said, shooting the sword wielder in the head. The corpse stopped moving. Master Guns shifted targets.

The firing slowed, and then stopped. "Lieutenant, hold your position. I'll move forward with the Ghost Hunters and see what's left."

"Yes, sir."

We advanced to the edge of the clearing, and then moved across, pausing to dispatch any still writhing corpses. They were a mix, mostly Japanese, but there were a few rotten French uniforms as well. I stepped around a tree at the far side of the clearing and knocked over a small figure that was trying to fire an AK-47. I dispatched the body with a single shot to the head before recovering the rifle from the twitching corpse.

"Looks like daemons know squat when it comes to modern firearms," I said, clearing the jammed cartridge from the action.

"The possessed you shot probably had limited time with the weapon. At most a few hours of familiarization," Captain Trahn said before blessing the body. "He was probably just a villager that got handed a rifle."

"We're still short a bunch of villagers," I said, watching Wilson gather intel. "And where's Baird, if these are his troops?"

"Good question, Major."

"Hey, Major, you remember that patrol from 25th ID that disappeared about a year ago?" Anderson asked, walking across the clearing.

We'd thrown out listening posts around the clearing, just in case. I mean, the plantation was officially Middle of Nowhere, Laos, but you're never sure when a wandering giant or NVA patrol is going to show up, so better safe than sorry.

Even though we had a budget that was unlimited, Marines are by and large frugal, so we were stacking the bodies and weapons around the trees we were going to blow down for the LZ. The same det cord that will blow down trees will take the head clean off a corpse, and chop the body into convenient, bite-sized pieces if you throw a couple of wraps around it.

We'd brought a lot of det cord with us.

Most of the company had pulled in around the clearing. The charges had been set in the mad science lab in the processing building, and we were going to blow both sets of charges simultaneously, because sure as god made little green men—don't ask—the blasts would attract attention from nefarious forces.

"Yeah, something about them just disappearing near the border," I said, stuffing another handful of Japanese and French dog tags in a bag for later sorting.

"Well, we found one of them," Anderson said, handing over a set of dog tags.

They read Niedermeyer, Douglas C.

"Command'll be happy to ship the family one hundred and eighty pounds of sand in a sealed coffin," I replied, adding the tags to the bag. "Unless?"

"We can put what's left in a body bag, sir. But it looks like he was fragged before rotting in the jungle for the last six months."

"Yeah, something tells me we're better off listing him as deceased, body non-recoverable," I said.

"Yes, sir. We should have it all ready to blow everything up in about half an hour."

"Good," I said, dusting off my hands.

There was a brief spatter of rifle fire from the south.

"Sir, Lt. Fox reports contact," Wilson said.

"Just contact?"

"Yes, sir. That, and something large and grey moving through the forest."

I took the handset.

"Hammer Six to Hammer Three, what's your target, over?"

"Hammer Three to Hammer Six, target unknown. It's bulling over trees, however. Rifle fire is doing nothing, sir. Request you send the M67 team to my position, over."

The M67 was along in case we needed to break something in a hurry. Right now they'd stacked arms and were helping to drag bodies to trees.

"Master Guns, get Sargent White and his team," I said before responding to Fox.

"Sir," Master guns replied, sending a runner for the anti-tank team.

"Three, Six. I'll be bringing the anti-tank team to you, over."

"Roger that, Six. Three out."

"Large and grey, Major? Could be an elephant," Captain Trahn suggested, bringing his squad over.

"That's what I figure, but if Fox has been shooting it, it's probably pissed off," I said as a horrid, dry screeching started to the south.

"If it's an elephant, sounds like his nuts are caught in a tractor, Major," Huggins supplied as we started toward Fox's position.

"I always wondered what that sounded like, Master Guns. Thanks for completing my education," I replied.

"Happy to oblige, sir," Huggins replied with a grin.

What had been a few spatters of rifle fire escalated into a full-blown firefight. All the fire was from American weapons, which was unusual, although the weird, dry screeching built in volume and frequency as we got closer to Fox's position.

"What's going on, Lieutenant?" I asked, dropping down next to Fox behind a tree.

"There's a pair of elephants…well, they look like elephants anyway, sir. We've been able to keep them from advancing, but rifle fire is just pissing them off, and they're shrugging off machine gun fire and forty mike-mike, sir."

"Sergeant White, sounds like you're up," I said. "Command team will hold here."

White and his A-gunner Holmes moved toward the sound of the heaviest firing.

"Back blast area clear!" The A-Gunner's shout was almost drowned out by the solid THUMP of the M67 firing.

"Load HEAT!" White shouted.

"UP! Back blast area clear!"

A wet SLAP followed the THUMP.

CRUMP.

"Load HEAT. Shifting target. Christ, Miller, drive the fucker out from behind that tree, huh?"

There were three quick bursts of fire.

"That's it, you big bastard…Firing."

Nothing.

"Misfire."

"Misfire."

"Keep it off the M67!"

Firing rose to a crescendo.

"Up!"

"Firing…Misfire!"

"Misfire!"

Over the sound of the firefight, someone started screaming the Hail Mary.

"Hail Mary, full of grace."

It's weird the things you hear in a firefight. Most people think all you can hear is what's immediately around you—gunfire, explosions, the wounded screaming for a corpsman or their mother. I could hear all of that, and someone screaming the Hail Mary.

"Hail Mary, Full of Grace."

There was a metallic scrape as Holmes, White's A-gunner, pulled the dud round from the M67.

"The Lord is with thee. Blessed art thou amongst women."

Holmes slid a reload in and locked the breech with a clang.

"Up!"

"And blessed is the fruit of thy womb, Jesus."

"Firing."

CLICK.

"Misfire! Move!"

"Misfire!"

Something came charging through the jungle. White's scream ended in a soggy thump.

"Huggins, Trahn, let's go," I said, rounding the tree we were behind.

My dad took me to a museum one time, when he was home between trips to kill strange things in faraway lands. They had a painting that showed cave men killing a wooly mammoth. That's what we saw when we came around the tree—tiny humans trying to kill an unkillable beast.

I'll give Holmes credit—he'd recovered the M67 from White and was trying to bring it back into action.

"Shit, Major," Holmes said as I dropped to one knee beside him. "I told Sarn't White that batch of ammo was crap. Some of it was green when we uncased it."

"We'll deal with that when we get out of here, Lance Corporal. Is the weapon serviceable?"

"Sight got knocked around a bit, but I can hit that," he pointed at the elephant, "from here no problem. If the damn round will fire."

"What about beehive?"

"Those were a different lot, sir, but didn't do shit when we shot the first elephant broadside."

I'd read H. Rider Haggard as a kid. He talks about killing African elephants, but the shot placement couldn't be that much different on an Indian elephant.

"We're going to have to get in close, and you're going to have to put the shot right behind the front leg," I said.

"Yes, sir," Holmes said, handing me his ammo pouch. "That should be all the anti-personnel rounds."

It had been a while since I had functioned as an A-gunner, but needs must when the devil drives.

"How close, sir?" was all Holmes asked.

"Well, we don't want to shove it up his trunk," I said. "Missing his brain might be sub-optimal."

"Yes, sir," Holmes said with a laugh. "Two, three feet be close enough, you think?"

"Should be," I replied as we worked our way around to the side.

"You want to load first, sir? Nothing personal, but if I miss at that range, I'm going to drop the tube and run. You might be in the way."

"That might not be in our best interests, Holmes," I said, opening the breech and sliding in a flechette round. "Up."

Holmes closed to within three feet of the elephant before shouting, "Firing."

THUMP.

SPLAT.

Usually flechette makes a sound like a disturbed beehive when fired—thus the nickname 'beehive'. Holmes fired from so close the sound was barely audible before the flechettes struck. Twenty-four hundred steel wire flechettes at a range of three feet don't make a hole, they scour flesh from bone like a fire hose hitting soft sand before eating away the bone in a similar manner. The round Holmes fired was a final protective round against human wave attacks. At three feet from the muzzle of the M67, the flechettes had just begun to disperse, so they struck the elephant as a solid mass rather than dispersed as they'd hit the other elephant.

Haggard had been right about shot placement. Destroy the heart, and the elephant will drop. Holmes had done more than destroy the heart. He'd eliminated it, along with the muscle tissue supporting the front legs. The elephant collapsed on its front legs, a dry shriek of rage its final complaint.

"It's possessed," Captain Trahn reported.

"Figured. The HEAT rounds for the M67 are no good. You have any suggestions other than closing to contact range and hacking its head off with a machete?"

"Simply immobilizing it leaves it here for Baird to reuse," Trahn said. "One of my men used to work on a rubber plantation before the war. Let me ask him."

"Before which war?" Master Guns asked as Trahn walked away with one of his soldiers.

Anderson, the corpsman, came over to report on White. "He was dead when he hit the ground, Major. Couldn't have saved him in a major trauma center back in the world."

"Right," I said. "Let's get him over to the LZ so we can get the body back to the World."

White would get all the bells and whistles at home.

"Major, Vin says we can either hamstring the elephant and shoot it just above the ear, or just shoot it. I'd suggest cutting the head off with det cord once it's safe to do so," Trahn said after his quick consultation.

I looked around. "Baldwin, bring the Pig over here!"

Baldwin was a recent addition to the company, transferred from a line company where there had been a few 'issues'—mostly minor incidents involving aggressive behavior towards ARVN and locals; he'd handled the impromptu 'weird shit' course we put people through in Da Nang well, but this was his first major field operation.

"Sir."

"PFC Baldwin, this is Captain Trahn. One of his men is going to give you a very specific spot to shoot that"—I pointed to the elephant—"in. Do so, and we can get the hell out of here."

"Aye, Aye, sir," Baldwin replied before following Trahn and what I assumed was Vin over to a spot where they could get a good angle on the elephant's 'sweet spot'.

Anything else aside, Baldwin was an artist with the Pig. Two quick three round bursts, and the elephant shuddered and fell over on its side. One tusk held the head off the ground.

"Good work, Baldwin," I said. "Lt. Fox, throw a couple loops of det cord around that thing's head and blow it in place."

"Sir."

I turned back to Trahn. "Anything else?"

"Major, let's get the hell out of here," Trahn replied. "I'm starting to think we need to exorcise this place with an Arclight strike."

"Captain, I was thinking the same thing."

The afternoon rains had started by the time we had gotten the LZ cleared. When it stopped raining, a ground fog rose, obscuring the site.

"Aviation reports extraction is a no go due to conditions on the ground, Major," Wilson said, shrugging.

"Ask them if they've got a hook up there," I replied. "We can march everyone out, but I'd like to get White's body out of here."

"Sir." Wilson held a brief conversation with the air traffic controller, I could hear his O-1 Bird Dog circling above the trees.

"Yes, sir, one of the Sea Knights has a jungle penetrator and a hook. They'll drop it in the middle of the clearing."

You could tell when the big, twin-rotor Sikorsky started hovering—the downbeat from the blades stirred the gelid fog in strange patterns. Anderson and Trahn carried the bag with White's mortal remains to the hook and rigged it so the helicopter crew could recover the body. They winched White into the fog, and after a few moments, the Sikorsky flew off, leaving us to the gentle ministrations of the Tokay lizards.

I called a quick meeting of the platoon leaders. "We're thirty miles the wrong side of the Laotian border," I said as something exploded in the processing shed; they were burning nicely. I pulled out a map sheet. "We've got enough food for two days, three if we stretch it, and most of the ammo. We've got to get from here to here."

The second here was the alternate LZ, a good day's march away from our current position. "The only issue is, we don't know where Baird is," Major Trahn said. "We've destroyed his base, but he could be anywhere out there with his remaining…call them troops."

"Sir, the men have been reporting things moving in the fog," Lt. Fox reported.

"Things?"

"Yes, sir. No one has gotten a good look at them, so 'things'. Could be humans, could be rock apes," he replied.

"Right. Keep your eyes open, people. We're going to move in ten. Fox, your platoon has point."

"Yes, sir."

Five minutes later, we found out where Baird was.

All I can figure is that he had sent the elephants in as scouts—if they'd returned to him, he'd have known it was safe for him to come back to the site. Instead, we killed them, alerting him that someone was in the area. He probably closed the range to observe—daemon-controlled elephants might not make the best scouts, after all, they can't report back what they've seen—and we blew the site into low earth orbit just as the rains started.

You want to know the best part of the whole thing? Intel, going over the maps and crap we'd seized before blowing the plantation up, determined that the alternate LZ was where Baird was picking up supplies smuggled upriver to him. Based on the things we found in between the plantation and the site, he'd probably taken his giants and other daemon-controlled workers down to the river to pick up supplies while we'd marched in from the other direction to destroy his body farm. This job is a crapshoot on a good day. Missions like this are why MAC-V (SU 13) members drink, heavily.

Coonts, a runner from Fox's platoon, came up while I was going over the final preparations for extraction.

"Sir, there's a man standing on the trail leading to the alternate LZ with a white flag."

"Master Guns, Captain Trahn," I said, following Coonts back to Lt. Fox.

When we got back to Fox, there were two figures waiting a hundred yards down the trail. One, holding a stick with a white flag on it, was black—not African black, but a shiny, lacquered black, as if he'd been weatherproofed to prevent rot—his features were European, and he was barefoot, wearing the remnants of a French legionary uniform topped with a local smock. The other figure had the mellow skin and melded looks that indicated mixed Asian and European ancestry, looked like he had just stepped out of a 1950s Great White Hunter Film—he was wearing brown knee-high boots and khaki trousers, topped with a khaki bush jacket. Completing his ensemble was a light tan slouch hat with a wide white ribbon hatband. I could see the barrel of a rifle sticking up over one of his shoulders, its wide leather sling crossing his body at an angle.

"Is that Baird?" I asked, handing Trahn my binoculars.

"Yes, Major, that is Doctor Jean Baird," Trahn replied sadly. "I can speak with him if you'd like."

"We'll both go, Captain."

"Yes, sir."

"Master Guns? You have a handkerchief on you? Mine are all green."

Master Guns had been thinking ahead of me—he handed me a branch with some white gauze tied around the end of it. I handed it to Captain Trahn, and he and I started down the trail, coming to a stop at what C.S. Forester described as 'half pistol shot'.

"Trahn? Is that you?" Baird asked after a polite half second. "Did the government let you form your Tho san ma?"

"Yes, Jean, on both counts. They also sent me to put a stop to what you are doing."

"Why? I'm helping them win the war, aren't I?"

"Possessing people with daemons is farther than even the government in Saigon is willing to go to win the war with the Communists," Trahn said with a sigh. "The only way you could see to win this was necromancy?"

"When the idiots in Nguyen's orbit laughed at my other suggestions, yes. You don't know the powers involved, Trahn."

"Jean, I do," Trahn replied, opening the collar of his battle dress to show the white tab collar of a priest. "It's not too late for you to renounce the powers you are allied with. Show some contrition, and you can die with a clean soul."

Baird threw back his head and laughed, his hands on his hips. He looked like a tiny, khaki-colored version of the Jolly Green Giant. "Come crawling back to the light of the Church, in other words," Baird said. "Pray that I be allowed the boon of heaven after what I've done?"

"Something like that, yes," Trahn admitted. "Your penance won't be easy, but you can die shriven."

Baird looked at me. "Your part in this, American?"

The way he said 'American' showed he probably didn't like us that much. I think if he'd been able to go back in time and keep the French from aiding the Colonies in revolting against England, he'd have been a happy man.

"Doctor, I was ordered to put a stop to a series of attacks against villagers and American forces in the northern area of the Republic of Vietnam. I've destroyed your base, and killing you lets me mark my mission complete," I answered with a shrug. "However, if you are willing to release the daemons under your control and submit yourself to Captain Trahn, that would also be a successful end to my mission."

"So, my choices are to surrender, give up my power and submit to the gentle ministrations of Mother Church, or die?"

"Something like that, yes," I replied.

Baird drew himself to attention, giving me a French style salute. "Major, in good conscience, I cannot surrender. Therefore I will see you on the field of battle," he said before turning and walking into the jungle.

"He's kidding, right?" I asked Trahn as we walked back toward our position.

"No, sir. Jean's father died at the hands of the Japanese when the Americans wouldn't sell the French in Indochina supplies during World War II. Jean received a commendation from Ho Chi Minh during the struggle against the Japanese—it was only after Ho started openly preaching communism that Jean returned to the side of the French in 1949. He was at Dien Bien Phu with the Legion, and only escaped being interned in the North by virtue of having French papers."

"So he's rabidly pro-Vietnamese, and anti-everyone else?" I asked.

"Yes, sir."

"Wilson, platoon leaders meeting, now," I said when we walked back into sight of the command party.

The one good thing about having spent most of the day destroying the plantation was that I knew where I wanted to dig in. Either most of the fires around the plantation house had burned out, or the rain had put them out, because otherwise it was going to be a stone-cold bitch to survive the upcoming fight.

I gave my orders as quickly as possible. We fell back on the plantation and dug in around the smoldering remains of the main house. We raided the lone processing shed still standing for tin, to line foxholes and to cover an aid station near the plantation house, before destroying the remains of the shed.

The short jungle twilight was on us before Baird made his first attack, which we destroyed. Short, violent and brutal as night fell.

"Captain, I don't understand what took Baird so long to move against us," I said, counting the remaining ammo for my shotgun by touch.

"You have advantages he lacks," Trahn said.

"How so?" Of the hundred and fifty rounds I'd started with, forty-five remained. I'd been on the horn to Saigon, and they were laying a mission in to drop supplies on us in the early morning hours. Beans and ammo would be nice. Water was going to be a saving grace.

"You can tell me, Lt. Fox, or Staff Sergeant Davis 'do this' and reasonably expect the task to be completed, no?"

"Yes," I replied.

"Baird does not have that luxury. Depending on the size of his horde, he has either to lead them personally or hope that the daemons he's placed in charge will follow his orders. That's probably why he had to create the giants."

"You've lost me," I said, taking a sip from my canteen.

"Daemons are vain, showy creatures. A Vietnamese body might be a fine shell for an imp. A daemon who leads imps, however, is going to demand a finer body, and so on and so forth. The giants probably house the equivalent of his lieutenants."

"You've just said his forces don't operate along the lines of a military hierarchy, but you talk of lieutenants?"

"Yes. Think of them more as enforcers. He cannot give them orders that they carry out independently. He can tell them 'Force the minions to assault that hill' and they will do so. Usually in the most brutal and efficient manner, but if something changes that would require backing off, the minions won't, unless Baird is there to tell them to do so."

"I think I understand. If we kill Baird, the whole thing goes to hell, then?"

"Literally. Baird is the key. All the daemons are tied to him through the spells he used to place them in the bodies of the slain."

"He probably won't show up on the battlefield then?"

"No, Major, there is a very good chance he will. He has to be there to direct his minions. He also has to be there to show them that even though he is a frail mortal, he has a greater personal courage than they do—otherwise they will turn upon him and rip his soul from his body to torment in a hell of their own devising."

"That I understand," I said.

The night was quiet—if it hadn't been for the Tokay lizards and their mating calls, I'd have said it was too quiet. Just as the ground mist was burning off, we could hear the sound of rotors beating the air into submission. Air Traffic Control was back as well.

"Major," Wilson called. "ATC reports there will be at least one bird on site from now until we're able to extract. They also state there's a couple of fast movers we can call in."

Colonel Conrad had to have called in some favors to get that kind of support. "What're the fast movers carrying?"

"Mixed load of nape and five hundred pounders, sir."

"Right. Tell ATC thank you, and we'll put his birds to use as soon as we need them."

The first helicopter, a CH-53 with a sling load, came into a delicate hover over the X we'd laid out with aircraft identification panels. I could see the crew chief watching the load as the bird dipped toward the ground. When it was about three feet off the deck he released the hook, dropping the load, and the big bird rotated up and out, making room for the next drop.

Marines ran in from the sides and broke down the load as quickly as possible, while the second bird lined up on the X. Its drop was as textbook perfect as the first, but as it turned to exit the drop zone, something passed just in front of the bird.

"Major, they're reporting something on the ground is throwing rocks at them," Wilson reported.

"How much loiter time do they have?"

"Twenty minutes on station before they've got to drop everything and run for Khe Sahn."

I turned to Trahn. "Can your Tho san ma find whoever Baird has throwing rocks at the helos?"

"Yes, sir."

"Get the frequency for ATC from Wilson. Find that thing and see how well it reacts to napalm."

"Yes, sir," Trahn said, whistling for his troops. Wilson handed him a scrap of paper with the frequency for the circling ATC. Another rock flew into the air, this time aimed at the Bird Dog, who wagged its wings and circled higher.

It was ten minutes before Trahn called ATC, and a thin plume of purple smoke climbed into the sky from the jungle on the edge of the rubber trees. Two USAF F-4 fighters dropped down from the sky to just above the treetops. The lead bird thundered past the smoke, silvery canisters dropping from under his wings. His wingman, flying behind and to the left, pickled the bombs he was carrying the minute he saw the lead bird drop the napalm. The napalm and bombs went off almost together, a close, manmade thunder. Something screamed in pain over the thunder of the bombs going off.

"Tell Trahn to get back inside the perimeter," I said to Wilson, "then get on the horn to ATC to get the last of the sling loads down."

"Sir."

"That should make things harder for Baird," Master Guns said. He and I had discussed Baird's command problems over a breakfast of ham and motherfuckers washed down with coffee powder.

"Probably. I'll have to ask Trahn if the other giants will try to absorb the followers of the one we just killed, or if they'll just disappear."

Trahn was almost back into the circle of foxholes surrounding the ruins of the plantation house when Baird's forces attacked again, a stumbling, shuffling mass of bodies swarming out of the trees to engulf Trahn's Ghost Hunters.

"All ready on the left!" Staff Sergeant Davis shouted, lifting himself out of his hole.

"What the hell is Davis doing now?" Master Guns asked as Holmes went past with his new A-Gunner, a kid named Cornwall.

Holmes had all kinds of 'new' ammunition, freshly acquired from an Army stockpile somewhere.

"All ready on the right!"

Davis was walking down the line of his platoon, making sure all his troops had their heads on straight.

"With one round, lock, and load!"

Davis' Marines were into it—they'd all check their weapons to insure they were ready to fire.

"Open fire! Fire at will!"

"Which one is Will?" Baldwin shouted, jumping out of his foxhole and holding his M60 at waist level, firing into the crowd of dead things that were advancing on Trahn and our position.

Trahn and his men were becoming one with the earth—Davis's platoon could put a hell of a lot more fire on the incoming undead than Trahn's twelve sub-machine guns, and they did. There was an evil buzz as if someone had kicked over the largest beehive ever seen. A huge swath of the shambling horde just disappeared.

"Ninety mike-mike flechette, it isn't just for killing elephants," Wilson commented dryly.

The angry bees swarmed again. Holmes was taking it easy, firing about once a minute, something he could keep up—as long as he had ammunition—until hell froze solid.

The possessed didn't break as human troops would have. One minute there was a horde shuffling toward us, arms outstretched. The next, nothing except corpses for the bugs to eat.

I watched Trahn enter the perimeter, a bandage on one arm. "You ok?" I asked.

"Nothing major, Major. I was a little too close to one of the five hundred pounders when it went off and got knocked ass over teakettle. This," he pointed, "was the gift of the log that stopped my roll."

"Did you see Baird?"

"He's riding around on one of the giants," Trahn reported, taking a deep drag on a canteen. "We engaged the rock thrower to keep it in place for the airstrike, but the minute Baird saw the smoke marker go off, he had the giant he was on run like hell."

"Makes sense," I replied. "Where'd the horde come from?"

"Those were the possessed we didn't get with the airstrike. When we killed their leading daemon, they attacked to get revenge."

"Oh fun, fun, fun," I replied.

"Major, if you wanted safe fun, you'd have been an accountant," Trahn replied with a Gallic shrug.

I shivered. "Nah, numbers give me the willies," I said. "Monsters, not so much."

"Honestly, they have a similar effect on me," Trahn said with a smile.

ATC called to report he was swapping with another bird. I went around and checked on the men in their positions, making sure everyone was ok. There were the usual small injuries after any fight—mostly burns from hot brass flying into locations that God himself never intended it to go.

"Baird must be having command and control issues," Huggins said as we were sharing lunch—perversely enough, all the C-rations dropped this morning had been breakfast units, so we were enjoying green eggs and spam as we waited Baird out.

"The problem is, his minions are on an accelerated learning curve," Trahn said. "When they first possessed the bodies Baird made for them, they'd probably never seen modern warfare. Alternatively, if they had, it was WWII or earlier. The daemons that possess those giants aren't stupid, they will learn."

"So do you think Baird taught the giant to throw stones?" I asked around a mouthful of green eggs.

"Probably not. The daemon might have come up with that solution for the strange bird it saw on its own."

"Why doesn't that make me feel better about this?" Master Guns asked.

"It shouldn't," Trahn replied.

"There has to be a way to hold Baird in place and still pound the crap out of him. If we were closer to the border, we could call up artillery support from Khe Sahn and just grind them into goo."

"Wilson, how're your batteries doing?" I asked, a thought about Khe Sahn flickering across my mind.

"Good, Major. There were some in the sling loads this morning, why?"

"Get ATC on the horn. I've got an idea, but it's going to take someone with a lot of pull to approve it."

I was right. My request to bomb an entire grid square into dust required approval at the highest levels. Colonel Conrad later told me he'd had to wake some three-star Air Force general back in the States up, yesterday, in order to get permission to lay on the assets required. Part of the problem was, no one in theater wanted to approve dropping bombs that close to our position. I was asking for 'closer than danger close'. In the end the mission was approved, in part because no one wanted to call Conrad on his threat to wake up LBJ to get the mission approved. MAC-V (SU 13) having a direct line to the White House made some things a lot easier. Especially when officers far senior to Conrad remembered the photos of Conrad on LBJ's ranch in Texas.

While everyone from Saigon to Washington was arguing, my Marines were moving rubble and digging. The house had finally stopped burning—the outer wall of the foundation was stone rather than wood, and we were going to use that as the outer wall of the 'just in case bunker'. The platoons saw it as a competition, and dug like hard rock miners into the reddish soil around the remains of the house. The ad hoc bunker was finished just as the word came back from Saigon. Officially everyone thought I was nuts, but bombing the jungle around the plantation was approved.

We hadn't spent the entire time digging. Baird had realized we were up to something, so he'd sent in constant, spoiling attacks to keep us focused on him, not whatever we were planning, until one of those minor attacks cost him another giant—and almost cost me Holmes and his A-gunner.

The two were probably the single most effective weapon we had against mass attacks—the possessed came at us in waves, not even trying to get out of the way of outgoing fire. Holmes had hammered one side of an attack and was shifting position to kill even more possessed when one of the giants showed how fast their learning curve was.

"Incoming!"

Holmes and Cornwell dodged a hard-flung boulder.

"Load HEAT."

"Up."

"Firing!"

THUMP.

Holmes later told me it'd been a lucky shot—the HEAT round had gone home just as the giant started its windup to throw a second bolder. It had blown Baird's carefully assembled monster all over the jungle in fine chunks. Killing the giant leading the attack also caused the horde shambling toward our position to drop to the ground, dead, entirely dead.

"Interesting," Trahn said, observing the newly re-dead.

"How so?" I asked.

"If there had been another giant in range, the imps controlling these bodies would have stayed and charged us, similar to their actions this morning."

"Revenge?"

"That and to show that they were worthy of serving a different daemon lord," Trahn replied. "Without that support, they fled."

Baird changed tactics—instead of shambling possessed charges, which had to be eating into his supply of possessed bodies, it started raining rocks on our positions. That wouldn't have been bad, except the rocks were huge—some of them the size of a Jeep.

"Where the hell is he getting these rocks?" I asked, watching yet another one smash into the ground just short of our position.

"The river, probably. I'm surprised it took him this long to think of it," Master Guns said. "The only saving grace is he hasn't hit shit. It's harassing fire."

"I'd be willing to bet he moves in closer when the sun goes down," Trahn supplied helpfully.

"Which is both to our advantage and disadvantage," I said, checking my watch. "Start moving everyone into the bunkers around the house."

First Platoon had drawn the 'lucky' straw—they'd be riding out the upcoming airstrikes inside the bunker we'd turned the foundation into. Second and Third would be outside that safe zone, but as protected as we could make them.

Perversely, I'd be riding it out in a foxhole, just in case everything went to shit and we had to kill a whole bunch of possessed. That's why I had the gold oak leaves on my collar, though. The government paid me to take the biggest risks.

It slowly got darker and continued to rain rocks. Trahn was right—the darker it got, the closer the rocks fell to our center positions. I watched one smash into a foxhole in what had been our outer perimeter before it got too dark to see anything.

Wilson and I huddled in a deep foxhole on the south side of the house. Gunny had a radio operator borrowed from Davis in a similar hole to the east, and Trahn and his operator were hunkered down to the west.

Wilson nudged me and then handed me the handset.

"Hammer, Jackal."

"Hammer. Send it."

"Arc Light."

Somewhere above us, eight B52 bombers—four to the north and four to the south of us—had determined by the arcane magic used by navigators and bombardiers they were in position, and the pilots had agreed. Flying so high that we couldn't even see them, the bombardiers had hit the release for the seventy thousand pounds of bombs each plane was carrying. The planes were flying in echelon formation—widening the spread of the fall of the bombs to almost a mile on either side of our position. If the inside bird of the formation was off on his position calculations—well, if he'd been off, I wouldn't have been here to tell you this story, now would I?

We were at 'minimum safe distance' from where the bombs would fall, aka 'danger close'. I'd ridden out an artillery barrage at minimum safe distance in Korea. I'd been on a warship waiting to go in and make sure we'd killed the sleeping thing that had taken up residence at Bikini Atoll when we did the bomb test there.

Those were love taps compared to what happened next. Five hundred and sixty thousand pounds of bombs rained from the sky from east to west. Before the last bomb had fallen, the same thing happened on the east and west side of our position. We were nowhere near the impact zone of the bombs, but they threw so much crap into the air that it rained down on our position—rocks, trees, dust, and bodies, along with less identifiable bits and pieces. The earth moved in strange and interesting ways. Finally the earth stopped moving, and the weird rain ceased.

I could hear a tinny sound.

"Hammer, Jackal."

I'd forgotten I was holding the handset.

"Jackal to any Hammer Element, report."

My muscles were still quivering to the aftershocks of over a million tons of high explosives going off under a mile from my position. It took me a minute to convince my thumb to hit the transmit button.

"Jackal, Hammer. I think we survived. I never want to do that again," I said into the microphone.

"Understood, Hammer. Did we get the target?"

"Unknown, Jackal. Let me roust the troops and report back to you."

"Roger that. Jackal, out."

"Hammer, out."

It took ten-fifteen minutes to get everyone out of the bunkers and back into position—not everyone had followed orders, and a couple of Marines had tried to 'surf' the Arclight strike, resulting in bruises, contusions, and a broken arm. Fox's Third Platoon was in the best shape, so I led them on a quick patrol into the beaten zone.

Dad had nightmares about the things he'd seen and done in the European Theater. I'd seen the photos from Hiroshima and Nagasaki—including the ones the government had taken to show why those cities, and not Tokyo, had received nuclear death. What we found out beyond the rubber trees made those look tame. A swath of jungle roughly a mile wide was gone. Shattered trees and churned earth were all that remained. It took a while to recognize that the flies were gathering on hunks of flesh—although, like something out of the painting

Guernica, we'd come across a leg, or an arm, or a torso that was perfectly preserved, except for the missing limbs or head. We wandered through that wasteland for close to an hour before finding what was left of Baird. In one of those oddities of blast dynamics, his body was whole. He even looked peaceful, like he'd just laid down to sleep.

"Jackal, this is Hammer."

"Send it."

"Target is down."

"Roger that. Can you move to the extraction point?"

"Jackal, that's a negative. There is no way we can move through the landscape. Original LZ should be clear."

"Roger. Birds are on the way for extraction."

I watched as Trahn carefully composed Baird's body before sliding it into a body bag. He did an abbreviated form of the Last Rites, zipping the bag shut.

"Personally, Major, I'd prefer to leave the body here. However, my government requires proof that Doctor Baird is dead."

It was a long flight back to Khe Sahn.

Lloyd Behm II spends his days writing Sci-Fi, Urban Fantasy, Post-Apocalyptic Fiction, Steam Punk, and Fantasy, painting miniatures, and watching his two cats perform kitty parkour. He is a frequent contributor to Cannon Publishing, and his work can be found here on Amazon

Origins

Spy vs. Spy
Michael Morton

Prologue

Manila, Philippine Islands, 2 December 1941

Kasumi straightened gracefully from her crouch, carefully wiping the blade of the kaiken on a scrap of cloth. She cocked her head from side to side, examining the sigils carefully. The spell would go awry if even just one was off. After considering them carefully, she nodded, satisfied with her handiwork.

Slipping the blade into its sheath, she then blew a kiss to the man lying on the bed. A gentle breeze shifted the curtains in the window, and the scent of hot iron and sulfur filled the room briefly. Small motes of glowing green light passed from her lips and floated on the currents, carried into a small cyclone above his body. The sigils she had delicately carved into his flesh flared with reddish light, and both the breeze and cyclone died quickly. The motes of light fell onto his body, each unerringly aimed for a sigil. They were absorbed into his flesh, and the cuts healed almost instantly, with no scar to show they were ever there. So carefully had she done her work that not even a drop of blood marred his skin.

His eyes slowly opened, but they were dull and unfocused. She lifted her hand, a delicate thing with nails painted in a light pink, and he slowly swung his hips and legs over the edge of the bed. He levered himself up, moving with the slow, reluctance pace of a sleeper who does not want to get out of bed. Still, after several seconds, he rose to his feet.

He remained placidly in place as Kasumi replaced his undershirt and then the uniform shirt. Her slender fingers deftly buttoned him up, and she placed the field scarf around his neck. She smiled gently at him as she tied it, but his face remained unresponsive. The khaki tunic went on over that, silver eagles on the shoulders dimly reflecting the weak bulb overhead. She fussily adjusted the fit of his clothes until she was satisfied that everything was in place.

Leaning in, she whispered at his ear, "You had a wonderful time. All your needs were satisfied, and you worked so hard…" she paused, her eyes glittering red, and lowered a hand to hover near his groin. Abruptly she jerked her hand up, and he moaned in pain. "…that you pulled something."

Sweat began to bead on his forehead as she paced slowly behind him, but his eyes didn't track on her, and he didn't move. Her eyes still glowing red, she crooked her hands like claws over his back. Her mouth curled in distaste, and she said in a bitter tone, "A little something to remember me by, since you won't remember the rest, Colonel." Slowly, she mimed a raking motion across his back. He arched his back slightly, another moan escaping his mouth.

Kasumi closed the side door behind him, not even watching him fade into the night. Her spells would hold, and he would stumble to his rooms, not wakening until dawn. But he would be hers for the calling when she needed him. He was her creature now, he would do her bidding until she had no more need, and then she would discard him. Throw him aside as she had been…

Inhaling deeply, she forced herself to calm her mind and push the memories away. That woman did not matter anymore, nor did any man. She had power now, enough to take what she wanted from whomever she wanted, and leave their discarded corpses in her wake. Slowly the red in her eyes faded away, leaving only their normal brown color.

The Americans were easy prey, and so, so many of them deserved what was coming to them. There would be much death in the coming days, and many more would learn about true suffering. Not all the native people enjoyed being under American rule, and it was so easy to convince the aswang, the island witches and demons, to seeking out Americans for prey. This in turn helped to convince the natives that the Americans were not welcome here in the islands. She played no small part in that role, and it was easy for her to dominate the locals. Their petty spells and powers were no match for her knowledge, gained from over four hundred years of experience.

She slowly pushed open the door to the main living area, where four men were huddled over a shortwave radio. The room was lit only by the glow of the dials of the radio and a small lamp in the far corner. The radio operator had the angular features of a native of the Japanese islands, and held a set of headphones to his ears while he scribbled on a notepad. Two of the others were locals, pinoy they were called, and they watched anxiously. The fourth sat in an overstuffed chair, puffing quietly on a cigarette. His face was expressionless, and the hand that raised and lowered the cigarette was steady. The lights from the radio dial showed a strong Asian face, with thick, black hair and a Roman nose. Sweat beaded the face of the radio operator and the other men, but his face was dry and untroubled, as if the mere act of sweating was beneath his dignity.

Kasumi watched him from the shadows near the doorway, not bothering to disguise the hatred on her face. He held her true name, and thus had power over her. He was the only one who could defy her, who could defile her as she had been when she was human. So far he had not, but men were not to be trusted and always despised. They betrayed you sooner or later.

The radio operator leaned back and removed the headphones. He handed the notepad to the fourth man, who took it gravely and considered the message for several seconds while the cigarette burned unnoticed in his mouth. He turned to look at the other two men, ignoring Kasumi's presence completely. His gaze traveled over the two of them, as if measuring them. They squirmed slightly, until at last he removed the cigarette and blew smoke into the room.

"Niitaka Yama Noboru 1208," he read from the notepad, his voice deep and measured, courtesy of years of tutelage in public speaking and debate. "Translated, 'Climb Mount Niitaka', gentlemen. Negotiations with the American government have failed, and hostilities will commence on December eighth. You know your roles."

Origins

1

Manila, Philippine Islands, 5 December 1941

He gripped the broken table leg with both hands, tightening his grip against the slickness of the blood that smeared it. Twisting it as he pushed down, he rose up off his knees to get better leverage. The ribcage crackled, and he felt the vibrations through the wood. More blood fountained up from the pierced heart, and the creature that had been his wife jerked one more time and was still. He slumped down, breath coming in gasps, and oblivious to the carnage and destruction of his home. Then the body jerked up, once, twice…

The PBY Catalina seaplane skipped twice as it touched down in the water of Manila Bay, throwing up great sprays of water. Captain John Torres, USMC, jerked awake in his seat. The nightmare was the same as it had ever been, leaving him in a cold sweat and breathing hard. Rubbing his face with both hands, he pushed the memories to the back of his mind with an effort that was far too familiar, and equally fruitless. Three years still hadn't taken the edge off the memory, and he reached down into his musette bag, hands automatically finding the leather-wrapped metal flask. He hated it, hated every drink he took, but it was the only thing that masked him, letting him function with the rest of the people around him. The lightness of the flask as he pulled it out only made him shove it back into the bag with a tired sigh.

Bracing himself in his seat as the plane turned and slowed, preparing to taxi to the pier at the US Navy Base at Cavite, John turned his head to stare at the green water out the window. He was here to kill more things that caused nightmares, but he couldn't kill his own nightmare. Ignoring the preparations of the other passengers around him, he continued to stare out the window as the nightmare echoes continued to fade. Only the increased conversation as the hatch opened and the sultry Pacific air filled the cabin roused him from his reverie.

Last off the seaplane, he hoisted his sea bag with ease over his shoulder and carried the musette bag in his hand. Of medium height and stocky, with dark black hair, he looked like many of the local pinoys, with the exception of his crew cut. He followed the others off the wooden pier to the quay. Most of the rest of the passengers were boarding a military bus idling at the base of the quay, but John made his way to a private car off to the side. Seated on the hood of the 1939 Chevrolet sedan, smoking a cigarette, was a slender, good-looking blonde captain in an Army Air Corps summer uniform.

"Good flight?" he asked as he hopped off the hood and walked around to open the trunk.

"Sam, after five days travelling, and over five thousand miles, we didn't crash on landing. That's a good flight." John tossed his sea bag into the trunk, but held onto the musette bag and got in on the passenger side. The other man got into the driver's seat and started the car.

"I've got us a secure room at the headquarters and made contact with the Unit's man on the ground here. You can see what we've found out…" He trailed off as John held up his hand.

"No, just to the hotel. Let's keep this quiet for now. No official visits or anything of the sort." He looked out the window at the buildings passing by. "Quite frankly, we don't care what classified is missing or what the Japs know about the defenses."

He paused, his nostrils flaring. "We're here to kill the…things that've been working them over."

The pilot glanced over at his friend, concern in his blue eyes. "Maybe you should rest up first. A long trip like that is certain to tire a man out."

Shaking his head, John turned to stare out the window. The storefronts flashed by, and the sidewalks were crowded with the daytime shoppers. None knew or suspected what the Japanese agent had unleashed here, and even worse, there were plenty here who would be just fine with Americans suffering under their attentions. "I'm fine. I just want to find Takeshi and the things he brought and force feed them my forty-five."

Origins

The conversation lagged a bit until Sam asked, "We're sure he's here in the Philippines? I haven't queried the G-2 shop on this yet. They're still trying to verify my clearances."

Working the clasp on the musette bag, John pulled out a manila envelope. It was sealed with heavy packing tape. He used a penknife to carefully slit the layers of tape and opened the envelope. "On October twenty-seventh, Naval Intelligence verified that Takeshi boarded a liner from Yokohama harbor bound for Manila. It's about an eight to ten-day journey, putting him here no later than November sixth. That means he's had almost a month to establish his network and contact the local supernatural talent."

He slid a black and white photograph from the folder and held it up so Sam could see it. The man in it was in his early 40s, with thick black hair. He had strong features which, combined with his piercing dark eyes, proclaimed him a man who held uncompromising principles. "Nakano Takeshi. Businessman on the surface, but in reality, a key agent of the Black Dragon society. He's worked mostly in China and Manchuria against the Russians, and they report that he is ruthless and utterly committed to the cause. Plus he has a business degree from the University of California, of all things."

Sam nodded at the picture. "Committed enough to employ things that go bump in the night?"

"Apparently, so are most of the Black Dragons. Their agenda for Japanese prominence in Asia and the Pacific region is flexible enough to consider using all means available, especially those of Japanese origin." He slid a second photograph out of the folder. This one was much older, with yellowed edges and several creases. The quality wasn't good, but it showed an open field with mountains in the background. Several men in Russian army uniforms were clustered around three bodies, all of which had been torn apart. Legs, arms, and heads were scattered about, and the only reason to believe there were three victims were the three visible heads. A third photograph followed, showing the inside of a hotel room. The simple bed was strewn with gore, and the body of a disemboweled man lay on the bed. Cyrillic letters were drawn in blood on the wall next to him.

Glancing over, Sam swallowed heavily. "He doesn't mess around, does he?"

"Nope. The first group was a Russian counterintelligence team, who apparently got a little too close to exposing Takeshi's activities. His pet spooks apparently either enlisted or coerced some of their Russian counterparts and pointed them straight at these guys. The second was a Chinese government bigwig Takeshi bought. The man then decided to go to the Russians and tell tales for more money." John put the pictures away and stashed the folder back in the musette bag.

"These are just the ones our Siberian counterparts are willing to share with us. Evidently Takeshi's supernatural activities over there have really stirred up the Russian spooks, no pun intended, and they're having a hell of a time containing them."

As Sam turned into the hotel parking lot and parked, John pulled out a leather-covered ID holder. Tossing it to him, he said, "The Boss got us these, which will hopefully get us through the red tape and allow us to requisition help as needed."

Opening it, he found an ID card listing one "Samuel Greaves Hawthorne, III, Captain, USA", and the title of "Investigator, Counter Intelligence Corps". Opposite the ID was a pocket with a folded, mimeographed sheet of paper. Pulling it out, Sam saw that it directed the reader to render all assistance as required by the holder, and was signed by the Assistant Chief of Staff, G-2 (Intelligence), for the Army. Whistling low, he glanced over at John. "You got one too?"

John tapped his breast pocket. "Except mine is from the Office of Naval Intelligence. Between the two of us, we should be able to get access to whatever information we need, and even some backup. Now that the Fourth Marines are here, I should be able to requisition a squad or even a platoon if, when, we need some real firepower."

The hotel was a simple affair, and each of them had their own room. They weren't adjoining, but at least they were across from each other. John unpacked his bag while Sam went down to the lobby to call the Unit's man here and have him meet them. This guy was an expert on the local supernatural lore, and was a local himself, Sam had said.

His uniforms hung neatly in the armoire, John pulled out a cheap bottle of bourbon from where it was nestled amidst his undershirts and socks. It was only a quarter full now, and filling the flask took care of almost all the rest. He hid the flask in the nightstand drawer under his skivvies, and considered the lone swallow remaining in the bottle. He was still standing there looking at the bottle in his hands when Sam knocked and came through the door.

"Ron's busy right now, but he'll be down before supper and…" he paused, looking at John looking at the bottle.

Tossing him the bottle, John turned back to his bag, glad to be able to hide his face. "Found it in the armoire. Guess someone didn't want the last swallow." He turned back to the chest of drawers and began to put away his clothes. "Help yourself."

Sam shrugged, twisted the cap off, and tipped the bottle up. Swallowing, he grimaced. "Blech. Rotgut whiskey was fine enough at the fraternity house, but that was then." He capped off the bottle and set it down on the rickety side table near the door. "Let's go down to the bar and get a real drink while we wait for Ron, and you can tell me more about our boy Takeshi."

Smiling in what he hoped looked like agreement, but was in fact relief, John said, "I thought you'd never ask."

Takeshi sat at the sidewalk café in downtown Manila, tea and local pastries on the table. He was reading a local paper with ease, apparently fluent in Spanish, and occasionally raising an eyebrow at the articles. There was certainly enough anti-American sentiment on the political front. This Ganap party definitely wanted freedom for the country and removal, by force it seemed, of the Americans. It appeared the country was ripening quickly, and would soon be ready for the plucking. With its sugar and timber industries, it would be a fine addition to the Dai Nippon Teikoku, the Empire of Great Japan, as well as providing a vital forward military outpost against American and British imperialism in the Pacific. In this way the Greater East Asia Co-Prosperity Sphere would grow into the Pacific and provide a secure forward base against Western imperialism.

He was still reading the paper when his second, Koga, strolled up to the table and sat down, as if he had just stepped away for a few minutes. Pouring himself a cup of tea, he said in a casual but lowered voice, "Our local talent reports that an American meeting the description supplied by your…asset arrived a few hours ago by seaplane at Cavite. He met another American already in place here in Manila. They did not go to the base, but instead are staying at the Hotel Elegante."

As Koga sipped at his tea, Takeshi considered this information. It was not unexpected, and perhaps given the length of time it had taken him to arrive, indicative of a slowness in the American intelligence apparatus. "Do we have identification?"

Koga shook his head. "The new arrival was wearing the uniform of a United States Marine Corps officer, while the one he met was a pilot officer in their Air Corps. Without access to our files back home, it will be difficult to specifically identify either of them as Special Unit agents."

He folded the paper neatly, smoothing the creases, and withdrew his wallet to lay some pesos on the table. "No matter. In the game of Go, one must plan for the future moves your opponent makes, so you may effect the capture. Come, let us put our contingency plans into play. If they are Special Unit, we will be prepared, and they will play into our hands. If they are not…" Standing, he shrugged. "What's a few more American deaths?"

John and Sam sat at a simple table in a corner of the hotel bar, which itself was nothing more than a few tables inside and on the sidewalk in front of the hotel, and the bar itself. Given that sugar was a major part of the Philippine economy, rum made up a significant part of the selection. Sam tried to get John to try the basi, or wine made from sugar cane, but after one taste, the Marine pronounced that he wouldn't use it to clean his weapon. After that he stuck to some of the local beers.

"Ron's been tracking the activities of the local spooks. People have started reporting more and more of their activity in the past few weeks. All sorts of stories are flying around about things that go bump in the night. People are going missing, and lots of business in charms and protective spells. Also, church attendance is up." Sam sipped the glass of basi, glancing at the bartender. The local was focused completely on some program coming over the radio and paid scant attention to them. Indeed, aside from themselves and a couple of tourists at a table outside, the bar was empty.

John turned his beer bottle in a circle with his fingertips. "Just about the time Takeshi arrived. Seems like he's back to his old tricks, pulling in the native talent for his work. We gotta figure there's much more going on than just missing classified documents." The beer was settling his nerves, although this was his third bottle in less than an hour. Better slow down. Not the time to get a load on. Once we take care of Takeshi, though…

"They have to be building up to something. He's here, the classified is missing, and we've left China. You think the Philippines might be next?"

Shrugging, John lifted the bottle to his lips for a swallow. "Don't really matter much. Our job is Takeshi's creatures and Takeshi himself, whatever they're doing. Man like that, what traffics with the spooks, he's too dangerous to let live."

He paused and looked Sam square in the eye. "Director himself told me to make sure we finished the bastard off. That's half the reason we got them badges and letters. 'Do what it takes, John.'" His voice grew harsh, and his eyes bored into Sam's. "Well, I aim to do anything and everything it takes."

Sam frowned, but then his eyes lit up as he looked toward the entrance. He gave a short motion with his head and said, "Ron's here."

John looked up from his beer at the new person. Or persons, rather. Ron was a slight pinoy with prematurely grey hair. He looked to be in his early 40s, and wore a plain white linen shirt and pants. With him was a tall Westerner, blonde with a military crew cut, wearing the tan shirt and brown pants the locals wore for everyday walking around. They walked up to the table and took the remaining two seats that Sam indicated.

"John, meet Ron." He grinned at his creative alliteration.

Ron held out his hand. "Ronaldo Ocampo, actually." His voice was soft and cultured, with only a trace of his native accent. He indicated the man with him. "This is Robert Hammeler, whom everyone calls 'Ham' for some reason."

Ham nodded in greeting, but didn't offer his hand to shake. Giving Ron's hand a brief shake, John asked, "Want a drink before we get started?"

Ron shook his head. "I don't partake. But it doesn't bother me that others do."

Ham said in a west coast accent, "Maybe later. After business is concluded."

Waving his hand at Ron, Sam said, "Anyway, Ron's the foremost expert here on…local customs."

John put his beer down and looked at Ham, then at Ron. "I assume your friend knows something of why we're here, even if he isn't…with us."

"He does. He has some personal reasons for getting involved, as well. I will vouch for him." Ham frowned at the last, but didn't say anything.

"What does he bring to the table, besides being a warm body who's seen something?"

Ron smiled slightly. "Ham is well-connected around Manila and the islands. If we need something, or to talk to someone, Ham can make it happen." He paused, then added quietly, "Also, he saved my life once. From something that is best left undiscussed."

Leaning back in his chair, he examined Ham. There was something about him that said 'military' besides the haircut, but John wasn't about to push on that. It would come out later. He saw the man's hard eyes also taking his measure. The Marine let his eyes drop, willing to let Ham take him in without turning it into a contest of wills.

Leaning toward Ham, John tapped the table gently. "Ron's one of us, so I'm going to take him at his word. You've obviously seen the other side of the coin once. Why see it again?"

Ham shifted in chair, his head twitching as he controlled his impulse to look around. "I've seen some strange shit, but nothing as strange as what went after Ron. Stuff like that I thought was only in the comics and dime store novels. It ain't supposed to be really real, ya know? Then after he told me what you guys do…well, I thought, somebody needs to do it. I mean, I ain't figgering myself as no hero, but shit…" His voice trailed off, and he looked down, embarrassed.

John looked at Sam, who smiled and shrugged. "I can't say that's any better reason than I have."

Taking in all three men, John said, "Then you're in. Ron, any reason we can't talk here? Should we go up to our rooms?"

He shook his head, but he was grinning. "People are talking a lot about the increased supernatural activity.

Origins

You can't pass by a teahouse or bar without hearing twenty different thoughts on why it's happening and what to do to protect yourself. It's fascinating, sometimes. I've heard more 'Lola always says…' tales than I knew existed. If the threat wasn't so real, this would be a great opportunity to write another book."

John motioned for him to continue. "You can write as many books as you want after we get this thing taken care of. And run you-know-who out of town, or preferably into a shallow, unmarked grave."

Sam's eyes slid sideways briefly at John, but returned to Ron as the other man begin to speak.

"There are many different creatures that comprise Filipino lore. Many are parts of cautionary tales to unwise travelers, and often tied to specific geographic features or specific sites, like a grave. These wait for a traveler or wandering local to pass close enough that they can employ their magic. The ones that are really dangerous to people, though, often seek out villages and towns to get their victims.

"These are called aswang, which can mean witch or demon. The arrival of Catholicism somewhat muddied the waters about their origins, and the cautionary wisdom of the lolas has become so intertwined with biblical references that finding their true roots is extremely complicated."

John's expression had grown thoughtful. "Can these…aswang be killed?"

Ron shrugged. "I suppose so. There is nothing to indicate they are immune to damage from a machete or bullet, although they can be very tough. And some, even though they are in human form, do not keep their heart or brain in the same place as a human would. Trial and error will be a better guide to these matters than lore, I'm afraid."

Sam snorted. "Too much error and there won't be a trial. Just a casket."

"So no special immunities or vulnerabilities, like silver or holy water?"

Ron shook his head. "Those are tied to Christian values. These creatures grew out of the pagan fears of the early islanders. Strength and wisdom were heavily favored by the tribes that birthed these creatures, and so it stands to reason that a warrior would need both to defeat them. Tricking the aswang into giving up its prey was a favorite tactic, but that takes time. The speed at which the incidents are growing suggests we don't have much time."

John emptied his beer bottle. "Sounds like prime recruiting ground for our opposition, then. Any suggestions on where to start?"

Ron looked at Ham, who spoke in a low voice, "I have people in and around town who keep me in the know for…special business opportunities. They've told about a group of two or three Japanese businessmen renting an apartment here in town, ostensibly to buy sugar cane. They've been there not quite a month and don't seem to have travelled to any of the local farms."

The two Westerners looked at each other. Sam spoke first, his voice low, "It could be a trap. If our friend is as good as you say, this would be a setup for any busybodies."

John rubbed his chin. "I really don't want to go in through the front door if I can help it."

Ham grinned. "I have some friends in the Manila PD. I also know some coppers who aren't my friends. For some easy dough they'll take the first knock, and whatever comes after that."

John nodded. "We have an operating budget. Let's get this set up for tomorrow night, if we can. Sam and I will be nearby, and either the police will bag Takeshi or, more likely, they'll flush him out into the open. Then we can either take him ourselves or pay them off again to give him to us."

As the trio separated in the hotel lobby, none of them noticed they were being watched. Of course, it would have been extremely hard to for them to see the semi-translucent form half-in, half-out of the ceiling near a dark corner. It watched until all three were gone from sight; Sam and John upstairs, and Ronald out the front door. It slid horizontally through the ceiling toward the stairs they had used. The white kimono it wore was undisturbed by the passage through wood and plaster.

It cautiously followed Sam and John as they went to their rooms. As their doors closed, it continued down the hall toward an outside wall. Its task was complete, and it longed to be laid to rest. Once it reached the wall, it continued its progress much more slowly, carefully passing through the wall. Though this was only a hotel with very little threshold, it had been owned by the same family for over fifty years, and they lived here. A creature such as the yūrei would suffer if it tried to force even such a threshold as this too quickly. Once it was clear of the hotel, it would return to the one who had summoned it with the locations within the hotel of the two rooms.

Origins

2

Manila, Philippine Islands, 6 December 1941, 1800 local time

John and Sam watched from across the street as the Manila police officers entered the apartment. Ham waited further down the alley with the car. As the last of the four officers went through the foyer, they left the concealment of the alleyway across the street. With Sam holding a sawed-off shotgun tight against his leg, they crossed the street to the alley next to Takeshi's building. Once covered by the dim shadows, Sam brought the shotgun to his shoulder and flicked off the safety, while John drew his M1911 and held it low. He whispered, "Don't use that thing unless you really need to. We want this guy alive if we can."

The pilot snorted. "Yes, mother."

Before they'd made it to the back of the building, they heard shouts from inside. There was the sound of wood shattering, and then a gunshot.

Picking up their pace, Sam glanced worriedly over his shoulder at the building. "Shit. The party started early."

"That's fine. They can hold Takeshi and his goon's attention while we sneak in the back way and bag him." John's voice had that grim tone again, and Sam gave him a worried glance as they carefully made their way down the alley.

They reached the back corner of the building, and John peeked around the corner. The rear entrance of the apartment building was less than ten feet away, and it was dark and quiet, with a three-step concrete stair leading up to a single door. Several metal garbage cans lined the back fence, and an old Ford Model T was up on blocks off to the far side. He felt his heart speed up as he anticipated the possibility that Takeshi could come right through that door.

Looking back, he began to motion the pilot forward, when the door burst open. Light spilled out into the alley as a screaming body in a police uniform went flying into the garbage cans near the back fence. It hit with a dull crunch and slid to the ground, unmoving. A human-sized figure followed under its own power, shrieking at the night. Its nightmarish face sported a dog-like muzzle, except the teeth revealed in the light were sharp fangs. The light also revealed claws on the hands, and the shredded remains of a woman's dress covered its body.

Without hesitating, Sam continued around the corner, brought the shotgun to his shoulder, and fired in a single motion. The muzzle blast illuminated the creature's face, a garish, blood-red countenance. The double-ought buckshot slammed into its body, knocking it off the steps and briefly out of their view.

The Marine swung wide around Sam as he chambered another round, trying to get a bead on the creature. It was writhing on the ground, snarling and yowling like some massive cat. He fired twice as soon as he had a good shot center mass, and the body went limp.

Sam altered his aim point to the open doorway. The door was half-broken, attached only by the lower hinge. Nothing moved in the short hall beyond, but they could hear more screaming and furniture breaking inside the building.

"What the fuck is that?" Sam said hoarsely without taking his eye off the doorway.

"Beats the hell out of me. All I know is it can be ki—" John's words broke off as the creature rolled to its feet with the lithe agility of a cat and swung at him.

His jacket acquired four slashes in it as he dodged back, but not quickly enough. The claws left a cold sting behind as they grazed his chest. As the creature came in for a second swipe, he went limp and dropped to his back on the ground. Its swing sliced through open air instead, and he fired up, putting two shots through the bottom of the creature's chin. One fang shattered as the heavy bullet hit it, pieces flying into the night air. Brains and blood splattered against the wall behind the creature, and it collapsed like a puppet with its strings cut. He fired three more rounds into the body from where he was lying on the ground, and the slide locked back on an empty magazine.

Sam hadn't changed his coverage of the doorway, knowing that the shotgun would be more hindrance than help in the close-quarters fight. He had, however, altered his position to move out of the direct line-of-sight of the door. As his colleague picked himself up off the ground and began to change magazines, he said, "You were saying?"

John finished the magazine change and motioned at the lifeless body. The remainder of the face was shifting from its frightening visage into that of a middle-aged pinay. "Ron was right; they can be killed. Looks like it might take a head shot, though."

"You'd better hope those claws weren't poisoned. Looks like you took a good hit."

Wincing as the adrenaline rush subsided, John peered under the jacket. The wounds pulled with every motion, and he could see that his shirt was sliced through under the jacket and slowly soaking with his blood. Gently he probed the wounds. "Christ, that hurts."

"I am NOT kissing your boo-boo. Hurry it up."

"I'm good. Just scratched me. It's not serious." He pushed the pain to the back of his mind, just like in training, and focused on the mission. "Let's get this sonofabitch and find out what other weird hoodoo he brought with him. This is about more than some stolen classified documents now."

Carefully they went up the stairs to the interior hall. With the shotgun tucked in close, Sam took the lead. The noisy activity within had stopped, and they heard a faint moaning from the front of the building.

The hallway stopped at an interior doorway after about ten feet. The door itself had been thin, cheap wood, and had been shattered by the creature. Pieces of wood lay scattered across the floor, while the frame of the door itself was still mounted to the hinges. Beyond the door was another short hallway leading to the front door, with two doors on either side leading to apartments. Two police officers lay lifeless in the hall, one with his head at an odd angle, while the other lay with his throat sliced open in a pool of blood. The coppery smell of blood filled the small space, as well as the shit-stink of recent death.

They took up position on either side of the doorway as a new sound came to them. The faint moans had become words, unintelligible but with a pleading edge to them. Whoever it was, he was pleading for his life in the left-hand apartment. John motioned with his head, and Sam went through the hallway door and flattened himself against the left-hand wall next to the apartment door. He peered at the open doorway on the right side and shook his head.

His 1911 held in two hands in front of him, John rushed the left-hand apartment door. It opened into a studio apartment, with a simple kitchen on his left, and a living room/bedroom on his right. He caught a brief motion out of the corner of his eye, but his attention was on the scene in the middle of the room. The fourth policeman was impaled on an overturned wooden chair, with two of the legs piercing his chest and abdomen. One of the doglike women was bent over him, one hand gripping him by his hair, while using her claws to carve bloody lines in his chest. As her head whipped around at his entrance, John fired twice into her chest.

She flinched and shrieked, the sound like a locomotive's steam whistle, but it cut off as Sam came through the door and put a blast into her chest. Staggering and off balance, she was unable to react as John lined up a shot and put a single round through her temple. Her face ballooned with hydrostatic shock as the blood painted the bed behind her a wet scarlet. She sank to her knees next to the bed, and then collapsed in a heap.

As Sam covered the creature's body with his weapon, John checked on the policeman. His breath came in quick gasps, and his eyes were glazed with pain. Checking the position of the body on the chair legs, he snapped, "Sam, help me get him off these things!"

Laying the shotgun on the floor well away from the creature, Sam helped him rotate the chair ninety degrees, allowing them to get the policeman into a sitting position. The man's breathing was slowing, the gasps becoming less forceful. John supported his shoulders against the pull of the chair legs impaling him. Blindly, the man grabbed at John's chest, taking a huge handful of his bloody shirt. Pulling with surprising strength, he gasped into John's face as his eyes tracked upwards. "Aswang! Aswang!"

John followed his gaze up to see another aswang crawling across the ceiling with cat-like grace. This one had a face like a pig, he noticed, as she dropped to the floor, knees bent to absorb the shock.

Both men reached for their weapons, but she thrust both hands at them. A cloud of dusty particles shot forth as if propelled by something. It enveloped them, and John felt his skin tingle briefly and then go numb. His arms felt like lead, and it was an effort to even breathe. He saw Sam collapse backward, gasping for breath.

She stalked forward, a piggish squeal of glee coming from her fanged mouth. Flexing her claws, she muttered something in a language John didn't understand. He could tell, though, that she was looking forward to whatever she had planned.

His balance finally failed, and he also slid backward to the ground. His head contacted the floor with a heavy thump, although it didn't hurt like it should have. She shuffled forward to stand over him, and an evil-looking tongue, shaped more like a mosquito's proboscis, unrolled from her mouth.

A dull thumping sound reached him through his numbed ears, and blood spattered his face and body. Wounds blossomed from her body, and she stumbled backward with each one. Ham came into John's field of vision, a long, heavy rifle at his shoulder as he continued to hammer rounds into the creature. Finally one split her head like a melon, and she collapsed in a puddle of blood.

As soon as she died, John felt life coming back to his body. He heard Sam give a great gasp, as if he was surfacing after being underwater for a long time. His arms and legs began to tingle like they did when they recovered from falling asleep. Ham walked over to the witch and nudged her body with one foot, rifle carefully pointed at her. When she didn't move, he checked the other one. Only then did he come over and kneel down by John and Sam. By this time they were struggling to rise on their own, and he gave each one an arm to grab on to.

"Know you told me to stay with the car, but what with all the gunfire, I thought you might need some backup."

Sam croaked, "Fine by me."

John only nodded, saving his breath. He looked instead at the policeman, whose breathing had slowed. They were shallow breaths, and his eyes were fixed somewhere in the distance. John pulled himself over to the man and croaked out a question, "Who else was here? Did you see anyone else?"

The man didn't answer. He took one final, shallow breath, and then he stopped breathing. His eyes stilled, fixed on some point in the distance. John looked over to the other men. "That sonofabitch Takeshi. He really did set us up."

"Knew we were here and after him. He laid a trap designed to take us out. Guess he didn't count on the cops taking lead."

Ham looked around the room and shook his head. "These guys were mean sonsabitches, dirty as hell, but even they didn't deserve this."

Standing with an effort, John began to look around the apartment. Sam also stood with difficulty and retrieved his shotgun. They all heard raised voices from the upper floors, calling out in questioning tones. Motioning at the door, Sam said, "We have to go. The neighbors will be here soon, and more cops. I doubt Takeshi was here at all, and if even if he was, he's gone now."

Holstering his pistol, John ran one hand through his hair as he glanced one more time around the room. He winced as the motion pulled at the wounds on his chest, and he sighed in frustration. "Dammit. I'm really starting to hate this guy."

Keeping the shotgun tight against his leg to conceal it, Sam led the way to the back door. The body of the creature was still in the position in which it had fallen, and they quickly made their way to the alley, and then across the street to where their car was parked.

Sam and Ham helped John sit on the bed in his room. The scratches on John's chest had soaked the shirt and jacket completely, and he was moving very stiffly. His friend went to the bathroom sink and soaked a hand towel with water.

"Let's get that shirt off you and clean that out. No telling what was on her claws."

John winced and gasped as the motion of pulling his arm out of the sleeve stretched the torn muscles and skin. "Forget it," he panted. "Cut it off. It's ruined anyway."

Sam hesitated, but Ham pulled a slim, pointed dagger from a sheath on his wrist. He stepped forward, but stopped at the looks from the other two. "What? You guys ain't never seen a knife before?"

"I shouldn't be surprised at you having a knife like that." John smiled tiredly and lifted his arms slightly. "I probably assumed it would be a switchblade. Cut away."

"What the fuck is that supposed to mean?" Ham asked, but used the slim Fairbairn–Sykes to start slicing away the sleeves. The jacket fell away from John's shoulder, and then he set to work on the shirt. Once they were gone, Sam went to work on the wounds.

Ham watched the whole affair with measuring eyes. "You boys get cut up like this a lot, going after these things?"

Sam looked at John briefly. He smiled back at his friend, true amusement in his eyes. Turning back to Ham as he cleaned the wounds, he said, "It varies. John more than most."

"Fuck you, Airedale," John said in a tired voice. "What was that you were toting back there?"

Ham smiled. "Cut down BAR. Figgered if it was good enough for Clyde Barrow, it's good enough for me. Makes it easier to carry, too." suspect NIS

Several minutes later, the towel was stained red, but the wounds were clean and bandaged from a kit Sam had fetched from his room. "Boy Scouts are always prepared," he proclaimed to John, who only grunted assent. "I prescribe lots of bed rest and plenty to drink. Water, that is. And you won't listen to me, and you'll be dragging us onto the street bright and early to hunt down you-know-who."

Ham pulled a chair out and sat backward on it. "Yeah, about that. Who's this bigwig you're—we're hunting."

John motioned to the musette bag sitting in the closet. "Show him the pictures, Sam."

As Ham examined the photographs, John explained about Takeshi and the mission. When he was done, the blonde man looked him in the eye and said, "I ain't no assassin. Not a triggerman neither."

From where he was lying on the bed, propped up by several pillows Sam had appropriated from other rooms, John replied calmly, "Yeah, but you swore an oath to defend the Constitution from all enemies. This isn't an assassination or murder; it's war. A conflict with supernatural and unholy powers that has been going on since before the United States was founded. These things don't respect human life. We're just tools, or playthings, or even food. As you said before, we have to stop them, because we're the ones who can do it. And humans who consort with these creatures? They've given up their humanity and made common cause with the side of evil."

A heavy silence followed his words as Ham looked from him to Sam. The pilot's face was solemn, and he nodded once. Ham blew out a long breath. "Wow. You sure know how to hit a guy in the gut. And how'd you know I was in the service?"

John smiled. "Just a gut feeling. Army or Navy?"

"Navy. Mustang, with five years enlisted, then commissioned from the ranks. Currently serving in the Cavite Quartermaster shop."

"Where you have access to all kinds of things."

"Yeah, I know some people who can get things. I take care of my people, and I take care of other kinds of people." He paused, then laughed. "Okay, you got me. And yeah, I'm in for putting the fix on this Takeshi guy. What the hell, we're gonna be at war with Japan sooner or later."

Kasumi stood over the sleeping form, tasting his dreams. *His morality is so delicious. If I only had a month to work on him, oh, the fall to depravity I could bring him to.* But she didn't have a month. Nor even a week. No, she had to have something she could use today, right now. This one was not suitable. *Perhaps the other one…*

Gaining access to the hotel the Americans were staying in was child's play. A simple spell of familiarity on the clerk so that she looked like someone he expected to see. Then up the stairs to the rooms her spirit had found. Another spell on the simple locks, opening them with ease. The American pilot was her first target, and she had hoped he was like the ones from her homeland—young, cocky, full of themselves, and ready to prey on any reasonably attractive female. She could have worked herself into his dreams, an exotic woman to entice, attract, snare, and learn his weaknesses. But this one, this Samuel, he was that rare quality of man. Nearly pure in thought, conscientious of his family and friends, and considerate in deed.

She shuddered in revulsion at the touch of his mind, even though a small part of her, the lonely remaining human part, reveled in the find. *If only one such as he…*

The demon in her quashed that thought before it finished, pummeling the human frailty within with images of her past; rape, violence, abuse. The things that pushed her to seek her revenge. Then the demon brought back images of the revenge she had inflicted on those men. Men bloodied and beaten, forced into postures of submission and subservience. Bodies mutilated and flayed, and their blood used to power her spells. The human part shrank from all of it, back into the mental box she had constructed to keep it hidden away.

Kasumi breathed deeply, composing herself. She still had work to do tonight. Silently, she left Sam's room, the door enspelled to close silently and lock again. The lock and hinges on John's door moved just as easily, and the scent of his blood hit her as she entered. Though it was dark with only a bit of moonlight coming in through the small window, she unerringly crossed the room to the small bathroom. There, in the tub, was the bloody shirt and towel.

His blood was cold and lifeless now, but she still brought the shirt to her lips and tasted it. It would make her connection to him stronger, and she could do more in his dreams. She sucked lightly on the fabric, drawing more blood into her mouth and sampling the taste. After a few minutes, she reluctantly dropped the shirt back into the tub and moved over to his bed.

He stirred restlessly in his sleep, his wounds obviously paining him. The bandages on his chest were spotted with fresh blood, and he lay on top of the sheet and blanket, wearing only boxer shorts. She drew in a breath, cupped her hands, and blew gently on them. A shower of blue sparks, gently glowing in the darkness, cascaded down to land on his face. His skin absorbed them quickly, and she closed her eyes, linking her mind to his with the spell.

Immediately she was assaulted with waves of terror and pain. He was reliving a memory in the form of a dream. A creature with leathery skin and needle-sharp fangs was bent over him, going for his throat. She watched as he got his feet between them and pushed sharply, sending the creature flying backward into a wooden table. The table shattered under the impact, pieces of wood everywhere, and the creature rolled back to its feet and charged at him.

They fought in the dream, wrestling back and forth until he was able to grab a sharp piece of wood, a table leg, and thrust it into the creature's chest. He twisted and ground it into the creature's heart, and it struggled weakly against the mortal wound. Amazingly, he was crying as he did so.

The creature's face changed after it died into that of a pretty young Western woman. Her eyes were fixed in death, all vestiges gone of the evil influence. Kasumi recognized the type of creature, if not the specific kind. The poor woman had likely fallen under its influence, and it had captured her soul and changed her into one of its kind. Killing her was a mercy. Ironic that she was lucky enough to have someone who cared enough about her to perform that mercy. And that gave her what she needed.

Chant in a soft voice, barely a whisper, she began to cast her spells. His dreams changed, subtly so he would not recognize it. She softened his pain, but intensified his sorrow, and started changing the face of the woman to hers. When the time came, if she needed to immobilize or even incapacitate him, she could change her looks to that of his dead woman, the one he'd killed, and he would recognize her from his dreams. The shock of seeing the person he loved—whom he thought he'd killed—come back to life would be enough to ensure he hesitated at the very least, or did not act at all.

Before she was done with the spell, he gasped in his sleep. It was almost a sob, a cry for help. She froze, her motions incomplete, as she waited to hear what his outburst might bring. The door across the hall creaked as it opened, and she turned her spell into one of concealment. In the shadows she would remain unnoticed, and she quickly but quietly moved to stand next to the dresser, where its bulk would provide cover.

However, it was hard to find any shadows when Sam swung open the door and switched on the light. Several things happened at once. John awoke with a start, hand diving under his pillow. Kasumi ran for the door, her demon-enhanced speed turning her motion into a blur. Sam was knocked aside as she fled through the door, and John was left with no target as he aimed his pistol around the room.

"What…what the hell was that?" Sam gasped as he rubbed his shoulder. "Are you okay? I heard you cry out."

John's heart was racing, first from the dream, and then from the startlement of how he was awakened. "Yeah, I'm fine. I was just having a bad dream."

"About Anna?"

He nodded. "At least, I thought I was having the dream. With that creature here, something seemed different than before." He swung out of bed and headed for the dresser. At this point, he didn't care who saw. Pulling open the drawer, he fished out the flask and took a healthy swallow.

He wasn't surprised when Sam took the flask from his hand, but that Sam only took a swallow himself. Perhaps not as big as his. Handing it back to John, his friend patted him on the shoulder. "Come on. Let's check those bandages. Knowing you, there's probably more bleeding."

Origins

3

Manila, Philippine Islands, 7 December 1941

Sam looked up from his breakfast as John walked into the room. Despite being freshly showered and shaved, his gait was slow and his demeanor distracted. He absently grabbed a cup of coffee from the urn at the counter and headed toward Sam.

"Did you get any sleep after…" Sam paused, at a loss for words to describe last night's encounter with the supernatural.

John set his cup down on the table and sat heavily in the chair. "Not much. Between that and this"—and he waved a hand at the bandages on his chest—"it's a wonder I got any sleep at all. But I'm okay."

Sam pursed his lips as if to say more, but nodded and motioned toward the door. "Speak of the devil."

John turned to see Ham walking into the dining room, dressed in civilian clothes as well. He headed straight for their table after getting a cup of coffee for himself.

"Mornin'. You two look like you slept like shit."

Sam snorted. "We had some unexpected company last night." He briefly relayed the night's encounter to Ham.

"Damn. That's…they can do that? Walk into your dreams?"

Sighing, John massaged his face with his hands. "Apparently so. She was trying to play some tricks on me with…people I know. Knew. Anyway, we now have some idea of the kind of magical muscle Takeshi is using."

"Now if we only knew where your boy is hiding out."

"Yeah. I think the plan today is for Sam and me to drive around this morning, looking for likely places that Takeshi would hole up. Places that might not attract too much attention."

Ham spun the coffee cup around on the counter. "You might wanna be careful of that. Plenty of normal people in not-so-nice businesses fit that bill, and they won't be happy with you snooping around."

"We'll be careful. We're not looking to engage him at this point, just find him, or some likely places we can stake out. Ham, if you could touch base with your people, maybe they've noticed something. We'll meet back here after lunch and talk about what we've found."

Three frustrated men sat around the hotel dining room table later that day, staring morosely at the food there, untouched.

"I hate ta be the one to say it, but this guy is good." Ham sighed. "Ain't none of my fish got a nibble on nothing. It's like he's a ghost." There was a pause. "He ain't, is he? A ghost, I mean?"

John shook his head tiredly. "No, he's as flesh and blood as us. He's just got some real horsepower under the hood of his operation. Namely his tame spook. If she can get into our dreams, what else can she do? We already suspect she's teased out some classified information, probably on operational plans and deployments. And she was doing it for weeks before Ron suspected there might be something spooky. The guys she…spelled, entranced, whatever, they didn't even think they were doing anything wrong, even when confronted by evidence otherwise."

"So where does that leave us? We don't even know their timeline." Sam toyed with his fork, but didn't eat anything.

"Right where we started." They all looked up as Sam's name was called, but it was only the desk clerk, motioning him to the front. As Sam went to see what he wanted, Ham started shoveling food onto his plate.

"Well, I ain't givin' up. This little rat bastard is on my territory now. He can hide for now, but I got connections all over this city. They'll find him."

"Yeah, but I got the feeling we need to do it soon. Takeshi's pattern is that he doesn't show his cards until he's ready to clean you out. With his spook operating in the open, I think he's almost done with his game."

Sam came back and dropped an envelope on the table. "Desk clerk had this for us. No name on the outside, and he doesn't remember who left it with him."

The Marine considered the envelope as if it would bite him. Finally, with a sigh, he picked it up and opened the flap. It popped open as if held by the tiniest amount of glue, and inside was single, folded slip of paper. He slid it out and opened it.

Old Manila Café
5 pm

There was no signature, but also no doubt in John's mind who it was from. He showed it to the others. "Thinks pretty highly of himself, if he thinks we're going to fall for that. Not after last time."

John considered the note carefully. "I think I'm going to meet him."

"Are you crazy? What if he's got a hit squad ready?"

"In broad daylight on a crowded street? Besides, he could have had us both whacked last night by his creature." He tossed the note onto the table. "No, I think he wants to gloat in front of us. To show us that he can walk the streets by day with impunity, that there's nothing we can do about it."

"Well, there is nothing we can do about it, right?"

"Maybe there is." Pushing the note to Ham, he asked, "What do you know about this place?"

He read the note and shrugged. "It's near the main drag. Fairly popular place, 'specially at suppertime. You thinking of meetin' up with him? Get his measure?"

"That's about right. You say you have people all over the city. I assume you mean locals. If they got a look at Takeshi, could they follow him, or even track him back to wherever he's using for his base?"

Ham smiled. "You bet. Then we put paid on him and his spooky friends?"

"Close. I'll head out to the Fourth Marine encampment before we go in and round up some heavier firepower. After last night, I don't want to go in unprepared. As far as they'll know, it's just a Japanese agent the Office of Naval Intelligence wants apprehended. Anyone or anything that gets in the way is fair game."

John glared up at the lean Asian man in a neat white suit who sat down at the sidewalk café table across from him. He suspected Takeshi wanted to evaluate his opposition, so he decided to give him what he expected. "You've got some big balls, wanting to meet like this."

The man smiled faintly. "And you, despite your education, talk like a common enlisted soldier. I'm disappointed." His English had a West Coast accent.

"Really, if this is the best American Naval Intelligence can send, this escapade won't be much fun."

"Fuck you, it's Marine, not soldier. That low class enough for you?"

Takeshi laughed softly. "Oh, you do have fighting spirit. But a warrior needs more than just bravado in face of the enemy, Captain Torres."

"I've taken down three of your creatures already." John glared back, his body hunched forward over the table.

Leaning back in his chair with an air of nonchalance, the Japanese agent waved his hand dismissively. "Merely the least of our assets. Local talent, not worth much." He motioned at his jacket pocket, and when John nodded, pulled out a package of cigarettes and a lighter. He held out the pack to John, who shook his head curtly.

Lighting the cigarette, Takeshi waved it at the people passing by on the street. "Look around you, Mr. American Marine. Do you really believe these people want to be under the thumb of the American government? How many did your military kill in the Filipino Insurrection? Tens of thousands, to be sure. Your Military Governor General Otis condoned the use of rape, torture, and theft by American soldiers. That was less than forty years ago. Plenty of time for hatred to simmer and bubble. First the Spanish, and then the Americans. When do they get out from under Western rule?"

"And being under your rule would be better for them?"

"The Emperor cares deeply about all his subjects. The Greater East Asia Co-Prosperity Sphere will bring benefits for all." He puffed on the cigarette and blew smoke out his nostrils. "Instead of being American slaves. With not even the chance for statehood."

"Beyond my pay grade. Decisions like that are best left up to politicians. My only responsibility here is to stop you."

"I can see that. Your dedication to your duty is admirable. In duty, there is honor. But are you willing to risk death for your duty? That is the true measure of the samurai." He stubbed out the cigarette and rose. "You're out of your depth, Captain. You've had all day, and you still don't know where to find me. I control when and how we meet. I control the battlefield, as it were. Goodbye, John Torres. The next time we meet, it will be for your death."

"Bastard. You can try." John forced himself to sit and watch his opponent walk away. In moments he was lost in the passing mass of people, but he made no move to follow. Sam walked up a few moments later.

"Ham gave me the high sign. His crew is on him like white on rice. We'll see where he takes us. Think he'll be dumb enough to lead us straight back to his base?"

"Not directly. But yeah, he's plenty smart. Remember, he got a degree from the University of California. Not only is he smart, but he lived among Americans for more than four years. He's got a pretty good idea of how we think and work." John sipped from the coffee, now going cold, and smiled. "But we have assets he doesn't know about. He's feeling pretty good about himself now. We'll wait, and watch. Sooner or later, he has to get back to his base and coordinate things. A man like that doesn't leave too much to underlings."

It was approaching seven o'clock before Ham's people got word back to them where Takeshi had gone to ground. He was at a rented house on the north side of town, and it covered extensive grounds. There was a wrought-iron fence facing the front of the property with a gate, and a dirt road that wound its way through the numerous trees to get to the house. However, the fence didn't extend the full perimeter of the property, so it would be a simple matter to travel by foot around it.

It took John a couple of hours to get cooperation from the commander of the Fourth Marine Regiment. With the majority of the regiment stationed further west to guard the naval bases at Subic and Mariveles, there were a limited number of Marines available for 'other duties'. Only with prolific use of the Naval Intelligence identification and the associated letter—and the cooperation of the United States Far East Forces G-2—

was he able to pry loose a squad. After that, it was still more than two hours to travel to Manila from Subic. The entire time Ham and Sam had watched the house, but hadn't seen anyone else enter or leave.

However, Sergeant Joseph Keller, the squad leader, was far more cooperative. Once he realized that John was in fact a real Marine officer, all was right in his world. He took in the mission phlegmatically, only replying, "Aye, aye, sir. We'll catch that Nip bastard for ya. Squad's down one man, though. Malaria."

"That's fine, Sergeant Keller. We'll make do without him. We'll drive to within a half mile, and then we're going to march overland to the house where they're holed up. If they fight, return fire, and otherwise defend yourselves. If they flee, attempt to capture first."

The tall, thin sergeant nodded once. "We expecting heavy resistance, then?"

"Frankly, I don't know what we're expecting there. I asked Colonel Howard for a platoon, but he was…reluctant to part with that many men."

Keller laughed briefly. "Hell, sir, the regiment's in a tizzy since the move from China. Most of the men didn't land here but a few days ago, and there's been fuck-all transport to move most of our shit around. They got guys filling sandbags, digging foxholes, and ain't nobody knows shit about when the Japs are coming."

He paused and then said soberly, "Since those yellow bastards ran us outta China, most of the guys got a mad on about them. We all agreed on the drive over here that we got lucky, sir."

John looked the other man in the eyes. "Sergeant, I can't say how this is going to go. But I will say if you and your men see any kind of hostile act, don't hesitate to fire. No matter how unusual it may seem."

The trip overland to the house was without incident, although it was almost midnight by this time. They met up with the other two men, and they informed the Marines that the people in the house had dragged a fifty-five-gallon barrel into the backyard. They were now in the process of dowsing the wood inside with gasoline.

"My guess is they're getting ready to burn important papers. Which means they're getting ready to leave, and in a hurry," Sam said. "Although midnight isn't exactly the best time for driving on these roads, and the fire will give away their position."

"Unless they figger something else is going to distract people," Sergeant Keller said.

Silence fell as the group considered that action. In the distance, shouted orders in Japanese could be heard from the backyard, and a dull thump announced the ignition of the fire.

Ham peered over the bushes they were crouched behind. "Won't be long now. Maybe ten, fifteen minutes at the most before they start burning shit. What's the call, Cap?"

John looked around at the assembled men. "We don't know how many of them are in there, or how they're armed. If possible, I want the leaders captured alive, but whatever you do, don't let any escape."

He turned and motioned at the house with a knife hand. "Sergeant, I want you and the BAR man covering the back entrance of the house from the tree line. Corporal Hauser, take two men and put yourselves in the woods where you can put a crossfire on the back entrance, and otherwise support Keller's team."

He looked at the sailor. "Ham, you want to come with us when we knock?"

"If it's all right with you, I'll hang back some and cover you. Might be you need to dive for cover fast, and I can cover pretty well with this beast." He patted the side of his cut-down BAR.

Turning to the remaining Marines, he motioned at the front of the house. "Lance Corporal Holmes, you'll cover us at the front entrance with Lieutenant Hammeler. Captain Hawthorne and I will take the other two men and…knock on the front door."

Sam had his shotgun, and John had borrowed a trench gun from Ham and had his Colt Automatic on his hip. The two Marines with them, like the others, had the Springfield bolt-action rifles. John had them fix their bayonets, because sometimes the supernatural respected only cold steel.

He gave Keller and Hauser twenty minutes to circle the house and get into position. The Japanese agents had started burning their documents, but they had to feed it slowly to ensure all the paper burned. They counted three men, none of them Takeshi, going in and out of the house to burn before they headed for the front door.

"How do you want to play this, John?" They crouched in the bushes near the front, watching Ham get set to cover the front door.

"I want them to run, preferably straight into Keller's arms. So let's make some noise and spook the spooks."

The four of them approached the door from the side opposite Ham's position to give him a clear field of fire. There was a single window on the front of the house, and John motioned the two privates to one side, away from the door, while he and Sam took the side nearest the door. As they got into position, they could hear men talking inside—questions shouted and answers returned, some in Japanese, and some in the local language.

John mimed to the privates to use the butt of their rifles on the window and held up three fingers. He pointed at the door hinges for Sam to shoot out, and then took a position a few steps from the door. With one hand he counted down from three.

At zero, the two privates smashed in the window and then ducked back. As the shouts rose from inside, John nodded to the pilot. He raised his shotgun and plugged each door hinge. They shattered easily, the old wood and cheap hinges no match for double-ought shot from a twelve gauge.

Before the report of Sam's last shot had sounded, John ran at the door. He kicked the hinge side and it fell inward, and he followed it in. The front room had been a living room at one point, but now it held a large shortwave radio on a table in the middle of the room. Most of the furniture had been moved to the walls, except for one armchair that sat next to the radio. A man, local by his looks, was entering the room from the opposite side, from what looked like the kitchen. He yelled as the door fell inward and fumbled at his belt for a pistol.

John shot him twice, the trench gun sounding with a dull thud as the short barrel sprayed the man with heavy shot. He screamed in pain, shirt shredded and bloodied, and staggered backward about two steps before collapsing to the floor.

The Marine continued into the room, and he heard Sam enter behind him. There was another door in the living room, but it was shut. From the kitchen he heard more shouts and running footsteps. Moving quickly, he put his back to the doorway to the kitchen and motioned for Sam to cover the other door. Shots rang out as the two privates entered the house, striking the wood by the door frame with dull thuds, but not hitting anyone. One private went to a knee, shouldering his weapon and returning fire with slow precision. The other came to John's side, his Springfield held at the ready.

Kasumi started out of her trance as the sound of glass shattering and gunshots echoed through the woods. She frowned in annoyance; her activation spells were not yet complete. More time, just a few more minutes was all she needed. Quickly she took a sheet of rice paper from the inside of her kimono and tore it in half with a quick jerk. Instead of tearing like paper, it shrieked like a person dying. A cloud of yellow smoke emanated from the two halves, coalescing quickly into a seven-foot-tall creature. It was shaped like a man, but with blue skin, huge tusks, and sharp, pointed teeth. Its arms were grotesquely long and simian-like, and it growled fiercely as it solidified.

She spoke a command in Japanese and pointed in the direction of the house. It grunted and took off at a fast lope, using its long arms to propel itself faster than a man could run. Taking up her activation spells again, she smiled. The oni would at the very least give her the time she needed to complete her tasks, and if there were any intruders left, she could have some fun for herself.

John counted five shots from the private by the door, and then tapped the Marine next to him. The man dashed forward into the room, rifle leveled, and John followed him. Someone appeared out of the darkness from behind a cabinet near the far doorway, bringing a pistol down from the raised position they'd held it in. Before he could even level the weapon, the private had run him through with the bayonet, stepping into the lunge and pushing the man away from the doorway out of the kitchen. His opponent gasped at the impact, and he dropped the pistol to fumble at the blade in his gut.

Shouts came from the backyard in English telling someone to 'halt', and exclamations of surprise and anger in the local language. There were several pistol shots, and then the BAR opened up. Its heavy drumbeat of fire echoed loudly in the house, and screams of rage and fear followed the fire. Rifle shots followed closely after, both the heavy bang of the Springfield and a lighter caliber weapon.

John briefly wondered if Takeshi would stand and fight, or attempt to escape. The man's ego wouldn't like being surprised like this, but he was a professional's professional. The more logical option would be to escape and start again. The other door in the kitchen led to the backyard, so he wouldn't be that way. That only left the door Sam was guarding.

Back in the living room, Sam, Ham, and the Marines were gathered around the door. John took advantage of the pause to thumb two more shells into the trench gun as he looked at the others.

"Oxborough, take your team around the opposite side. Watch for any leakers from the windows. This looks like the last part of the house our target could be hiding in."

Corporal Oxborough nodded and took the other two at jog out of the house. Looking at the other two, John nodded at the door. "Time to end this thing. Ham, get ready. I'll open it and you be ready to spray the other side."

But before they could act, a huge roar sounded from outside in the backyard. A man screamed in terror, a loud, agonized sound. Then the back wall of the house shook as something impacted on it. The BAR started up again, short bursts at first, then a long, sustained roar of fully automatic fire. Something out there roared back, and there was the sound of wood shattering.

Ham looked at other two, a question on his face. Sam shrugged, and John motioned at the door. "They'll have to deal with whatever is out there. We have bigger fish to fry."

He readied himself to open the door as Ham positioned himself to one side, modified BAR at his shoulder. John tested the handle, found it unlocked, and nodded to Ham. He then whipped the door open and stepped back quickly. Ham swept the hallway with his weapon, but didn't fire. He lowered the heavy rifle and stepped up to the door frame.

"Sam, you take the left, I'll take the right."

Sam nodded, and they proceeded into the darkened hallway. There were three doorways opening off the hall, with two on the left, and one on the right midway between them. The first door was half open, and John peered carefully around the doorway. Seeing nothing but a bed and a dresser, he nodded to Sam, who stepped quickly into the room. Seconds later he came back out, shaking his head.

The sounds of the battle outside continued, rifle shots hammering away in rapid succession. The BAR had fallen silent briefly after one agonized scream, and then started back up again as someone else had picked it up. Still, the number of weapons still firing was dropping steadily.

The door on the right was closed, and John motioned Ham to come up and cover the last door while they forced this one. Sam kicked this door open, and John charged through. It was a bedroom as well, with the bedding in disarray, and a half-packed suitcase on the floor. There was no one in the room, however.

Carefully they approached the last door, Ham in the lead, and the other two men a few steps behind him. The hall creaked slightly, barely audible over the sound of the firefight outside. Ham stepped over to the hinge side of the door, preparing to enter the room after someone opened the door.

Motioning Sam back, John stepped up and kicked in the door. Ham sprang through, weapon coming up to his shoulder. It was fortunate that he did so, as something struck the wooden foregrip with enough force to kick the barrel up and to his left. His finger tightened on the trigger, sending a round into the ceiling. Ham paused in the doorway, realigning his aim on whatever had attacked him.

John had no clear shot past Ham, and he yelled, "Clear the door!"

Ham continued to bring the heavy rifle around, and this time the barrel intercepted the blade of a sword that swung from the room's interior. The screech of metal on metal filled the hallway. The Navy man attempted to muscle the blade back the way it came, but a foot lashed out and caught him in the right knee. It buckled, and he collapsed to the floor, giving John a clear shot.

He fired once, even though he didn't see a target. Charging forward, he leapt over Ham's writhing form into the room. A man clad in black seemed to bounce upward from where he had been lying on the floor. He'd obviously anticipated a shot from the hall and had dropped to the ground as he was taking Ham down. He held a short-bladed sword in his hand, and as his head came around, John recognized Takeshi's profile.

Bringing the trench gun up, he tried to line up a shot on his nemesis, but the man slapped the barrel in the direction it was already going, sending it spinning past him and spoiling the shot. Takeshi continued his own turn, using the momentum to bring the other hand with the sword around.

John had no choice but to duck back out of the way of the sweeping blade, which left him open to a kick from Takeshi. A solid blow struck him on the shoulder, sending his already off-balance form falling backward into the door jamb. Sam looked up from where he was helping Ham, and tried to bring his own shotgun to bear.

Instead he had to use it with both hands to block the downward sweep of the sword. It impacted on the weapon, and Sam struggled mightily from his crouched position to keep the blade away and maintain his balance. John attempted to bring his trench gun around, but Takeshi, without relenting the pressure on Sam, kicked the weapon out of his grip and sent it skittering across the floor.

"Arrogant gaijin. I told you that you would..." His words cut off as Ham lifted the BAR from the floor and fired a single round upward through the Japanese agent's stomach. The force of the gases from the barrel sent him stumbling back, and he wobbled on his feet as he tried to fight the force sending him away from his targets.

John used the wall at his back to stand up, pulling his Colt from his holster. Takeshi was coughing now, one hand at his chest, but the other still holding the sword. John raised the pistol and fired once, straight into Takeshi's chest. The heavy bullet struck him high on the chest, and he collapsed into a sitting position like a puppet with his strings cut.

Walking carefully over to the man, John kicked the sword from his nerveless hand. Blood sprayed over the floor as Takeshi continued coughing. He crouched down in front of the man, carefully avoiding the sprayed blood. "Who dies now, fucker?"

Takeshi coughed weakly, but as John listened, he realized his enemy wasn't just coughing; he was laughing. Takeshi raised his head, only it wasn't Takeshi's face anymore. "Stupid... gaijin..." said the man, the rictus of a smile on his face. He took one final, rattling breath and slumped to the ground. John froze, a look of disbelief on his face as his world came crashing down around him.

"John." Sam's voice was urgent.

John motioned him away, desperately searching the body for some clue, some indication that this really was his target.

"John!" It was a hoarse yell, pitched low. John looked over at Sam. "The shooting outside; it's stopped." And then something growled from the front of the house, the eerie sounded echoing down the hallway.

"Fuck fuck fuck," whispered Ham, painfully scrambling to shift his body so he could aim down the hallway. Sam slid to one side to give the other man a clear shot, and raised his shotgun to his shoulder. John looked desperately around the room for his trench gun.

A large shape limped into view at the far end of the hallway. It was taller than the door frame, and it had to bend slightly to get through. It growled again and took a step forward. Which was enough for Ham and Sam.

They both fired in earnest, emptying their weapons in a matter of seconds. The large shape at the end of the hall swayed, took another step, and then crashed to the floor, shattering several boards as it did so.

And the window behind John shattered as a body came flying through it.

It struck him full on, sending him crashing to the ground. He was pinned underneath it, and he struggled to get free. Another form leapt through the window gracefully, landing lightly on her feet in the room. She was barely over five feet tall, but her skin was red in the moonlight streaming through the window, and small horns grew from her forehead. Her eyes glowed a bright red, and a tattered and torn kimono hung about her.

Ham fumbled in his pocket, attempting to pull a fresh magazine out. Sam was rapidly thumbing shells into his shotgun, and John struggled to move the dead weight of the body off of him. She stalked forward to Sam and snatched the gun out of his hands with such speed and force that the friction burns on his hands made him cry out. Raising the shotgun, she broke it over her knee as if it were nothing more than a twig.

As John rolled the Marine's body off of himself—he had belatedly recognized the poor private as he was struggling out from underneath him—she kicked the BAR from Ham's grasp, sending it tumbling back down the hallway. He cried out in pain, cradling his right wrist in his left hand.

Struggling to his feet, he looked up to find the demon woman facing him. Her heart-shaped face, despite the horns and red skin, was still beautiful, with delicate lines and high cheekbones. Her long, black hair was in disarray around her, and seemed to wave about as if in a slight wind, despite the fact there was none. She stared him straight in the eye, smiled sweetly, and raised an empty hand toward him. He controlled a flinch, but then his eyes widened as she gently blew on the empty palm. A cloud of fine gray mist sailed forth to envelop his head.

Immediately the room faded away. Or rather, the room he was in faded, and was replaced by his own bedroom back in North Carolina. And he wasn't facing the strange Japanese witch, but instead his wife, Anna.

His dead wife Anna.

She stood there, face still human, not the monstrous creature she had turned into, but a broken table leg still protruded from her chest, and blood spread across the front of her blouse. She was smiling sadly at him.

"John, why did you have to kill me?"

His mouth gaped open. He had no words for her. Just seeing her again, even like this. It wasn't like his dreams, all terror and confused violence. Her face, whole again, human again. He involuntarily took a step toward her.

She nodded and held out her hand. "Yes, come to me, my darling. We'll be together again, like before. Nothing will ever separate us again."

Something in the back of his head was screaming at him, telling him that Anna was dead and this was a trick. Not real Not real Not real, his mind rattled at him, but his heart was breaking all over again. It made him yearn for her touch, to feel her skin, her lips on his…

He took another step. The pistol dropped from nerveless fingers, and his right hand started up, fingers stretching out to hers.

"You'll have me again, John. No more nightmares. No more drinks. Just the two of—," her voice broke off as the side of her head exploded outward, blood spraying into the air.

He seemed to come back to his own body as if from very far away. His bedroom fell away as if pulled from his vision, and the dingy living room in the Manila suburb reappeared. Corporal Oxborough, his face scratched up and with one eye a bloody mess, hung in the window, rifle braced on the sill. He smiled grimly, and it was a gruesome sight.

John looked back at the woman. She swayed in place and seemed to have difficulty focusing her eyes. He stepped forward and caught her as her knees collapsed, lowering her to the floor more gently than he would have thought. Thick, black blood continued to ooze from the head wound, and he could see pink and black brain matter through the exit hole.

"Where is Takeshi?" he asked with a quiet urgency, his voice hoarse.

Her smile was fading and her eyes unfocused, but at his voice she weakly turned her head in his direction. Her voice came out as a soft whisper. "She was very, very lucky. Not all of us are that lucky."

He could feel tears on his cheeks now, and wondered how long they'd been there. One drop splashed onto her cheek, and he asked again, "Where…is Takeshi?"

"Men…always betray…and leave us. Always." There was bitterness, even though her voice was soft and weak. Her eyes stared off into the distance, and the blood ceased oozing from the wound.

4

Manila, Philippine Islands, 8 December 1941

The cleanup of the scene took several hours, what with the injuries and deaths. Corporal Oxborough was the only surviving member of his squad. His eye was still intact underneath all the gore, just swollen and bruised. He would have a beautiful shiner for the next few weeks. Ham had a broken wrist and bruised right knee, and Sam's hands looked like they'd sat out in the sun for hours.

On the advice of John and Sam, they burned the bodies of the Japanese agents and the two creatures. After the aerial bombings started later that morning, they figured one more smoke column wouldn't be unusual. The Marines were loaded into the truck they had come in, and the rest of the bodies were left where they fell. Hopefully, with all the destruction the creatures had wrought, people would figure the house had been bombed or strafed.

Exiting the base hospital, the three officers watched the frantic damage control and repair efforts. "Welp, it's finally kicked off." Sam carefully placed his pilot's cap on his head with bandaged hands.

Ham balanced next to him on a crutch. "Shit's gonna be dicey here now. Ain't too many who think we can hold off the Japs."

John shook his head and said, "Not our problem now. We have to get back and make our report to the director. Especially since Takeshi got away."

"Yeah, but he didn't complete his mission, did he?"

Looking around at the burning wreckage and the smoke columns on the horizon, John mused, "Didn't he? Doesn't really matter, though. We got his spook. He can't have too many on the payroll, can he?"

Slapping Ham lightly on the shoulder, he said, "By the way, sailor, pack your bags. You're coming back to DC with us to give your part of the report. And join a new unit."

Ham looked down at his leg and then around at the destruction the Japanese aerial attack had caused. "I dunno. Might be I'm safer here."

Sam shook his head. "Stuck between heaven and hell, sailor boy. Better choose one."

Michael Morton is a retired United States Air Force major, having served for 20 years and worked as am ICBM launch officer and in space operations. He currently works as an Air Force civilian at Air Force Space Command on the next generation of space command and control systems. He started writing fanfiction with friends and recently took the leap to publishing his work. His work can be found here on Amazon.

Origins

Devil Dogs
Chris Bast

The President of the United States takes pleasure in presenting the SILVER STAR MEDAL to

LANCE CORPORAL JONATHAN B. LAKE
UNITED STATES MARINE CORPS

For service as set forth in the following

CITATION:

"For conspicuous gallantry and intrepidity in action against the enemy while serving as a rifleman, 3rd Platoon, Company C, First Battalion, Seventh Marines, Regimental Combat Team 6, FIRST Marine Division (Forward), I Marine Expeditionary Force (Forward), in support of Operation ENDURING FREEDOM from 13th July 2009. Lance Corporal Lake was the driver for the lead vehicle when they were struck by an Improvised Explosive Device which flipped the vehicle onto its side. Lance Corporal Lake began administering first aid to their turret gunner who was wounded by resulting shrapnel from the IED. During this time Taliban opened fire on the convoy and the stricken vehicle with overwhelming small arms fire and rocket propelled grenades. Immediately, another Marine was wounded, and Lance Corporal Lake again rendered aid. While stuck in the kill zone of the ambush, Taliban forces began maneuvering and closing in on the stricken vehicle and the pinned down Marines. Lance Corporal Lake, in complete disregard of his own safety, dismounted and employed the M240 machinegun from the disabled turret. By use of machinegun, hand grenades, and rifle, Lance Corporal Lake repelled the Taliban assault, resulting in seven enemy killed and three enemy wounded. By his bold initiative, undaunted courage, and complete dedication to duty, Lance Corporal Jonathan Lake reflected great credit upon himself and upheld the highest traditions of the Marine Corps and the United States Naval Service.

FOR THE PRESIDENT,

Raymond Mabus
Secretary of the Navy

PART ONE

S o yeah, that was my Silver Star citation. So many dry words that can never tell a story, but you get a reputation. That was before all this, though, before things got weird.

I'd deployed to Afghanistan before, back in 2009. That deployment had also been relatively quiet. We had a few incidents with IEDs and sniper fire; York even got a Purple Heart for taking a round in his bicep. We had one major firefight following a roadside bomb, and I thought I was as good as dead. I'd accepted death in that moment and figured it was the time to simply fight until something killed me. That second deployment was different though, and I'd have done anything to do my first one over again.

My name is Jonathan Lake, and at the time I was a twenty-one-year-old corporal of Marines who'd probably gotten promoted earlier than I should have. I had little experience as a squad leader, or even leading, for that matter. But when you're given a Silver Star, officers think better of you. There were more suitable Marines for the job who should have been given the position. Instead, they made me a non-commissioned officer, then gave me twelve Marines to lead into combat. When I objected, my platoon leader and company commander dutifully laughed and attempted to encourage me about my abilities.

So what did I do? I took the position and immediately took a big bite of humble pie. I went to the team leaders and sergeants who had led me before, and I asked for guidance. Whatever words of wisdom they poured, I drank in mouthfuls. I must have filled an entire notepad with knowledge and expertise. When I tried to put those things into practice, there were successes and failures. I asked my Marines and my leadership how I'd messed up and how I could improve. It was hard work. Sometimes I failed miserably and got an ass chewing; other times, we shined, and I silently basked in the praise, knowing I'd tried my best and won. Soon, my Marines began to trust and respect me, not because I had the medal, but for my capabilities. For how I treated and led them. The squad became my family, and my weapon.

I managed the squad through the fire team leaders, and they in turn oversaw their individual Marines. I didn't micro-manage; if a fire-team or a Marine messed up, I went to the responsible team leader. That gave the team leaders more freedom and responsibilities. It was a system based on trust and respect, and for us it worked. Lance Corporal Reid commanded the first fire team, Lance Corporal Evans the second, and Lance Corporal Petty had third. These three Marines were my counsel and spear. When I commanded, they pushed for mission accomplishment. When they brought me concerns, I listened and heeded their advice. This mutual respect became the foundation to our friendship and lethality.

Reid was always a joker. No matter what the environment or situation, Reid could crack a joke and make everyone laugh. He was a little younger than I was, and he'd also been with me at the ambush where I'd earned my Silver Star. We were close friends then, and he was always quick to call me on my bullshit or mistakes. It wasn't out of spite or malice, simply because he cared. I'm certain if Reid hadn't set the example, our squad wouldn't have had the dynamic it did.

Evans was the oldest in our squad, twenty-four. He'd enlisted after working as a deliveryman for UPS. The job had kept him in his local area, but he knew there was more to the world. Evans was always level-headed and calm; he was probably a little more mature than the rest of us.

Petty was a character in his own right. He was a gambling man and self-proclaimed entrepreneur. Every matter of disagreement Petty would try to settle in a bet, and every week was a new business venture that was never fulfilled. Sometimes the behavior was an annoyance, and the phrase "wanna bet?" would make our eyes roll. But admittedly, Petty was a good Marine, and dependable.

These three Marines helped me keep my sanity on that deployment. It was now the spring of 2011. The second tour had been much like the first so far. Our area of operation was quiet and peaceful. IED threats were few and far between. We had an occasional spotter with binoculars and a radio, but it wasn't enough per our rules of engagement for us to fire on. Patrols became known as nature hikes. Instead of hunting the Taliban, we conducted census patrols among the Afghan locals. When we asked them if they'd seen any Taliban, they simply shook their heads no. The activity around us indicated that as well. It was beginning to look like the end of the fighting in Afghanistan.

We trained the Afghan National Police, or ANP, so they could take over when we left. That was a nightmare. Most of them had absolutely no training or qualifications to begin with, not even a screening to ensure they were mentality or morally capable. Getting them to patrol with their weapons in both hands and not accidentally pointed at us was an accomplishment in itself.

As Marines, we hated this. I'll admit it, I wasn't itching for another gunfight. I'd seen and felt what that could be like. But I also wasn't against it; that was why I'd enlisted into the Marines and became a rifleman. I wanted to fight. And so did my Marines.

Instead, we conducted more nature hikes into the villages, helped build a bazaar, talked to the elders, and handed candy to the kids. We once patrolled with rifles at a low ready and ever vigilant. But after three and a half months of nothing, complacency set in. I still trusted my

Marines, we still acted and looked like professionals, but our rifles hung a little lower. Our minds wandered more while outside the wire. Sometimes we'd have open conversations and debates while in formation. Who had better chicken, Popeye's or KFC? What console was better, Xbox or PlayStation?

When we weren't on patrols, we lived in a tiny Tactical Checkpoint, or TCP. Made from a combination of an abandoned mud hut, HESCO barriers, sandbags, and wood planks of two-by-fours. TCP 2 lodged not only my Second Squad, but also our First Squad, as well a small contingent of ANP. Just enough Marines to keep out on patrols and post security at the TCP. Why we were numbered "Two" I'm not sure; the rest of our platoon was at TCP 4 a few kilometers away. There was no TCP 1 or 3, and the rest of our company was at a combat outpost even further away. We were pretty remote, standing alone and unafraid against our worst enemy, boredom.

TCP 2 was planted firmly along one of the major roads of the area. However, for Helmand Province, Afghanistan, the standard for major road was relatively low. It wasn't paved, just a hard-packed dirt strip, and just barely wide enough for two vehicles to pass each other as long as they veered to the banks. Our TCP's main entry was adjacent to the road, surrounded by a mazework of spiraling concertina wire. The ANP manned the road and searched everyone coming up and down it.

Our Post One stood towering over the street and covered the area with a M240 medium machinegun. The post was wide and thick, with the protective barrier of HESCOs, sandbags, and cami netting. A second post, creatively named Post Two, was only fifty feet behind it in similar form. Its machinegun pointed in the opposite direction. Around the posts were built fighting positions that were used more for smoke pits and satellite phone conversations. Open farmlands surrounded us, and fifty meters away was the local bazaar we'd helped construct for the Afghans.

It wasn't much, but it was home. When we weren't on patrol or standing security, we smoked cigarettes, played board games or cards, watched movies on laptops, or slept. Our platoon sergeant, Gunny Alvarez, was with us and served as the TCP's commanding officer. That allowed us to slacken some of our discipline. We didn't shave constantly or worry about haircuts. We rolled our sleeves and never bloused our boots. In a twisted way, this was a haven from the rigid Marine Corps.

But we were still bored out of our minds. The only real danger we felt came from something the Taliban hadn't laid for us. The dogs. The Afghan dogs were massive, territorial, and aggressive. The locals cut their ears and tails so they couldn't be bitten or used against them in a fight. The Afghans called them Kuchi; we called them bears because of their size. If you came anywhere near one, they took up that tense stance dogs do and started barking and howling. We couldn't turn our attention away from them—if we did and they charged, the dog could easily knock us off our feet. Then there was the risk of rabies or infection. I used to love dogs, but these things were just mean. Sure, they were great and protective of their Afghan family, but us they saw as the enemy.

Now for the most part, the kuchis left us alone. It was mostly barking; sometimes they'd creep closer and closer toward us. But that was usually it. When the dogs watched us pass by, they lost interest. However, there were a couple of times they charged, and that resulted in gunfire. Reid had tried to back away from an aggressive beast, only to have it sprint toward him. I could see the Marine step forward and make himself bigger at an attempt to scare the dog back. Instead, it snapped its jaws and kept coming. At the last second Reid fired his M16 into the hound's skull, and it tumbled end over end to a stop.

Another time in another village there was a massive black dog that charged our point man through the thick stalks of a corn field. Again at the last moment, the Marine saw the animal and pulled the trigger of his rifle. Five rounds snapped in quick succession, and everyone tensed up. Those of us who hadn't seen what was happening expected Taliban. When we turned to look, we saw the huge canine limping away. There was a round in two of its legs that ran bright with red blood, another round had pierced its torso, and the fur was turning wet and matted. The kuchi whimpered in pain. Our point man, feeling sorry for it, put another round into the dog's skull, ending the pain.

Each time we killed a dog, the nearby village elders rushed to our TCP demanding payment. At first they asked for tens of thousands of dollars. In the end, I think Gunny Alvarez gave them a couple hundred bucks. With that, the elders walked away pleased.

It wasn't much at all. Afghanistan seemed like it would be quiet and uneventful.

Evans had noticed it first, on another nature hike by a village led by elder Abdul Malik. Abdul was one of the few Afghans we genuinely liked to deal with. The man always seemed to be smiling. He'd invite us in, and I'd drink tea and have short conversations with him through our translator, Aarash. Malik spoke about how he loved Americans. A couple years ago they'd killed the Taliban that had oppressed his village. Americans bought cigarettes from him. He would make them food, and soon the Americans gave him gifts as well. To keep up with the rapport, I'd try to bring him American cigarettes like Marlboro Reds, and bottles of water or candy for his children. Malik would then have his wife make food for my Marines.

I told Malik about a Key Leader Engagement, or KLE, that was occurring at the TCP. All the local elders were invited to participate, and Gunny Alvarez would try to build rapport. Malik gave his bright smile and said he'd attend.

Just after that visit, Evans pointed out a particular kuchi. Evans simply stopped in his tracks and faced the canine. "Woah." We all turned to look.

Once you've seen one Afghan dog, you've kind of seen them all. But this one was…different. It just seemed—dark. Its eyes were a blur of black and emptiness, of red and hate. The canine bared its teeth, which seemed more akin to a row of daggers. They looked like pure ivory, clean and polished. Its coat and fur weren't matted or dirty, or tanned with Afghan dust. Instead, it was pristine and black as night. Four powerful legs stood tense and ready, with dark sharp claws that dug into the ground. It growled, deep and guttural, and the noise seemed to boom and carry on the wind. Just looking at it sent a chill down my spine. Had I not seen it, I never would have believed anyone's description of the beast. But that's what it seemed like, more beast than dog.

It kept its distance from us. We never approached it, and it didn't approach us. We just stared at each other for a moment, unsure who was the more dangerous. I kept my eyes on the beast, then motioned for our point man to lead us further; we still had other villages to visit and patrol. We moved away, and the dog stayed there.

Origins

We were approaching the second village when we came across it again. We heard it first. The bark dominated the air, louder and deeper than any dog we'd heard before. I admit, it even made me jump. We faced the source and saw it, then realized it wasn't the same canine. It stood, defiant and angry, on a berm across a wide canal. This dog looked identical to the first, but instead its coat was a rich and full brown. Still the same rows of dagger teeth and claws, and the same empty, hateful eyes. Just different fur. It, too, eyed us and barked until we passed.

It made me nervous. I walked with my rifle a little closer. I think we all did. It seemed crazy, how unnaturally evil these two kuchis appeared. Nobody said a thing, though I'm sure we all thought the same. I'm sure we were all just a little bit scared, but we were Marines, and nobody wanted to admit to being afraid of a dog.

We visited the last village, then made our way home to TCP 2. That's when Petty saw a third hound. This one, however, had more of a greyed coat. This dog followed us for some time, its daggerlike teeth snarled, and its eyes glared contempt into each of us. It kept a good thirty meters away from our patrol, but it just followed. Evans noticed as we approached other properties, the other kuchis would bark at us, then at the trailing beast. The beast ignored them, didn't even give them a sideways glance. The other dogs seemed to back away and keep their distance. We had to keep a Marine constantly watching it, his rifle ready, in case it came sprinting. After twenty minutes, it stopped and turned away.

The rest of the patrol went on without incident, and nobody spoke until we were inside the protective walls of the HESCO barriers. I slid out of my gear and couldn't help but think of those three dogs. Another chill ran down my spine. I shook them from my mind, but still grabbed my M4 and kept it close.

Reid broke the silence first. "That was weird."

We laughed and chuckled. I could always trust Reid to break the tension. Soon, I had the squad going about the usual post mission routine. Cleaning and readying their rifles, ensuring their gear was set, drinking and replenishing water, then relaxing. The rest of the day the squad had to themselves to eat and sleep before taking over the TCP security duties at midnight. We would then rotate with First Squad, who were then on post. The next day First would be on patrol, while my Marines stood watch.

I made my way over to see Gunny Alvarez to debrief him on the patrol. Though nothing had happened, it was still customary to do so. He and Sergeant Mason, First Squad's leader, were in our Combat Operations Center, or COC. It was a small room inside the mud compound filled with tables and folding chairs neatly displaying a military laptop, radios, maps, chargers, munitions, and everything else needed to keep our TCP running. They were both sitting and smoking cigarettes.

"What's the word, Lake?" Gunny Alvarez asked as I came through a small doorframe. Immediately, the platoon sergeant extended a pack of cigarettes for me and I eagerly took one. The look on my face must have been enough, because he waited patiently while I nervously lit the tobacco and took a deep inhale. On the exhale I practically fell back into the wall.

"What happened to you?" Sergeant Mason asked, his eyebrows up in curiosity. He knew something had to be up for me to act like this.

"I'm not sure you'll believe me," I started, then took another pull at the cigarette. "There's some fucking wild dogs out there."

Sergeant Mason started to lean back and wave his hand as if gesturing the idea away.

"I'm telling you, Sergeant, we ran into these three dogs. Could pass for straight demons. These things were creepy; I've never seen anything like them before." Their expressions debated amongst themselves.

I peered through the doorway and locked eyes with Aarash. "Aarash, come here for a second," I called to him. The small, thin Afghan came and entered. "Aarash, you saw those kuchis, right? You ever see anything like that before?"

Gunny Alvarez and Sergeant Mason turned their attention to Aarash, and I could see the interpreter shiver slightly. "No, man. Never. We do not have dogs like that in Kabul." His English came out heavily accented. "This is some backwoods country shit. That was some scary shit, man."

I motioned with my hands to the interpreter to prove my point to my two senior Marines. They still looked confused, and I described the three incidents. By the end of it, they simply leaned and said, "We'll keep an eye out."

I couldn't blame them; what could they do? What was I expecting them to do? In that moment, I felt silly and ashamed. Like I'd shown myself as a coward. But I think they believed me as well; the Silver Star I'd earned proved I was a warfighter and wouldn't scare easy.

The rest of the day passed like any other. Reid and I teamed up to play Evans and Petty in a game of Spades. As usual, Petty put money on the line, and Reid agreed. Evans and I simply rolled our eyes and played. I've played so many times I can't recall if we won or lost, but I know that was the last time. Later we tore through Meals Ready to Eat and traded the foods we liked and disliked. As the sun was setting, we gathered around my laptop and watched a movie. Some of the other guys from the squad joined us, and we smoked cigarettes.

At midnight I took over the COC, and my Marines started their rotations on post. Nothing different, business as usual. The night was silent, and I couldn't help but think about those dogs. I was certain we'd end up having to shoot one within the next few days. Or maybe Sergeant Mason's squad would. Either way, they'd see them soon enough, and they'd know what it was I was talking about.

Without realizing it, I had my pistol in hand. The smooth contours of the M9 Beretta felt comforting. I knew I was only an average shot with the thing; Sergeant Mason could outshoot me any day, but it made me feel safe. To be perfectly frank, part of me wondered why I needed it, but Gunny Alvarez said all the squad leaders in the battalion got one. I imagined myself shooting one of those dogs with it, one coming too close and I'd draw the pistol fast like in the movies. Hopefully the magazine wouldn't cause a notorious jam.

My rotation lasted for eight hours, long enough to wake First Squad and Sergeant Mason so they could get ready to step on their patrol. They had an easy one, just a quick hike around some of the nearby villages and back before lunch. They'd be around to help man the TCP when all the Afghans showed up for the KLE.

As morning came and went, the locals began to gather just outside our TCP. Almost all were elder men with long white or salt-and-peppered beards. They wore their traditional Afghan garb. Some wore black vests and battered dress shoes. Their faces were stoic, hard wrinkled, and strangely nervous. There were a couple younger guys, the old men's bodyguards. They had AK47s slung behind their backs and chest rigs lazily wrapped around their bodies. I hated that. The ANP and one of our Marines approached the group, there were quick and hasty searches conducted on everyone, and the bodyguards were told to remove the magazines from their rifles. They complied, and this went along smoothly enough.

Gunny Alvarez and I met them in front of the ANP's section of the TCP. We exchanged greetings, both Afghan and American. I offered cigarettes and water, while another ANP made tea. For the most part, I liked these KLEs. Sure, some of the demands or conversation points were ridiculous, outlandish, and strange. But I got to sit down and converse with these people. My last deployment, Reid and I watched from a security post as these were being conducted. I felt important; I could already hear the conversations I'd have with friends and family back home about this.

When we all finally sat down in a large circle, I recognized all the faces. But one was missing. Abdul Malik. I searched the faces again and only saw anxious and nervous expressions. "Malik's not here," I said in a quiet whisper to Gunny Alvarez. I saw the gunny's eyes scan and come to the same conclusion. "He told me he'd come."

"Maybe he's late," Gunny Alvarez said. Then he started the meeting.

Immediately, the Afghans began speaking. They seemed more organized than usual. One spoke at a time, his words spewed quickly, and the others nodded along. When he finished, another immediately began. Aarash tried to slow them down, his hands shot forward motioning for them to wait, but the elders kept going. Each one spoke more earnestly than the last.

"Aarash, what the hell are they saying?" Gunny Alvarez asked calmly. He was the pillar of professionalism, and I considered the staff non-commissioned officer a role model.

"Gunny," Aarash spoke with a slight turn of his head to the Marine, but his eyes stayed glued to the elders. "These dudes keep asking when you will leave."

My eyebrows furrowed and my head rocked back in confusion, I remember this because Gunny Alvarez stayed cool; he didn't flinch or show any signs of emotion. He simply heard the words and began processing and solving. We had good rapport with the Afghans; no, we weren't best friends, but we had working relationships. We gave them food and money and supplies. Now they wanted us out? It didn't make sense.

"They say your job is done here. You can go. You should go. They tell us to go home. Even me, they want me to go back to Kabul," Aarash said, his face visibly becoming more and more concerned.

I found myself hovering my hand near my pistol. I kept it tucked in the small of my back against my belt when I wasn't wearing all my gear and holster. "Ask them where

Malik is," I said to Aarash. Gunny Alvarez's eyes darted at me, and I remembered my rank and place, but instead of reprimanding me, he nodded his head in agreement.

Aarash spoke in Pashto.

Something was wrong; the elders didn't speak. Their eyes darted back and forth to each other, and there was a long moment of silence. Finally, one cleared his voice and spoke. I didn't know what was being said, but it wasn't right. Just moments before they had spoken without pause or any equivalent to an "um," but this guy kept tripping over his words. His wrinkled hands shook.

"Malik is sick," Aarash said, his own face expressed his confusion.

"Why do they want us to leave?" Gunny Alvarez asked.

Pashto went left and right. We waited patiently for Aarash to translate. "They keep saying the same thing again and again. Marines should go home. Job is done. They are asking us to leave. They really want me to go back to Kabul."

There wasn't much more progress than that. After twenty minutes of the same thing, Gunny Alvarez offered them some more water bottles and cigarettes, then said goodbye. The elders once again nervously eyed each other, got up, and left. I didn't wait for them to leave. I got up and went to the COC, where Sergeant Mason was waiting with a cigarette.

"That was weird," I said, my mind still very aware of my pistol.

Sergeant Mason, who hadn't seen any of the KLE, simply shrugged his shoulders. "Sounds like another day in Afghanaland."

I chuckled nervously. "How'd your patrol go?"

"No weird dogs." Sergeant Mason leaned back and folded his hands behind his head. His tone said he'd believed me, he simply hadn't seen them. Part of me wished he had, while another part of me thought he was lucky. Just thinking about those eyes and teeth sent another chill up my spine.

Gunny Alvarez came into the COC then, and immediately lit a cigarette.

"What do you think that was about, Gunny?" I asked, reaching for my own pack of smokes.

"I think we may be looking at Taliban activity coming into the area." Gunny leaned back against the cool mud wall and exhaled a cloud of tobacco. "The fighting in Sangin is still going pretty strong, might be enough to encourage some jihadists to start making moves down here."

Sangin. The Marines in Third Battalion, Fifth Marines were getting into gunfights almost every day there. The casualties were mounting. I'd be lying if I said I hadn't wished I was there. But the rational me was thankful I wasn't.

"Alright you two, don't fuck around on your patrols. Keep an eye out. Lake, I want you to head south tomorrow and investigate closer to the river," Gunny Alvarez said and pointed to a map hanging on the wall. His finger circled around a bend in the Helmand River. "If I were going to try and get fighters in this area, it'd be here."

"What about Malik? Shouldn't we check him out?" I asked.

Gunny didn't budge; his eyes stayed glued to the map. "Nah, you were there yesterday. We can't form a pattern for the Talibs to hit us with an IED."

"Roger that," I said. He was right.

So when the following morning came, we suited up. The sounds of velcro and buckles snapping into place became the soundtrack to our opening. Marines donned their heavy plate carriers and uncomfortable Kevlar helmets. Bolts slide back halfway to ensure there was a round in the chamber of their rifles. Radio checks were conducted. I inspected the corpsman joining us, Aarash, and the team leaders. The team leaders then checked their teams.

"COC, this is Headhunter," I said into the handmic of my PRC-152 radio. Headhunter was the callsign the Marines had collectively decided to name our squad. I wasn't the biggest fan, but the name stuck. "Radio check."

"Lima Charlie, Headhunter. Happy hunting."

With that, I motioned for Reid to get his team moving. Reid then turned and waved his arm for the point man to step. Everyone became serious and tense. Rifles were held a little higher, and eyes scanned harder.

The first hour went by quickly. I think everyone being on edge made the Marines focus more on their surroundings than the passing time. We'd made our way through fields, over canals, and through villages. Everything felt the same. The women tended to things around the compounds, some of the children were playing outside with sticks and stones, older boys worked the fields, and dogs gave the usual barks and growls we were accustomed to.

Hour two went by much slower. The heat was starting to get to everyone this time; it was hotter than usual. The sun was beating us down and draining everyone's energy. For the most part we were used to it, but today it was much more prevalent. I gulped down one of the two water bottles I carried, crushed the plastic, then stuffed it into a cargo pocket. I saw Petty pour some of his water down his neck. I found it amusing that his wet combat top looked no different from the sweat-soaked uniforms of the other Marines.

By hour three, everyone was starting to feel tired and sore. Heavy equipment-laden plate carriers dug into our shoulders and made our backs ache. Each piece of gear was slowly turning against us. We continued our patrol. We'd reached the bend in the river and set up a small

LP/OP, or listen post/observation post. We would stay here for about another hour or so in hopes of seeing distant Taliban movement.

Hour four wasn't too bad. The Marines were hidden in the shade of brush and trees. We weren't standing on our feet anymore. Some were laid out in the prone with their rifles out, while me, the corpsman, Aarash, and Evan sat central to the squad. We leaned back against our gear and could, for the most part, relax.

When it turned to hour six, I gave the signal for us to start moving again; it'd be another long walk back. I'd partially planned for this; though doing this longer and harder patrol was necessary, it also meant that on our next patrol day, we'd get an easier mission.

We were halfway home when we heard it. A snarling bark so loud it made us all jump. Rifles raised and heads turned. I couldn't believe how loud it was, and I've been blown up before. Again I felt my spine shiver. I gripped my M4 tight.

The dog walked up to the crest of a high berm, then sat on its hind legs. I thought it was one of the three we'd seen earlier, but its pristine coat was a mixed color of black and brown. Still those soul-crushing, empty, hate-filled, black and red eyes. The knife-like teeth seemed sharper. Its claws looked like razors. It snarled and eyed us.

Luckily there was a ten-foot-wide canal between us. The water ran deep and fast, and the rumbling it produced could have almost been peaceful, had it not been for the canine at its bank. Feeling relieved that we were safe from the kuchi, we began to move again. We'd leave its territory, and that would be the end of it. The hound stood on all fours, then effortlessly leapt across the canal. My heart stopped.

"Holy fuck!"

I'm not sure who said it, but the Marine summed up everything we thought and felt. The dog stood still for a moment, and that's when I realized just how big the thing was. It's spine alone was four feet high. It had looked big before; up close it was massive. Then it snarled at us once more. One of Evans' Marines was the closest to the dog, and in a blur it charged. It was fast. Too fast.

The Marine cursed and raised his M16 to fire, but he was too slow. The rounds dug into the dirt, harmless, in front of the beast. The dog kept coming without fear or care.

Three more shots rang out in quick succession. It was Evans, he'd sighted in on the dog with his rifle as soon as it had landed on our side of the canal. The animal's body jerked, and it gave out a hiss like noise before tumbling end over end, dead.

"Jesus fucking Christ!" the Marine yelled, his adrenaline running. He fired his rifle into the carcass a few more times just to be sure.

It had happened in an instant. I have no idea how many seconds had passed from that first bark to the final shots, but it couldn't have been more than thirty. I couldn't believe it. Before we could even inspect the dog, we heard yelling. It was one of the village elders from the KLE; two other men were at his flanks, and they were running toward us.

"What the fuck is going on here?" I said out loud. "Reid, search those guys! Evans, Petty, get us security! Aarash, what the fuck are they yelling about?" I never heard him answer me; My radio sparked to life with transmissions from TCP 2, they'd heard the gunshots. I responded, and we left the carcass behind.

When I was done, the Afghans had been searched, and Reid had brought them to speak with me. They spoke quickly and loudly. Aarash was about to begin translating while they yelled. "I know, I know, they want us to pay for the dog, right?" I said to Aarash with more irritation than I intended.

Aarash shook his head no. "No, man, they just want us to leave. Now." I could tell the interpreter was getting scared.

"What?"

"Dude, I have no idea. They do not want money. They do not want anything. They are demanding that we leave." Aarash began looking around nervously. "Dude, let us just go."

At this point I was tired, exhausted, slightly at my whit's end with the insane dog, and still concerned about Taliban activity. "Fuck it. Reid, get us out of here!" I yelled and immediately went for my pack of cigarettes. I lit a smoke and took a deep inhale, and we started to step off, when I noticed the Afghans placing a blanket over the dog. Maybe it was the heat messing with my mind, but I could have sworn I saw wisps of smoke and ash coming off the carcass.

At the end of hour eight I was finally stripping off the weight of the plate carrier. It was instant relief. I peeled the sweat-soaked combat top off my skin, and immediately went to work on my boots. In less than a minute I was in nothing but my skivvy shorts and sandals, with a cigarette hanging from my lips. Reid was much the same way, but he flopped onto his cot and let out a loud exhale. Everyone was beat. I wanted to do the same. A debrief stood between me and relaxation.

Gunny Alvarez was my savoir. He made his way over to me, and we knocked out the after-action report quickly. He was already tracking on the incident with the dog and had heard the situation reports I was sending in. I started to describe the jump the kuchi had made with no effort.

The other Marines were listening and joined in to tell the story. Gunny simply nodded his head. I know he believed us, but let's face it. We were talking about a dog, and Gunny had Taliban to worry about. In the end, Gunny simply said, "Well good shooting, Evans. Still no Combat Action Ribbon."

We laughed; everyone wanted the ribbon to show they'd been in combat against the enemy. Only I and a few of the senior Marines had one. The joke was well received, and it seemed to remind everyone that we were causing a big fuss about a dog. We went back to business as usual.

I ate then, finally, and let myself melt into my cot. I was asleep within minutes. I dreamt about home and meeting a girl. It was the kind of dream that lingered in my mind long after I awoke. I didn't have a girlfriend or wife waiting for me in the States, but admittedly I wanted one. I hadn't dated while back in California, I was too focused on becoming a squad leader. Now I wanted to return and find a girl. Maybe that was childish. Oh, well, it was an escape and a goal. She had long black hair and brown eyes, and her features were soft and beautiful. The dream was just about to get good when Reid woke me up.

"Bro, the ANP just bounced," Reid said in a harsh whisper.

I was rubbing the sleep out of my eyes, still envisioning the girl from my dream. In a more than annoyed tone I asked, "What happened?"

"The ANP, they just up and left."

I was awake now and turned my gaze to the COC. I could hear Gunny Alvarez and Sergeant Mason on the radios. It was night now, and only a few lanterns combatted the dark inside the TCP. I leaned up and swung my legs off the coat. I couldn't help but continue to rub my face in an attempt to wake up faster.

Reid kept talking. "A local came and talked to them, then they just hopped in their truck and fucking left." Reid was anxious, his rifle slung in front of him.

"Alright, alright. I'm up," I said.

"Dude, are you fucking listening to me?"

I could tell Reid was spooked; he wasn't referring to me by rank. Though in private I didn't mind, the Marine knew he needed to when others were around. I got up and made my way to the COC.

Sergeant Mason saw me and glanced at his watch. "Lake, you still got like two and a half hours left. Get some sleep."

I lit a cigarette and leaned against the door frame. "I heard the ANP bounced."

Sergeant Mason extended a hand, asking for one of my smokes. I gave him one, and he answered, "Yeah, no idea why or where to. Classic Afghans. But you get some rest, we've got this."

I nodded my head and went back to my cot. Maybe I'd be able to dream of the girl again. I went back to sleep. Instead of the her, the dog visited me. I was walking alone, and there it was, staring straight at me. It stood there, and I could feel its gaze pierce my soul. It didn't bark or snarl. It just stared.

I woke up in a cold sweat. Taking a glance at my watch, I saw it was twenty minutes until midnight, and my turn for COC watch. I went for a piss and gulped down a bottle of water before heading to the COC. Gunny Alvarez was there, and I told him I could take the watch now. He thanked me and left for his sleeping bag. I began waking my Marines for their turns to stand watch.

There was a pot of coffee in the corner, a gift from someone back in the States. The coffee maker had become one of the few luxuries we had in TCP 2. With a canteen cup filled with the black brew, I sat and smoked, and monitored the laptop. On the screen was a display feed of our thermal camera. The camera was placed high on top of Post Two, where it could rotate and scan the surrounding area. The display was set to "White Hot", and heat signatures showed in bright white. I pivoted the camera around and as usual, and saw nothing.

The TCP was quiet, except for the subtle rustlings of the Marines switching with each on post. I could hear them and their quick conversations, heard the velcro of gear coming on and off, the carbonated pop of a Rip-It energy drink opening. I reached for my book and began reading. It was military fiction, Airborne Rangers in Vietnam on long range reconnaissance patrols against the North Vietnamese Army. I'd found it on the shelf of used books selling at my local library, and I'd bought it for seventy-five cents. It had become my favorite read and my best investment. I'd read the thing at least ten times.

Origins

Every half hour I grabbed a black Motorola radio and called for a communications check with Post One and Two. The Marines replied back, their voices filled with boredom. I'd ask if there was anything they needed— coffee, water, a snack—then obliged any requests. Sometimes I'd visit the Posts, stand with the Marine on duty, and we'd talk to help pass the time. Standing Post was soul draining; they did rotations of four hours on, four hours off, eight hours on, eight hours off. They would have to wear their gear and helmets and just stand there, keeping vigilant in an area that had been quiet and peaceful.

I was climbing down the ladder of Post Two when we heard barking. No, not the air-shattering roar of one of those beasts, but the barks of the kuchis we were more accustomed to. It was a bit unusual, but nothing too far out of the ordinary, so I paid no attention to it. I simply cursed at the reminder of the beasts we'd seen and the one that had haunted me in my dream. I went to check on Post One, and the barking continued in the distance, the sound so low it wouldn't have disturbed anyone's sleep.

In contrast to Post Two's ladder, Post One had a long, wide, railless staircase made of two-by-fours. Evans was on duty, and he casually sipped on an energy drink. His PVS-14s hung in front of his face, and the green glow of night vision illuminated his left eye.

"How's your war?" I asked when I reached the top of the stairs.

Evans offered me a sip of the Rip-It. That was a testament to his character; I was sitting on boxes of the beverages down in the COC, and he still offered some of his to me. I waved it off, and he spoke quietly and with some cheer, trying not reveal just how dull things were so far. "Another day in paradise."

I chuckled and made my way inside the post. The floor was a sheet of plywood on top of dirt filled HESCO barriers. More HESCO barriers formed the walls, and wooden posts rose up from the barriers and held a wooden roof, where dirt and sandbags gave some overhead protection. Cami-netting hung from the roof and over the entry, and partially over the firing port. More sandbags filled the empty, vulnerable spaces around us. There was an M240 medium machinegun and two cans of belted 7.62 ammunition, pen flares, binoculars, Motorola radio, and, strangely enough, a machete. Why it was there I have no idea. A trash bag hung from the corner, and beside it was a stack of water bottles and some MREs to snack on. A piece of cardboard had been nailed to the wall with a drawing of a range card on it, the range card showing specific features and/or buildings and the distances to each. This was where the Marines spent twelve hours of their day, every other day. I was glad I didn't have to do it anymore; I had freedom in the COC.

Evans was a quiet guy, and for a minute we stood there in silence, then I lit a cigarette and offered him one. He usually didn't smoke, but this time he accepted, and together we blew small clouds of tobacco into the cool night air. The barking was still going on.

"You gonna get yourself a dog after this?" Evans asked suddenly.

The question seemed random for only a fraction of a second. "I'm not sure. That one today kind of ruined the fun." Evans nodded along in agreeance. "You?"

Evans thought for a moment before answering, "Sure, today was a fluke. I've seen plenty of good boys and good girls. Only the past couple days have I seen those…things."

I smiled to myself; Evans was always the levelheaded one.

"I'd like to get a husky or a German shepherd. Something big you can wrestle with, ya' know?" Evans continued, and we discussed pets until the cigarettes burnt to the filters. I asked if he needed anything, then made my way down the stairs and past sleeping Marines. With a look at my watch, I saw that it'd be time to wake the next pair of Marines for watch soon.

Reid was one of the Marines up next. I woke him up with a shake, and he cursed before forcing himself up. The next Marine woke up in similar fashion, and I waited in the COC. As they dressed, the noise of putting on gear was drowned out by the barking. I finally realized that the dogs hadn't stopped, they were getting louder—or was it closer? I worked the controls for the thermal camera and scanned around. At first there was nothing, just empty Afghan countryside in the dead of night. No one was out. The four other Marines and I were probably the only ones awake.

I kept moving the camera around, completed a full pass, then started a second. The camera panned toward one of the open fields next to a compound with long, high exterior walls. From the corner I saw a dog run out, turn around, then start barking. The way the kuchi moved and stood told me it was defensive. It was barking at something hidden, away by the compound. Another dog rounded the corner in similar fashion, and it too began to bark at something unseen.

I panned the camera around the compound and its surroundings. I saw the heat signatures of other kuchis, all barking and snarling at the same concealed thing. I was beginning to consider that maybe the cause of all this was inside the building itself, until another dog emerged from behind the corner. As it came into frame, the other dogs darted away to get their distance before once again turning around to bark and snarl. This new canine was massive compared to the already large hounds. Then another appeared.

And another. And another.

More and more of these massive beasts were making their way into the field. It was a pack. I couldn't believe it. The pack of massive beasts slowly walked through the field. All around them, smaller kuchis kept up their relentless, useless yelling. I estimated there were about thirty of them. I tried to count them all, but the heat signatures distorted their images and made it difficult to differentiate them all.

The heat signatures themselves were strange. The beasts in the pack shone at a brighter intensity than the orbiting dogs. They seemed to radiate heat. With slow determination, the pack walked, patient and stern. They were making their way toward us.

The chills were coming back, and I debated waking up Sergeant Mason and Gunny Alvarez. The pack came closer and closer. "Fuck it," I said to myself out loud and left the COC in a rush. I shook Mason and Alvarez awake and simply said, "You gotta see this."

The two walked into the COC in a haze. Gunny Alvarez didn't hesitate, he went straight for the coffee and poured a cup. After taking a sip, he finally glanced at me with this demanding look of curiosity. I motioned to the screen, and the two peered at it. It took them a moment to shake the sleep away and process what they were seeing.

"Alright, I'll admit it. That's fucking weird," Sergeant Mason said as he took the cup of coffee and drank some for himself.

"I think they're coming this way."

They both looked at me for a moment, then back to the screen. As if on cue, the Motorola radio sparked to life with Evans' voice. "COC, this is Post One."

I grabbed the radio and depressed the key. "Send it."

"I've got a huge pack of dogs coming this way." Evan's voice teetered between disbelief and professionalism.

Gunny took the radio from me. "Post One, Post Two, we're tracking it. Keep eyes on." He turned to Sergeant Mason. "Do me a favor, Sergeant, get our rifles."

"Hunting season's on," Mason said with a grin and a wink. I went for mine as well.

By then, Reid had switched out with Evans for post. Evans met us in the COC, with all his gear still on. "That pack is close."

Sergeant Mason ensured he had a round in the chamber. "Evans, let's go to the gate. I'll show you what it's like to hunt hogs in Texas." Together the two left the building and made their way to our entry point.

I decided I wanted some trigger time as well, and I went up to Post Two. I wanted the elevation to try to engage more of the beasts. I'd finally get some vengeance for the chills and shakes the dogs were giving me. I climbed up and met Harris there. He had his night vision down and was looking in the direction of the pack. His rifle wasn't shouldered, but ready. When he saw me leaning against the sandbags and leveling my M4, he did the same.

I hadn't gotten my night vision. I should have, but the skies were clear, and the moon was bright. Had it not been for this disturbance, it would have been scenic and beautiful. That was the only thing Afghanistan had going for it. I still think pleasantly about those nights, funny enough.

Evans and Sergeant Mason were out at the entry point, protected solely by the surrounding concertina wire. I watched Mason step ahead. He was excited and confident, but looked ridiculous. He was wearing only his skivvy shorts, boots, and helmet with night vision gear. An extra magazine was tucked into the shorts, and his rifle was slung over his shoulder. Finding a suitable spot, the sergeant swung the rifle into his hands and activated the infrared laser of the PEQ 15 device.

The pack was only thirty meters away now. "Sergeant's aiming at the lead one," Harris said. "Hey, can I get in on this?"

I remember smirking at Harris and told him, "Fuck yeah."

The pack sprinted forward. A giant mass of fangs, claws, and those wrathful eyes. Mason got a single shot off before they changed.

They weren't dogs or animals or beasts. That pristine coat of fur began to burn and illuminate. They became an inferno, a wall of fire, whirling faster and faster toward us. Fire that didn't create smoke. The bodies shifted and morphed into something human. Two arms, two legs, a head, but those same dreadful eyes of obsidian black. And they were armed. Burning with the same intensity and fire were the shapes of swords, axes, and spears in their hands. Some didn't even have weapons; their hands were opened wide to reveal burning razor like claws.

"Fuck!"

We had time to yell that. It's odd the things you remember. But between the time the pack sprinted forward and changed there was just enough time to vocalize our shock and horror. The moment after, Sergeant Mason was eviscerated. I've never heard a more bloodcurdling scream. His blood sprayed into the night air, steaming and sizzling and boiling from the fire. His body had been ripped and cut open, the flesh burning and cauterizing. Two more of the demons cut him down, instantly silencing his screams.

Evans had been able to snap off a few rounds before a demon with an enormous axe swung through his belly. Evans' upper half fell backward, and the man was screaming, but still trying to work his rifle. The demon brought the axe down on Evans' head, but the Marine had done something, his rounds had hit another demon. I watched it let out a roar before the flames went out, and an empty husk crumpled to the ground.

They could be killed.

Harris and I fired. Our rifles hammered out round after round in a chaotic beat of vengeance. I aimed at one wielding two curved swords, and hit center mass. I hit it again and again and again until the demon turned into a charred corpse.

I can't describe the noises. Marines waking up in horror. Demons howling. Gunshots, and the roar of blazing fires. Marines fought. Demons killed. It all mixed and tangled to create a symphony of death.

Reid was on Post Two, making any Marine proud. He grabbed the M240 and was firing the machinegun with both hands, the stock pinned under his armpit, the belt of 7.62 hung over his arm. Reid was fearless. He cursed and fired, and the machinegun held back the demons long enough for the other Marines to get out of their sleeping bags and reach their weapons.

I thought for just a moment that maybe there was hope for us. That with the two posts firing, we could strong point the TCP just long enough for the rest of the Marines to get their weapons in the fight. That's when a demon leapt at us from the entry point. Its flaming mass lit up the evening and crossed the distance. It landed in front of us, just at the lip of the firing port. Harris had the 240 ready. He let out a burst into the demon's face, killing it instantly. The body fell from view, and I thought we were okay.

Another demon reached in and grabbed Harris by his plate carrier. He screamed, not out of fear, but from the fire that was burning his skin. With an almost effortless show of strength, Harris was yanked out of the post. His legs knocked into me during the process, and I fell back down into the TCP.

I landed hard, the wind knocked out of me, and I gasped desperately for air while trying to recover my rifle. I was yanked up, and I thought that would be it; a demon was about to kill me. But I felt no heat, no fire against my skin. It was Gunny Alvarez. He fired his pistol and pulled me to my feet. Around us was nothing short of medieval. Marines were fighting desperately against the demons. I saw Petty empty his rifle and try to reach for his bayonet before being stabbed by a long-bladed spear. His wound burned, and soon the Marine was on fire, writhing on the ground. There were some black, charred husks, but not as many. There were more Marines lying dead. Their wounds were large, gaping, and cauterized. Blood steamed and boiled in the dirt.

Gunny Alvarez was pulling me backward. We started to fire our way through the demons toward Reid and Post One. Another Marine tried to join us, but he was torn apart by a demon. Gunny Alvarez fired and quickly got revenge.

Despite all the chaos going on around us, I could still distinguish the feel of my rifle bolt locking to the rear. My magazine was empty, and I hadn't put on my combat gear. There was an M16 on the ground, I'm not sure whose it was, but I figured the owner was dead. I threw my M4 down, grabbed the M16, and fired, thankful there were still rounds left. We passed another rifle, and I handed it to Gunny Alvarez just as his M9's slide locked to the rear.

TCP 2 was burning. We were dying. But damnit, we fought. None of the Marines stopped. It was obvious this would be our grave. We knew we were being slaughtered, but with rifle and bayonet, we stood defiant and proud.

Gunny and I were at the base of the stairs for Post One, and Reid was still hammering away with the machinegun. A demon rushed us, and Gunny put it down with the M16. Another came, and Gunny extinguished its flame in similar fashion. But then there was a third. It swung a sword and cut deep into the gunnery sergeant's thigh. He yelled and pushed me away as a final act of service. Gunny Alvarez died doing what a good staff non-commissioned officer does, caring for his Marines. I saw his face. He wasn't angry or upset or scared. He just wanted me to get to safety. I obeyed his wordless order and never saw the demon that killed him.

I ducked under Reid's gunfire. I grabbed at his extra magazines, replenished the M16, and began firing as well. There was comfort in the 240's death song; Reid wasn't working short, controlled bursts. He depressed the trigger in long choruses of hate.

Reid came to the end of the belt of ammunition, dropped the gun for his own M16, and fought back with that. The demons were swarming us, and before I knew it, my M16 was empty again. I backed up and felt something strange against my back. The Beretta. I had completely forgotten the pistol tucked into the small of my back. I reached for it and fired as the demons reached the stairs. Then they were in our post.

Reid screamed as a demon blade cut into his shoulder. The Marine grabbed for the machete we never understood why was there and swung with all his might. I couldn't believe it—the old blade tore through fiery demon flesh. The demon fell away as its flames were extinguished. Reid turned to me, the pain visible on his face. He dug into a pouch for the olive drab body of an M67 fragmentation grenade. He pulled the pin and released the spoon. "Watch my six, brother."

Reid shoved me out of the firing port. I tumbled end over end, landed against the hard ground of the road, and hit the back of my head. Everything looked blurry, and my skull was pounding. I heard Reid one last time.

"You can't kill me!"

My hearing cut out, the earth shook, and through blurry vision, Post One disappeared in a cloud of smoke and dust and fire. I felt very tired, though I knew I shouldn't; I needed to stay awake and keep fighting. But the blur got thicker and darker. I just wanted to fall asleep and wake up from this nightmare. My arms and legs attempted to push me up, but the weight was impossible. Stillness brought an undeniable pleasure. I closed my eyes, and everything went black.

PART TWO

My hearing came back first, to a distant, mechanical thumping. I tried to wake, but felt myself drifting off again. The noise stayed and grew louder and louder, until finally it became unavoidable. The sound encompassed me, and there was nothing else to be heard besides it. The wind shifted, and my face stung as if pricked by a thousand tiny needles.

Finally, I shifted. I tried to move quickly, but I could only muster a slow, drunken recoil. Coming out of the fog that was my head, the realization hit me. Helicopter blades. Large ones. I brought a hand up to my face to shield myself from the dirt and sand being thrown by the rotor wash. Looking up, I saw it against the still dark blue sky, the twin rotors and wide tail of an MV-22 Osprey. Its rear ramp was down, and two ropes were hanging down at an angle just before being released and falling to the ground. Then the twin engines rotated forward, and the Osprey was away, beginning to circle high and wide above TCP 2.

I gulped down saliva and dust before trying to get to my knees. I still had the M9 in my hands, and slowly I rose to my feet. I could hear shuffling and movement inside the TCP. I began to put one foot in front of the other. I gained my strength, and the fog cleared, allowing me to think and focus. There were harsh whispers coming from inside, I couldn't quite make it out.

"U.S. Marine! U.S. Marine!" I cried out, but my mouth felt like cotton. I tried to pool up spit to wet my throat. I yelled again. I needed to get all the way around the TCP toward the entry point. I saw Sergeant Mason. His body was twisted and open, and long stretches of his skin were burnt black. The smell of his blood hit me hard, and I recoiled and gagged. I couldn't look at him anymore. I passed him and told myself I'd deal with his body later.

I came toward the concertina wire and saw silhouettes forming along the tops of the HESCO barriers and on of what remained of Post Two. I quickly put the pistol in the small of my back and threw my hands up into the air, still approaching and yelling.

In the darkness I could see two men step out from the TCP and face me. One put his weapon up, and the other said, "Hey bud, stop right there."

I listened. I knew these guys would want to search me. I didn't blame them; this was everyone's procedure. The quicker I complied, the faster this would all end. I hoped. "I'm Corporal Jonathan Lake, and I've got a holstered pistol."

"Alright bud, do me a favor," the voice called back out to me. His tone seemed friendly, but cautious and confident. "Lift your shirt and do a little turn for me."

Origins

I couldn't help but chuckle quietly to myself. It was the same things we did to the Afghans to ensure they weren't wearing a suicide vest or concealing a weapon in their waistband. I complied, and told them again about the pistol.

"Okay, walking backward, hands in the air, come to me," the voice called.

Once again I complied, and hoped I wouldn't trip. As strange as it was, I felt safe. I hadn't heard any gunfire, so I assumed the demons were gone. There was no barking, howling, or snarls, just the hum of the orbiting Osprey. Then I did trip, on Evans' legs, which were detached from his torso. Any feelings of safety quickly disappeared.

The voice told me to stop, then hands were on me, the pistol was yanked away, and I felt the familiar routine of a search. Finally they turned me around, and I looked to see Americans in gear I had only seen Special Forces units wear. Their uniforms were green with M81 woodland camouflage, there were knee pads built into the pants, their plate carriers were thinner and streamlined compared to the bulky, cumbersome things we'd been issued. Even their helmets were more impressive than the Kevlar one I had, with IR strobes, flashlights, and battery packs for dual tubed night vision devices. There were thick headphones over their ears, and mics bent in front of their faces. The two had short-barreled MK18 rifles laden with optics, lasers, and lights.

Everything about these guys screamed nonconventional forces. Who, though, wasn't clear.

"Who are you guys?" I asked.

"The cavalry," one replied. It wasn't the voice who'd yelled to me earlier during the search.

"You're late," I said, a little more tensely than I'd intended, but the man's attempt at humor wasn't appreciated right after seeing so many of my Marines slaughtered and burnt.

"Sorry," he replied, and by his tone, he meant it.

"Is it just you?" the searcher asked me.

"I hope not." I had no idea who else could have made it. In that moment I said a quick prayer, hoping for the others to be okay.

"How many of you were there?"

"Twenty-three pax," I replied quickly using the military jargon for personnel.

The two looked at each other. The one who'd apologized turned away and left me with the searcher. "Mind telling me what happened here?"

Fire flashed in my mind, and I couldn't imagine this guy believing me. But I told him the truth. I told him about the dogs, the pack, the transformation, the flames and heat. His expression never changed. I expected him to give me a look as if I were crazy. Instead, he just listened and nodded softly. He dug into a cargo pocket, produced a bottle of water, and offered it to me. I stared at it for a moment before taking it and finishing the drink in one go.

There was silence between us then. I looked at the doorway into the TCP and started to take a step forward. "I should take a look." I felt guilt then. I knew most of my Marines were dead. Reid had saved me.

The man side stepped to block my path. "You shouldn't."

The second man exited the TCP, and the two exchanged looks. "I'm sorry to tell you, Corporal, but I've got twenty-two remains inside." The look was solemn. "Put up a hell of a fight, though."

I collapsed to my knees. The two gently knelt and followed me down. I was oblivious to the tears trailing down my face. "You guys got a cigarette?" They handed me one and lit the end for me. I inhaled and pictured my Marines' faces; Reid, Petty, Gunny Alvarez, even Aarash the interpreter. A third man with a thick black beard came up and spoke to the others in whispers; they had to lean into each other's faces and lift their earpieces to hear. "Who are you guys? MARSOC?" I asked again, realizing they'd never answered my question. Everything about them screamed Marine Special Operations Command.

Their eyes darted to each other before the searcher answered, "Sure."

I shook my head; they weren't going to tell me anything. "You guys think I'm crazy, huh?" I kept going at the cigarette, trying to stay sane.

"No, Corporal. No, I don't." It was the searcher again. He was back down to my level, and he also lit a cigarette. "I'm Captain King." He motioned to the second man from earlier. "That there is Master Sergeant Quince, and this one here is Gunnery Sergeant Carland."

Quince and Carland gave the captain a look of surprise.

"What you saw, Corporal, is what we call Djinn."

Quince spoke in surprise, "Sir…"

Captain King looked up at the two senior noncommissioned officers. "He's the sole survivor, let's give the kid a break, huh?" King gave me a look that told me I needed to stop feeling sorry for myself. "I'm going to be straight with you, Corporal. You guys got hit bad, and you're it. I can't afford to extract you right now. We've got to hunt the rest of those things down before they try to hit the rest of your unit."

I thought about the remaining Marines from the platoon at TCP 4. Where had they been? Where they about to get attacked like we had? The look on my face must have given away what I was thinking. "The rest of your platoon is fine; they haven't been engaged yet. Looks like you guys did enough damage to cause the Djinn to regroup." I think I sighed in relief. "But you need to come with us. Marines are warfighters. I need you to fight." His tone became more fatherly than anything. At his words, I nodded my head and stood up.

"What about my Marines?" I asked.

"I've got more Marines en route to handle the remains; we've got to finish the fight before we worry about battlefield recovery," King said matter-of-factly.

I tried for the doorway again. "I need to tac up." My combat gear was still inside, and I wondered if any of it had burned.

Gunnery Sergeant Carland got in my way this time. "I don't think you want to go in there, my man."

"I'll be okay," I told him. "I need my rifle, at least."

King nodded his head, and they let me pass. Inside I finally saw the damage that had been dealt. There were burnt marks everywhere. Marines lay dead, and mixed amongst them were the charred husks of the demons that seemed to crumble to ash at the gentlest brush of wind. The smell was horrid, and I struggled not to gag. Standing amongst the dead were the living, other Marines dressed in similar fashion to King, Quince, and Carland. A couple took photographs on digital cameras, for what I suspected would be used in an after-action report. Others stood security with their weapons and night vision pointed outward.

I went to my cot, ignoring the blood stains. I simply grabbed my plate carrier; it was still staged where I'd left it. There were a couple black marks where embers must have landed, but thankfully it was clear of any blood. My helmet didn't share that luck, however—the inner padding had burnt away, and the camouflage cover was dark and stank of copper. I left it behind and found my M4 where I'd dropped it. I slipped in a new magazine and chambered a round. A couple of the other Marines stared but left me alone.

When I was done, I returned to Captain King. "I'm sorry about your brothers, Corporal, but we're stepping out in one minute."

"Where do you need me, sir?" I responded. I appreciated his sympathy, but the need for revenge started to build within me. He'd said they were going to hunt these Djinn, or whatever it was he called the demons, and I wanted in.

"You'll be in the middle with me," he said, then continued, "Have you noticed any new faces or anything suspicious in the area since you've been here?"

I thought about that for a moment, and then I remembered Abdul Malik. "A local elder didn't show up to a KLE a couple days ago. Good guy, we had great rapport with him."

Quince chewed on his lip while he listened. When I finished, he spoke next, "Thinking the usual, King?"

I was surprised to hear him refer to the officer by last name only, but I'd heard the Special Forces community was much more relaxed.

"Yeah." King nodded his head. "Yeah, it does."

"The usual?" I asked.

King let out a long exhale, as if preparing himself for a speech. "The Djinn are something like ghosts or spirits. Shapeshifters, and made of fire. They don't usually hang out in our world. Unless they're summoned. That's usually through a deal, or sacrifice, or both." I suddenly became very sad for what that could mean for Malik. "But nine times out of ten, there's someone nearby and in charge."

"Like a necromancer?" I asked, cutting in, dumbfounded by what I was hearing. But hell, how could I not believe it at the same time?

"Nah, necros work with dead dudes. Djinn aren't dead," Carland said as he put a pinch of tobacco into his lip. "More like a sorcerer."

I was speechless. I wanted to believe I was being pranked. A bunch of Special Forces Marines playing a joke on the grunt. But I'd seen the Djinn.

"So we kill the sorcerer, we stop the Djinn in the area," King said matter-of-factly.

"Wait, if Djinn are ghosts, how were we able to kill them?" I asked.

Quince answered that one. The large Marine was in the middle of taking off his helmet to scratch his head. "They don't live in our realm, but when they cross over, they play by our rules."

"You guys are serious about all this?"

"It's the dumbed down version, but yeah." Quince put his helmet back on, then spoke into his mic. Immediately the other Marines began moving and exiting the TCP. There were fourteen of them in total, operating in what appeared to be two teams of six, with Captain King as the patrol leader, and Master Sergeant Quince as the executive.

I kept close to King and Quince; I must have stood out like a sore thumb. I dug deep into my memory to recall everything I'd learned and trained on. These guys were heavy hitters, and I was the weak link; I needed to make sure I did everything right, and not be the thing that slowed them down. King asked me where Malik had been from, and I pointed out the village in the distance.

"We've only got an hour and a half left before the sun starts to rise," the captain said with a glance at his watch. He motioned for the Marines to move, and we were off.

I was slightly surprised at the way they moved. It was almost like any other patrol I had done with my squad; they simply moved a bit faster and more efficiently. These guys were much more comfortable working with their night vision optics than my Marines had ever been. There was little need for communication between them, other than directions. They moved as one. It was hard to describe, but I could feel it. A part of me loved it.

Malik's village wasn't that far, and we were there in twenty minutes. The sky was still dark and filled with stars, the air was cool, and there was a slight mist coming from the Helmand River. Only the sounds of insects wandered in the air. There wasn't even the bark or howl of a kuchi. I became nervous and thought about what the three Marines had said about a sorcerer. I eyed the few small compounds that made up the village. There were only a few gates and windows, and I couldn't help but stare at their dark shapes through the night, wondering if there was a Djinn waiting for us.

I saw Captain King and Master Sergeant Quince speaking quietly into their mics but couldn't hear the words. Instead, the two teams split. The first moved to take up overwatch positions. I recognized where they were going, they were taking the same positions my Marines had occupied when we'd first arrived. Master Sergeant Quince took the second team and advanced into the village. Captain King motioned for me to follow him.

We moved toward the overwatch team, kneeling just behind them. One of the Marines began to set up the bipod of an M240 machinegun, only this one seemed strange. To my amusement, I realized this one had a small collapsible stock and shortened barreled compared to the long, encumbering thing my Marines had. It was really beginning to sink in that these guys were a different breed of Marine, and I craved to be them.

"Which house is your guy's?" Captain King whispered to me.

I pointed out the central compound whose gate was always open. Malik was the friendliest, kindest man I'd ever met. Strangers were always welcome for a meal and conversation. Now, the gate was closed.

King nodded and repeated the information into his mic. I was about to ask something when another voice cut in.

"Heat signatures to the south, three of them," a Marine laying in the prone said, just loud enough for all of us to hear. His right eye peered through a long scope that led into a secondary device, a thermal optic, atop a M110 Semi-Automatic Sniper System. No one but King budged; the other Marines continued to eye their own sectors.

Captain King leveled his own rifle in the same direction as the sniper. I tried to do the same, but without any sort of night vision, I could barely make out details within fifty meters. "I got 'em," King said, his voice trailing off just a bit as he sighted in. "Corporal Lake, peer through that glass and tell me what you see."

The sniper rolled to his side and allowed me to take up his position behind the rifle. As I shouldered the weapon, he began to whisper the direction into my ear. "Hundred fifty meters out, just before the corn field."

I spotted them before he finished. Not based on my own skill—the signatures were just that bright. Three of those damned dogs were walking in front of the field, slowly making their way toward us. Unlike when they'd first come toward TCP 2, they almost seemed relaxed. There was no mistaking it, those were the Djinn. "That's them, alright."

Captain King relayed the information over their communication gear. Then he spoke to the overwatch team, "Pierce, Sanders, Wilkes, get eyes on the pooches in the field. Be ready to engage as soon as Carland makes entry into the compound."

Two more Marines shifted their aim; they both had large tan Mk17 rifles chambered in 7.62. The weapons mounted thermal optics and suppressors.

"Djinn still wandering around means the sorcerer is up somewhere," King whispered to me, and I looked back to the other team getting closer and closer to Malik's compound. They were moving along the outer wall now and made it to the gate. I could just barely make them out; they were dark shapes against the wall. One appeared to take off a ruck, lean it against the wall, and climb up—it was an assault ladder. The Marine quickly rose above the wall, clearing the area closest around him, then the distant spaces. I realized he was then not only setting security for the other Marines to enter, but he'd also gotten a visual clear of the gate. The other Marines pulled at the metal door and wordlessly entered the compound. I couldn't hear anything but the Afghan night. I was tense for them, my hands white-knuckled around my M4. The next second the Marines were inside the building, and we could only wait.

There were three hushed snaps that caused my heart to jump into my throat. It was Pierce, Sanders, and Wilkes engaging the distant Djinn. "We got 'em," one of them said. After my nerves settled, I was once again overwhelmed with admiration for these guys. The execution had been perfect.

"Dry hole," King said suddenly. I turned to face him; Master Sergeant Quince must have transmitted their find. "They're gonna hit the other compounds. Pierce, we're linking up with them."

"Roger that, skipper," a Marine with one of the Mk17s said.

"I fucking hate that."

"I know, skipper."

Captain King rose up and pulled on my plater carrier's shoulder straps. "We've got to secure Malik's building while Carland clears the others. I've got to warn you, it's not going to be pretty."

I accepted that Malik was dead then. A part of me had hoped he was still alive. "Let's go."

We made our way to the metal gate, King in front, and me close behind. Another Marine met us, opened the gate, then directed us inside. It was a slightly wasted effort. I'd been here plenty of times before and knew the layout like the back of my hand. In the courtyard's opposite corner, where Malik would gather most of his trash, I saw the legs of his wife and family. I didn't give it a look or even more than a glance. It was just something out of the peripheral of my vision, and I would keep it at that. We went inside, then hit a wall made up of the scent of rotten decay and death.

Origins

In what would have been the living room where I often had tea was Malik's lifeless body. There wasn't much different to the room, no circles, strange runes, or candles like I'd envisioned. Just Malik on his back, arms and legs straight, throat cut, empty eyes staring at the ceiling. He was grotesque; his corpse had been baking in the building for the past few days. I wished I hadn't seen him like that, but it made me more resolved to hunt down this sorcerer.

Master Sergeant Quince met us, then Gunny Carland took his team and began their hunt. "We got lucky, fucker left his phone," the master sergeant said and presented the cell phone in a zip lock bag, already labeled with a date, time, and location for evidence.

"Same group?" Captain King asked and took the bag before putting it into his assault pack.

"Looks like it," Quince said, then motioned with his head toward a kettle. "He can't be far, the kettle's still hot."

"Can I ask questions?" I blurted out. I should have probably been more tactful in the situation.

King and Quince looked at me for a moment. "Shoot," King said.

"What the fuck is this?" I asked, then quickly added, "Sir."

King took another look at Quince. The master sergeant simply chuckled and lifted an eyebrow. "You already told him about the Djinn."

The captain motioned for us to leave the building. "Let's talk outside. Sorry, Lake, but your friend here stinks." We exited, and I made sure I kept my back to the bodies of the remaining family. Once outside and settled, I could hear the rustling as Carland's team began clearing the other compounds. "So, the Djinn are…"— King paused to think of his next words carefully— "interesting." The words hung in the air for a moment before he continued, "They're normally not threat, or even a concern. For the most part they live in their space, realm, dimension, spiritual plain, whatever you want to call it. Texts say they're jealous of humans and our relationship to God; how true that is, I don't know. Sometimes they can be summoned, or they'll strike some sort of deal, or in the cause of Malik here, they're brought in by a sacrifice. Once they're here, it's not hard to convince them to wage war against us."

"Because of jealousy?" I asked.

"Like I said, interesting," Captain King said, then continued with his explanation, "There's a Taliban cell that's been attempting this sort of thing all across Afghanistan. Usually we're able to intercept in time."

I couldn't help but feel bitter at that last bit. "Usually?"

King's eyes stared into mine, and I began to feel bad about my remark. I could see he was just as bothered as I was. "I'm sorry, Lake. This one blindsided us; we came as quickly as we could."

Master Sergeant Quince cut in, "This is also the biggest incursion we've seen. Usually there's no more than ten or fifteen."

"I think we got hit with thirty of them." I had a strange sense of satisfaction, knowing it had taken so many to bring down our TCP.

"There were the twenty-seven Djinn corpses, plus the three in the field. There're bound to be a few more," Quince said, while rotating his head and massaging his neck.

"But what that means is the sorcerer here knows his stuff."

I found myself massaging my neck as well, then put my hands back on my M4. At the feel of its cold steel, I resolved myself to finding this sorcerer. Quince put a hand to his earpiece and stepped out of the conversation. As quickly as he'd done so, Quince was back. "Carland's got nothing."

"Goddamnit." King kicked at a rock with his boot, and we followed him out of the compound. In a minute the overwatch team met up with us, and the squad was reformed. There was cursing and small talk; they were obviously upset about missing the sorcerer. King was next to me, and I could overhear his radio transmission. "Archangel, this is Nighthaunt, we've got nothing here. What's the status of ISR?" He waited, and then spoke again, "Roger that, two mikes."

That left us waiting. I kept examining the Marines around me. They held their security positions with relaxed confidence and professionalism. Two of the Marines carried on a quiet conversation about something I couldn't quite make out. During the talk, they kept their heads and eyes locked on their sector. I'd heard before of the "big boy rules" a lot of Special Forces communities lived by; as long as there was mission accomplishment, the strict rules of the military became more like guidelines. Again the desire to become one of these guys intensified within me.

Soon enough there was the low hum of an overhead drone. Captain King received a radio transmission shortly after, then spread the news to the rest of his team. "We've got something in the next village over." He looked at his watch. "Sun's coming up soon, we need to hustle."

"Do the Djinn avoid sunlight?" I asked Carland quietly.

"No, they ain't vampires," Carland said to me as if I was a child, "but the sorcerer's still human." He motioned to the night vision on his head. His team started to move, and I fell back into my position between King and Quince.

I knew the village we were heading to; it wasn't far, and there was only a wide canal we'd have to cross as any real obstacle. I whispered into King's ear about a crossing point not far off. The bridge was nothing more than the twisted trunk of an old tree. It wasn't the easiest thing to walk over, especially at night. In my naivety, I thought I could show off a bit by being able to cross without issue, but the Marines traversed the bridge without a problem. I guess the only thing I did well was not slowing them down.

Once we were over, King kept the Marines moving to one of the larger compounds. There was something about the building...I couldn't remember. We were moving quickly again. They really didn't want to be out when the sun came up, but the night sky was turning a light blue. I wondered what they would do if this became another dry hole and the daylight came.

They stacked up on the outer wall of the compound. The Marine with the assault ladder once again peeled it off his back and leaned it against the mud barrier. Captain King turned to face us. "Quince, stay here with strap hanger." I knew he was talking about me. His words were harsh and tense. They were about to make entry into the building, and I needed to stay out of their way. I moved away from the stack and found a corner to pull security on.

As much as I wanted to, I didn't watch the Marines go in. Instead of watching the Marine climb the ladder and the others stealthily work the gate, I kept my eyes peeled on my sector, determined to play my part. I could just barely hear them, the shuffling of boots and fabric swaying against each other.

There was the muffled shot of a suppressed Mk18 that caused my stomach to jump into my throat. My heart raced as combat was waged just on the other side of the wall. There was the unmistakable sound of a fire catching and engulfing something. Then there was the howl of the Djinn I'd heard so many times now. I knew this compound; I'd been in it multiple times before. While I kept to a knee and held my rifle, I envisioned the fighting inside. Which corners the Marines hit, how they navigated around the center well, the tractor on the wall, the inside of the main building, the rear door. "Oh, shit."

I jumped up and turned, my body instantly going full tilt into a sprint. "Top, there's another door!"

"Wait!" I heard the Master Sergeant yell after me. I think he meant for me to wait so he could radio the rest of the team, because he was right behind me when we turned the corner. As if on cue, the slender wooden back door burst open, bouncing off the wall and creating a resounding crack. Fire exited first; a Djinn, then an Afghan.

The Djinn roared at us in angry defiance; the Afghan had a look of shock on his face.

I tried to pull my M4 up and get a shot off, but in my haste the rifle was at my hip. I'd been too focused on sprinting instead of being able to level my weapon. Master Sergeant Quince was fast. His rifle barked five times, sending rounds into the chest of the Djinn. It crumpled, and its flame extinguished.

Origins

My momentum sent me past the dying Djinn toward the Afghan. I desperately reached out my hands and leapt with my legs. I grabbed his shoulders, and we both tumbled and rolled to a stop. The whole thing unraveled in slow motion for me. I didn't recognize the Afghan. He wore the brown and baggy perahan tunban that most Afghans wore with a black vest over it. A necklace with an intricate jewel hung from his neck. He dropped a rifle with the short profile of an AKS-74U. I distinctly remember seeing the weapon was still on safe. The coward never even attempted to fight the Marines coming in.

The Afghan was on top of me. At first he tried to pull himself up and away to keep running, but I had a firm grip on his baggy clothing. I pulled him close, and his hands started to punch and swipe at my face. I thought the Marines would want to detain the guy, so I attempted to subdue him, but he pulled a knife, its long, curved blade glinted in the dawn sky. It came down at me, and the blade struck center. My eyes went wide, and I prepared myself for pain. Nothing came. He'd brought the blade down on my plate carrier, the ballistic plate easily stopping the fatal blow. The Afghan pulled at the knife trying to free it, and I struck him with the heel of my left fist, while my right reached for the Beretta.

The knife came free, and the Afghan lifted his hands to bring the blade down on my throat. I saw his expression, the young face contorted with pure hatred and disdain for what I was. There was a thick, black beard now covered with dust and dirt, and clean white teeth snarled at me. I saw him for what he was, and I saw the man responsible for the death of my Marines. I'm sure I gave him the same look as I remembered Reid and his sacrifice for me.

"You can't kill me!"

I pulled the trigger, and the pistol bucked in my hand. The nine-millimeter round hit home. He was coming for my throat, so I went for his as well. Blood burst, and he fell back, dropping the blade into the dirt. His hands clutched at his neck as he desperately tried to stop the bleeding, but to no avail.

There was a loud cacophony of shrieks. I pushed with my heels and elbows to create distance between us. Suddenly there were Djinn all around us, and as soon as they appeared, the fiery ghouls were diving and plunging into the Afghan. They tore at his soul, and he burned, unable to scream. The horde began to dissipate into wisps of embers that blew away in the breeze.

They were gone, the Djinn and the Afghan. There was simply the spilled blood turning the dirt to mud, the burnt marks of a struggle, and the necklace with the jewel. Silence filled the air.

I let myself go limp so I could take lungfuls of air. My mind was a storm of emotions, from relief and confusion, to anger and sorrow. The Afghan had tried to kill me, and I'd killed him instead. He'd been devoured, and I was fine. The fighting was over. My Marines were still dead.

I didn't notice Master Sergeant Quince taking a knee beside me until he spoke, "You got him, Corporal. You got him."

I think I may have had tears on my cheeks. I got up and saw that the other Marines were gathered around us. "Is everyone okay?"

King nodded with a small grin.

"What just happened to that guy?"

King's voice came, familiar and almost comforting. "That was our sorcerer. It appears he made a deal with the Djinn. His soul for their service."

"You guys are pretty calm about all this," I said with a soft chuckle, trying to calm my nerves.

"It gets old," Carland said as he handed the necklace the Afghan had been wearing to Captain King. I left that question unvoiced. I could only handle so much for right now.

"So now what?" I asked quietly.

"We've got a bird coming in," Quince said, and I could hear the familiar sounds of helicopter blades.

"And I go back to my company?"

Captain King looked at me with piercing green eyes. "Corporal Lake, I'm sorry, but you won't be returning to your unit. You'll need to come with us." I nodded in understanding, and rose, no complaints.

The Osprey landed, and we ran up its lowered ramp. I took a seat closest to the ramp and looked out at the Afghanistan countryside lighting up with the rising sun.

The Osprey pitched upward, and there was still smoke pluming from TCP 2. I said my goodbyes and turned back to Captain King and Master Sergeant Quince. "Sir, how do you do your recruiting?" My question caught the officer off guard. "I want in."

Origins

Troll
J.F. Holmes

Chapter One

It seemed to go on forever. The confusion, the gunfire, the up and down of adrenaline rushes. The darkness, punctuated by the strobe light of muzzle flashes and the screams of dying men. Staff Sergeant Richards had hurt his ankle when he came down hard on the paved road, jumping way lower than they were supposed to. Thousands of acres of pastureland, and the wind had carried him right onto a hard surface. Well, that's the fortunes of war. At least he was alive and had some of his own unit around him as the sun came up, and they knew where they were. Twelve paratroopers from the 82nd Airborne were nothing to mess with. The night's terrors had passed with the faint glow of dawn on the horizon, as it had for men for thousands of years. He lay quietly on the knoll above the road, the horizon turning lighter as dawn approached.

Major VanKoop lay next to him, trying to match what he saw through his binoculars with the map hidden under a poncho and illuminated with a red light. Richards lay, patiently waiting. Pulling security around them, Sergeant Simmons held the other end of the line. Between the two NCOs lay the nine paratroopers, half sleeping, half on guard. Rest was a weapon, and the hour they got was enough to keep them going for another day. They were young, and after their textbook ambush of a German patrol, invincible. It was dawn, June 6th, 1944, and the rumble of the great guns pounding the coast of Normandy twenty miles away lent urgency to their mission.

"I can see a roadblock; call it four men, one machine gun." VanKoop paused, turning to the left, looking across the road. "That's Saint Remy there, I recognize the church steeple."

"We were supposed to be interdicting the road to Caen, but you make do when the devil dances, Sir. You're the boss." They'd been kicked out of the plane miles from their drop zone and objective, but paratroopers were trained to make mayhem wherever they landed. Their officers and most of their platoon were nowhere to be found, but the battalion S-3 had stepped in and taken charge of their little unit.

"Yeah, well, this bridge is a D+1 objective for the Brits. If we can blow it early, we need to. The road is one of the main routes for the Panzer Lehr Division to reinforce their 21st Armored."

"Damn. Well, I don't want to take on tanks with my piano," said Richards, referring to the Thompson that lay across his chest.

"Should be simple enough, if we hurry. Let's take out the guard and blow this thing."

"Yes, Sir. Thank God we have the bomb and Private Soblowski."

VanKoop grunted. On the ground behind them lay a battered five-hundred-pound aerial bomb, a dud dropped from a B-24 earlier this week. Like any battlefield, unexploded munitions littered the ground; as a kid Richards had found live Civil War mortar rounds every now and then, heaved up out of the ground at his parents' farm outside Vicksburg. This one had been sitting almost right where they lay, part of a string of bombs that must have been aimed at the bridge. A series of craters gaped silently on the far hill, attesting to how hard it was to actually hit anything with a bomb.

"Still gives me the willies, even if he did pull the fuse. Not that any of us would know it if it DID go off." He shook off those thoughts, rubbed at his tired eyes, and said, "Gather the men and let's review the plan," and the word went down the line. Soldiers who had been deeply asleep snapped to alertness, and they formed a small circle around their leadership.

"OK," said the major, "just past the crest is a bridge over the Orne River. We're going to use that bomb to blow it, since we lost all our demolitions. There's one roadblock on the south end of the bridge—fortunately for us, on our side. It's about three hundred yards from here, and I count four men, one motorcycle, and an MG 42 pointed north to cover the bridge." As he spoke, he drew all this in the dirt, using rocks and twigs to indicate positions.

"Sergeant Simmons," the officer continued, "you and I will take three men and move to a position within about a hundred yards of the roadblock. There should be enough cover to get that close, then an open field." The young man nodded; he was a veteran of the Invasion of Sicily, and hard as nails at twenty years old.

Seeing that Simmons understood his part, VanKoop turned to Sergeant Richards. "You'll take the others and set up the BAR, giving harassing fire. If you can hit them, fine; if not, don't worry about it. I just want their attention focused on you."

The NCO looked at Private Orson, their BAR gunner. The kid was a wizard with the .30 caliber automatic rifle; Richards suspected he could take out the entire roadblock from four hundred yards. A plan with redundancies, though, was a good plan.

"Once the firing starts, give them a good minute of random bursts. Do NOT get into a machine gun duel with them; that 42 will eat your ass for lunch." Orson smiled, a 'yeah, whatever, Sir!' smile. It was, VanKoop knew, a smile of confidence, not cockiness. They were Airborne, after all.

"Then Sergeant Simmons' squad will assault through the objective," the major continued. "When we give the all clear, Staff Sergeant Richards and his men will carry the demo down to the bridge," summarized the officer. "Are you sure you can make this thing blow, Soblowski?"

Another confident smile. "Sir," he said in his heavy Bronx accent, "I was a miner before the war. Isn't anything I can't make go bang. Especially with that motorcycle battery."

"Except your wife," whispered Orson to him. The Pole ignored him, though the smile disappeared off his face. His Dear John letter in England had been a sore subject for weeks, and though he would give his life for his fellow soldier, it didn't mean he had to LIKE the kid.

"Any questions?" VanKoop made each of the men repeat back to him their roles in the plan, and when he was sure they hadn't missed anything, he turned them over to their NCOs to get everything in order.

It was a quiet time. Five minutes to psyche yourself up to do something that might get you killed or seriously wounded, and this far behind enemy lines, both were probably the same thing. Some drank water, others chewed on a chocolate bar, a few said quiet prayers. All checked their weapons and ammunition. Multiple prayers to God might save your ass, maybe, but an M1 Garand only gave you eight chances and a ping, so you had to make sure your equipment worked right.

Origins

They moved out slowly; the sun rising in the East had yet to clear the valley. Richards could see the four men hunched over as they moved down an irrigation ditch, but a row of hedges obscured them from the Germans. No traffic moved on the road, but high in the air overhead, contrails danced and engines droned. Always in the background was the thunder of big guns. They hardly noticed it anymore.

"OK, they're set. Don't worry about what the major said, Orson, give it to 'em good. No chances of return fire."

"You got it, Sarge," said the teenager, and he lined up the sight—already elevated for the estimated three hundred yards—on the two men sitting on ammunition crates next to the machine gun. He exhaled, muttered, "Jesus forgive me," and pulled the trigger.

Deep beneath the surface of the river, in a cave that arched up over the water level to provide a dark, gloomy cavern, the valley's oldest inhabitant felt the gunfire through the ground. He was a creature of nature, attuned to the earth around him, and the bombs earlier in the week had greatly disturbed him. He knew of the modern world, had watched it develop over the last five hundred years, and didn't like it. The bridge, his bridge, the one he was inexplicably linked too, had felt the effects of war before, and the creature had raged and killed, devastating the countryside. The land had been quiet for more than a century, and he only took the occasional toll of a random life. The creature felt OLD, and this was too much to be borne. With a heave, he lifted his enormous bulk from the floor where he had been resting and slipped into the water.

The dead smelled, but you got used to it. Bodies ripped by bullets spilled guts, and blood had a coppery tang. The ragdolls of the dead Germans were sprawled in that boneless way only the dead can be. Three lay around the roadblock, another hadn't made it to the motorcycle, and an unseen fifth had been dropped as he ran across the field. In any other time, him trying to run with his pants around his ankles would have been funny to the young men, but each knew it could have been them in a different reality. Orson had killed four without changing the twenty-round magazine, and Private Compton had drilled the runner through the back from his position with Sergeant Simmons. The man who'd killed him draped a poncho over the half-naked body of the teenager, and no one said anything.

When Richards' squad came up, they were sweating from the exertion of hauling five hundred pounds of dead weight between them, along with their equipment. They collapsed on the ground, exhausted. There wasn't much time to rest, though. They'd barely sat down and started swigging water when Sergeant Simmons had them dragging it toward the bridge.

"Well, that worked," said Staff Sergeant Richards to Major VanKoop, examining the bodies. The officer just shook his head, thinking about where to place the bomb. Together they walked onto the span, toward the middle. Soblowski was already at work on the motorcycle, stripping out the electrical components.

"Set up a defense for both approaches while we get this thing in place," said VanKoop to the NCO. "Put the MG-42 here, and the BAR at the far end of the bridge. SOBLOWSKI!" he yelled, "HOW LONG?"

"FIFTEEN MINUTES, MAJOR!" he yelled back.

The creature felt the first footsteps on the bridge, felt them in his mind. It was his bridge, and no one crossed it without permission. For five hundred years he had exacted his toll whenever someone moved, and the French peasants had learned the price of his peace. He had slept for the last century, only waking briefly while the world moved on. Half aware the whole time, the creature was now awake, and enraged. The battle raging around the French coast had stirred up energies he hadn't felt in almost two decades, and for the past day he'd been slowly stirring. In his mind he could feel the intent of the humans above to destroy his bridge. Not even during the Revolution had there been such a threat. Reaching the low piers, the troll grasped the stonework and hauled himself upward.

Major VanKoop had just turned back to the south when a large, gleaming, wet form climbed over the stonework. What he saw would have been called a "Troll" by the Norse who settled Brittany, but had become known in French in later years as an "Ogre". The thing reached its full height, maybe twenty feet tall, and roared in an incomprehensible language.

"What the…" began the startled major, reaching to unsling his rifle, and the Ogre's open hand struck his head, ripping it completely off his shoulder. Staff Sergeant Richards turned to see the major's body dance for a few seconds, blood spurting from the stump of the neck, and then collapse.

Ken Richards had grown up on a farm, and had seen blood in plenty. He'd hunted the woods of the Roanoke

Valley, and knew the darkness that sometimes dwelt in the land and lived in the deep hollows of the mountains. His introduction to combat in Italy had inured him to the paralyzing effects of surprise, and even as his thinking brain stuttered, his animal brain reacted. The Thompson came up, the thing was in his sights, he aimed low, and the bolt slid forward, chambering and firing the first fat .45 caliber round. He held the trigger down as the full metal jacket rounds blazed from the barrel, letting it climb across the thing's body. The soldier let off the trigger after ten rounds, let the barrel drop, and fired again, emptying the magazine.

The creature staggered as if being pelted with rocks, shook himself, and roared as the bolt locked back, empty. From twenty feet away, Richards methodically dropped the empty, then reloaded. He stepped forward to lean into the rise and pulled the trigger again, this time not stopping. The majority of rounds hit, but the thing ignored the impacts and walked forward, an evil grin on its face. The paratrooper turned to run and slipped on the blood spilled on the bridge. With a laugh, the creature grabbed his ankle and dragged Richards toward its mouth. He twisted and drew his combat knife, stabbing downward. It was like hitting a piece of iron, and the monster laughed again.

With the characteristic buzzsaw sound of the German MG-42, his squad let off a massive fusillade. They probably figured Richards was already dead, and were as scared and surprised as he had been. The tracers skipped past him, hammering the thing's back, then stopped. That much firepower should have riddled whatever it was like swiss cheese, but it just stood and shrugged. Looking down at Richards, it grinned cruelly, lifted him by his ankle, and threw him off the bridge in the direction of the northern shore.

As he pulled himself from the water two minutes later, after struggling out of his gear and almost drowning, the 82nd Airborne NCO could hear shots and screams echoing across the river, accompanied by the monster's roars. Reaching the road again, he looked across the span as the thing picked up the discarded bomb in one massive hand and threw it a hundred yards. Around the end of the bridge lay the bodies of the rest of the American soldiers. One man, he couldn't see who it was, tried to crawl away, but the creature grabbed him and casually bit his head off, chewing vigorously. It waved to Richards and slipped over the embankment, dragging the body down with it, and disappeared beneath the water. Struggling not to slip into madness, the sergeant turned and started jogging toward the thunder of the guns far to the north.

Origins

Chapter Two

There were still shells dropping on the blood-soaked sand of Omaha Beach at 03:00 hours, but the men standing in the deep hole ignored it. It was no different than a thousand other holes on Omaha Beach, except that this was the command post for Task Force 13, and a radio operator fielded half a dozen high priority calls at once.

At first glance, all was chaos, but then a pool of calm settled off to one side. A man with hard features and grey in his close-cropped hair sat up against the wall of the crater, ignoring the commotion. Colonel Archer sat in the sand because the creature in front of him was a little over two feet tall, in the shape of a man, wearing a red cap. Between the two stood a slightly taller, but far more beautiful, golden haired woman, all of four foot tall.

"Tylwyth," said Archer, "it is very important that you translate directly. I need your word that you will."

The Welsh fae looked at him and rolled her eyes. In a high, musical voice, she answered, "You insult me. We have the treaty between yourself as the leader of your band, and my queen, Mab. And I am OF the Tylwyth, but that is not my name."

Origins

The human ran his fingers through his dirty hair. "Sorry, it's been a long day. I'm grateful for your people's help. What's your name?"

"Like I would tell you and let you have power over me. You may call me Angharad ferch Afrelia," she answered, and turned back to the smaller French sprite, blistering him up and down in a language full of consonants but few vowels. The Korrigan bowed deeply, grinned at Archer, and shot back something equally nasty. Then he actually vanished.

"Gods be damned rude French bastards," said Angharad.

Archer actually smiled. It was at times entertaining to see the—well, whatever they were—creatures, dealing with each other. "Do we have our treaty, or not? And I thought he was a Briton, like your people in Wales."

"Maybe a thousand years ago, mortal, when I was young. Now they are all stinking garlic eaters. You have your treaty. In return for one thousand ounces of gold and five hundred gemstones, the Korrigan people will, how do you say in America, 'gremlin' the Saxon machines where they can."

"German," the colonel corrected automatically. "Now I just have to get a thousand ounces of gold."

"Not my problem," said the Tylwyth Teg, and she, too, vanished. More like she moved faster than the eye could see, but he knew she would be back if the Allies needed help again. Say one thing about the supernatural, they didn't break their word. Just interpreted it to their best advantage.

"Colonel, Sir, I've got a BLACK ROCK priority situation south of Caen," said his RTO, handing over a scrap of muddied paper. It had come as a call from their liaison with the British 5th Parachute Brigade. "Says here an 82nd trooper showed up at their lines around half an hour ago, claiming that his squad had run into a troll at a bridge south of Caen."

The commander of Task Force 13 shook his head. They'd been getting reports like that all day long, and ninety-nine percent of them were complete bullshit. Tired men in combat saw all kinds of strange crap, but this might have to be checked out. "That must have been a hell of an off-course drop," said Archer, looking at the map. "Did they send us coordinates?"

"No, but the paratrooper says it's about here," answered his RTO, putting his finger on a bend in the Orne River. "Should we let the Brits check it out?"

His boss pondered, turned to a gunnery sergeant who was talking into a field phone, and said, "Who do we have back here, Jack?"

"Sir, Captain Miller just brought this team in from tangling with a Morvarc'h that took out a landing craft. They're pretty wet and tired; lost one man, two wounded. They're in a shell hole over that way," said the enlisted Marine, pointing over his shoulder.

"They'll do." He scrambled out of the hole, glad to get away from the blaring radios, trying hard to avoid the dead that were slowly being collected from the sands of Omaha Beach. He thought about calling in the Tylwyth to get information, but dealing with them was exhausting. How hard could killing a troll be, after all?

Captain Miller was sitting with his men, ten of them sleeping or eating. He looked up from the cold C-ration he was spooning into his mouth to see Colonel Archer crouching over him. Miller started to get up, but Archer slid down into the hole next to him.

"John," said his commander, "I want your team to catch a high-speed boat back to Portsmouth, get a plane, and drop south of Caen to take out a troll holding an important bridge on the Panzer Lehr Division reinforcement route. Take ten more minutes, and then go see Gunny Jones, he'll give you the necessary orders and passes. Have your men refit, but I expect you to be crossing the channel before dawn, and at the site within twenty-four hours." Archer then stood up and scrabbled back up the sides, slipping on the sand. Before he disappeared into the growing darkness, he stopped, turned, and said, "Good job with that water horse." Then he left.

"Well, doesn't that beat all," said Miller. "You heard the man, mount up, we've got a boat to catch."

There were a few grumbles, one "Aye, aye, Sir," and men were shaken awake. It had been a very tiring twenty-four hours, but hopefully they could sleep on the boat. Or on the truck ride to the airfield. Or on the plane. Hell, hanging from the risers on the way down. After all, how tough could a troll be? Yet here they were, caught between Heaven and Hell, as usual. "Gunny McCoy," he said, fighting the fatigue, "go steal another BAR, and did you get that Lewis unjammed?"

The twenty-three-year-old Marine NCO just looked at him with that solid, West Virginia coal miner silence, then spit some tobacco juice to mix with the blood on the sand. Then he nodded once and turned away. In a regular Marine unit Miller would have had his stripes for his insubordinate manner, but this was Task Force 13. You needed men who would spit in the face of an officer AND the face of the Devil himself. Miller sat down and started scanning a map of the area to their south, looking for drop zones close to the bridge and analyzing the terrain.

"You heard the man," McCoy said to the rest of the squad, making it almost sound like a series of grunts. "GIT!" And they did, two men climbing out of the shell hole to look for another BAR among the dead littering the beach.

"Jesus, look at that. Goddamn crabs are out already," muttered Private Thorson. He and Corporal Bodi were walking among the dead, looking for another of the powerful .30 caliber automatic rifles. Small clawed creatures moved in the glow off the red flashlights, ripping pieces of flesh from the bodies.

Bodi shrugged and said in his relaxed California accent, "Nothing we can do about it, and I don't think they care," meaning the dead. Still, each man took delight in stomping on the shelled creatures as they looked through equipment. They were both big men, as Task Force 13 members usually were. Firepower and ammo, and lots of it, was the creed of the men who dealt with the spooky shit, as they called it. "Surf's different here, you know," he continued. "Different than Cali. Lot longer, the water stays shallower further out."

"OK, got one," said Thorson, lifting a complete BAR, still wrapped in its protective waterproof covering. "Thank God it's only been a day, no time for this bitch to rust out on us."

"This ain't Guadalcanal, Thorson, and everything isn't going to rust on us in two minutes. That seawater, though…" He stopped. Overhead was the howl of night fighters going after targets, and above that the drone of the heavy British Lancasters going to bomb German positions. Flashes from the Navy ships offshore lit the beach, a ripping sound as the heavy rounds passed overhead, and the crash of the surf all combined to create a wall of sound and light that seemed to deaden the senses. That and the fact both men had fired hundreds of rounds that day, pouring lead into both Nazis and demons alike, made hearing almost impossible. Though they didn't know it, they'd been shouting.

"So what do you think of the Task Force? Seen enough to believe yet?" asked Bodi.

The private shrugged, picking up and then dropping a shattered weapon. He'd been a hasty assignment to the unit, added last week in preparation for the assault. "I've seen a lot of weird things on combat, some of them today, but you can't tell me there isn't an explanation for everything. World don't work that way."

"OK, Professor. I thought you Vikings were all about the supernatural; spirits, demons, heaven, hell, all that," said Bodi.

"I'm an educated, modern man, Corporal. I'm going to be a science teacher when I get out of the Corps. Evolution and all that. There's a scientific explanation to everything we saw today. Who knows, maybe the Nazis have been experimenting on people, like that super soldier stuff they always talk about. Like Captain America."

"Wait," said Bodi, holding up his hand, "can you hear that?" the corporal asked, turning toward the sea. Perhaps it was that he'd spent most of his life before the war on a fishing boat, plying the waters off San Diego, but Bodi could hear the soft singing that seemed to be everywhere around him. It rose early above the crash of the surf. "There's music, and singing. My God, it's beautiful!"

"I don't hear anything!" said Killain. He was fairly new to the Task Force, transferring in from the fighting in the Pacific after being the sole survivor of a patrol that had tangled with a Tamangori, the legendary Polynesian giant maneater. He still wasn't completely convinced he hadn't imagined the whole thing, but some of what he'd seen since hitting the beach was making him question his sanity. Now his NCO was talking about music that just wasn't there. His mind, focused as it was on science and the natural world, gave a ready explanation to everything around him, and he'd seen others crack from combat stress.

"Be right back," said Bodi, dropping his rifle and splashing into the surf, vanishing into the darkness.

Thorson stood there, opened mouthed, tired and stunned. For a second his brain didn't process what had just happened. Then he felt something touch his foot and looked down. A horribly wounded man, gasping and trailing his guts, was pulling himself across the sand toward the surf. The farm boy from Minnesota bent down to help, but then stopped as he heard more moans, and he looked up as a naval barrage started. In the flashes he could see a half dozen men, all wounded in some way, staggering or crawling toward the surf. Several were already in it, and he looked for his NCO, but the gunfire flashes were intermittent, making it had to get anything but snapshots.

He stepped forward into the water, yelling, "Corporal Bodi!" but then stopped. As soon as his leather boot went from dry land to ocean, he heard it. Faintly, like it was coming from a far distance, a song in a strange language, but one that was haunting and beautiful. Though he didn't recognize the words, he knew instinctively what they meant, and in the flashes the teenager saw…an impossibly beautiful woman, crouching atop one of the German anti-ship obstacles, almost as if it were a throne. At her feet huddled dark shapes, but he had no time for that, only her angelic song.

At that moment, one of the great battlewagons let loose with a full broadside, and the concussion made him step backward, stumbling, the guns going off less than a mile away. He fell almost comically, dropping onto the sand as the surf pulled away, and saw her again. This time, though, the beauty was gone, replaced by a hideous, scaled fish-like skin and razor-sharp teeth. One bare foot was pushing down on Corporal Bodi, shoving him down into the water, though he looked dazed and unresisting. A violent thought broke into his head, a remembered snippet from a briefing, and he knew he was seeing a Morgan, one of the sirens who haunted the coasts of Brittany.

All his doubts about the supernatural vanished, and a white-hot fury rose up in Thorson, an ancestral Norse hatred of the Fae who lured men to their deaths in the fields of the icy north. He bent down to the dead man crawling toward the surf, a sailor who must have been with the beach landing party. On the man's equipment belt was the bulky shape of a signal flare pistol, and Killain ripped it off, took aim in the direction of the song, and fired. The flare arced out of the gun with a loud pop and a whoosh and landed on the water in front of the Morgan. Shrieking, it leaned down and extended long claws at Bodi, aiming to rip his throat out.

In the flare light, Thorson went through the motions of loading the BAR automatically, ripping at the cover enough to expose the magazine well and trigger housing. Another tear as he slammed the magazine home, and his hand found the bolt, racking it backward. It was all automatic to him now, drilled into muscle memory at Parris Island, and in combat on Guadalcanal, where a second could cost a life. He lined the front sight post up on the center of the V formed by the two steel posts of the obstacle, the Morgan a pale white glimmer, and squeezed the trigger. Leaning into the burst, he watched as the bullets impacted into her and sparked off the steel, the muzzle flashes illuminating the thing like a jerky motion picture. He let the barrel drop between each burst, and poured all twenty rounds out in quick succession. With an inhuman screech, pounded by heavy 30-06 rounds from less than twenty feet away, the

Morgan was hammered off the obstacle and back into the sea, disappearing in welter of black blood.

Reloading, Killain stepped forward, but not far enough to touch the surf. "Bodi!" he yelled, "CORPORAL, GET OUT OF THE WATER!" The dazed Marine sat up, noticed the bodies floating all around him, and scrambled to shore.

"What the hell," said the NCO, staring at the BAR in the still burning flare light, "just happened?"

"Beats the shit out of me, but I ain't gonna doubt you again, Corp. Let's get the hell out of here."

Origins

Chapter Three

"What the hell happened to you two?" McCoy growled. In the light of the red shrouded flashlights in the shell hole, his craggy face looked demonic.

"Uh, we ran into a Siren or some shit," said Bodi, somewhat sheepishly.

"Did you kill it? Was that all that BAR fire I heard?" asked Captain Miller. He was always listening, though he rarely commented.

"I don't think so, Sir," said Thorson. "I put a whole magazine into it and stabbed it with my K-bar, but it seemed like the knife hurt it more than the bullets."

"Cold steel, boy, cold steel," interjected McCoy. "Hurts the Fae more than lead and copper."

"That reminds me, Gunny. Make sure we have some extra rounds for the anti-tank gun, if we can find them. Might still be lead and copper jacket, but it packs a hell of a punch."

"Aye, aye, Sir." The shell hole danced with the hooded lights as the ten-man squad opened up packing crates, oiled weapons, loaded magazines, sharpened knives, doing all the things soldiers have done to ensure survival over the millennia.

Origins

It was just before false dawn when they moved out, shuffling across the beach, past still burning tanks and landing craft. As the light grew, a breeze started to pick up off the ocean, clearing away the stench of death that was already rising from corpses less than twenty-four hours old. They were all conscious that the huddled forms, half buried by sand and tide, could had been themselves, but for the grace of God.

The ramp of an LCVP thundered down, and they waded through the small waves and up onto the boat. McCoy counted the men as they came on board, then gave a thumbs up to the captain, who was talking to the sailors operating the boat. With the thudding of overworked diesel engines, the craft pulled back and turned, churning over the waves toward a Destroyer Escort waiting offshore. Even though it was only a twenty-minute trip, and the small craft rocked as it lurched over the waves, all of the men sat tiredly on the floor, not minding the cool water sloshing around on the deck. They knew the Task Force rear detachment would have clean and dry paratrooper coveralls waiting for them, and rest was something the veterans grabbed every chance they could.

Only Thorson stood, trying to see the armada assembled offshore. Dawn had yet to actually break, and they were only massive darker shapes, sometimes lit by gouts of fire as their guns hurled heavy shells inland. As he watched, salt spray stinging his eyes, he thought he saw something just breaking the tops of the waves.

"Hey, Gunny, there's a—" he started to exclaim, but then a voice spoke from the darkness next to him.

"A U-Boat, yep. Don't worry about it," said the gnarled West Virginian. "It'll be taken care of."

"But…" the private said, then stopped. His eyes grew wider as he saw why the German submarine had surfaced before making its torpedo run. The hull seemed to twist in the water, and the propeller thrashed, briefly stirring up a wild foam, and finally spinning clear of the water in a wild blur. In the growing light, Thorson and McCoy could see the conning tower hatch fly open and small figures spill out. Then they saw a set of tentacles like flexible telephone poles wave in the air, flailing wildly, and then the sub rolled over and disappeared beneath the waves.

Behind the two men, a voice spoke, reciting a poem, a deep, melodious voice that had been made harsh yelling orders during years of seafaring.

Below the thunders of the upper deep,
Far, far beneath in the abysmal sea,
His ancient, dreamless, uninvaded sleep
The Kraken sleepeth: faintest sunlights flee
About his shadowy sides; above him swell
Huge sponges of millennial growth and height;
And far away into the sickly light,

Origins

From many a wondrous grot and secret cell
Unnumbered and enormous polypi
Winnow with giant arms the slumbering green.
There hath he lain for ages, and will lie
Battening upon huge sea worms in his sleep,
Until the latter fire shall heat the deep;
Then once by man and angels to be seen,
In roaring he shall rise and on the surface die.

From the back of the ship, the sailor steering looked at them with a huge grin as he finished the last lines. "The wee beasties don't particularly like the underwater boats, so we don't send out subs down this way. Jerry hasn't quite figured it out yet."

The captain had come up behind them to watch the final death of the enemy ship, and Thorson turned to him. "Sir, what was that poem?"

"That, Private, was Lord Alfred Tennyson, writing about a mythical creature called the Kraken. Sort of like a giant squid. More myth than reality, or so it was thought. Apparently not."

"Why aren't all the ships throwing depth charges or something?" the younger man asked.

McCoy made to shove him back toward the deck, growling, "You ask too many questions, kid."

"It's OK, Gunny," said Captain Miller. "Thorson, you just came to the Task Force a week ago, so let me explain. What did you see this morning when you and

Bodi had that encounter with the Morgan? What do you remember of it?"

"Uh, well, I remember the singing, and the guys crawling, and, and emptying the BAR. Not much else, I'm sorry, Sir."

"Don't apologize, son. That's the way it is," said his commander. "Hell, you're a veteran of the Pacific, right? How much do you remember about that?"

Thorson thought for a moment, then said, "Well, some things are really clear, some fights. Others, not so much."

"Well, that's the way it is, fighting the supernatural. You did good today; a lot of men would have left their buddy in the surf and run screaming. Your mind tends to blank out the horror, and in combat, guys tend to write off what they see and blame it on the craziness going on around them."

"Is that…" started Thorson, and continued on despite a growl from McCoy, "is that why it isn't in the papers? Because I've almost finished my degree, and I never heard of anything like that in the modern world."

"Boy," said the first sergeant, "you think Ernie Pyle is gonna write about ghouls eatin' the bodies of dead American GIs? They'd lock him in the loony bin. Now get your gear, we gotta climb up the nets into that boat." To emphasize his command, he gave the younger man a shove toward the front of the landing craft.

"You know, Top, someday they're going to find out you actually care," said Captain Miller when Thorson was out of earshot.

The dour hillbilly said, "I don't, Sir. Just a pain in the ass training new men to deal with the Fae."

"Uh huh," answered Miller with a grin. "You just keep telling yourself that."

McCoy put a pipe in his mouth and tried to light it, the sea spray putting out his match. He cursed and flung it over the side. "I did care, Captain. Till I saw shit that blasted my soul. Now I just hate."

They banged against the side of the DE, a long, lethal-looking ship that rode low in the water. The Task Force troops, exhausted though they were, scrabbled and grunted their way up the cargo nets, grateful to be leaving the blood-stained beach far behind.

Chapter Four

"So how did I get this gig again?" asked Thorson.

"You were in the 1st Marine Parachute Regiment, right?" The NCO grunted, pulling a strap tight.

Thorson did the same, making sure the parachutes were secure. Then they started checking their equipment. "Yeah, and then we got folded into the 5th Division. I was in the last class outta Hadnot Point, just got to the unit when they closed up. Whole lotta pissed off guys. We were supposed to jump into Kavieng, but that got scrubbed, and then all of a sudden I get orders to catch a PBY back to Diego."

"Who did you piss off?" asked Bodi with a knowing wink.

Thorson laughed, feeling welcome for the first time since he got there. "I might have punched some Army officer. I was a lance corporal, and, you know. We get back to Hawaii to train for the big push to Iwo, and well, here I am."

"There was supposed to be a whole platoon of you guys. I guess manpower is kinda short. Plus, you know, it ain't everyone who goes toe to toe with a giant and walks away without shitting himself."

"To be honest, I don't remember much. The jungle is kinda, I dunno, just a big green blur, you know? Just this hot, nasty, green hell. Jap snipers all around, fucking banzai charges, and maybe that giant thing was a demon or something. I kept telling myself it was just some big native that got mixed up in some shit, but after what I saw last night, I dunno."

"Well, someone saw it and sent up a report about you, and here you are. Jumpin' into France to save the doggies' asses from a mean old troll."

"Semper Fi, Corporal. Let's do this."

The C-47 sat waiting on the concrete runway, Marines lined up by the door. As each one reached it, two British soldiers almost lifted them into the plane. When Thorson's turn came, he stopped. The fuselage was riddled with jagged tears, and the floor was still wet from getting hosed down. Little rivulets of pink-tinged water ran out of the corners of the door, and a team of mechanics were neck deep in the engine, cursing at it.

He froze. A sudden, irrational fear seized him, and it had nothing to do with combat. Thorson had the requisite five jumps in school, and another nine in training. He'd flown all the way from Hawaii to England, making multiple stops, going through rough weather, and never blinked. Now he just stopped in the door, both hands locked on the edges of the doorway, unable to move his muscles.

Gunny McCoy was standing in front of him, and Thorson expected him to hit him, but he still couldn't move. Instead the NCO lit a cigarette, despite the no smoking signs inside the cockpit, and placed it in Thorson's mouth. "Deep breath, kid, take it in." The private did so, and slowly sagged forward into the fuselage. McCoy grabbed him by the harness and shoved him into a seat.

"Thanks, Gunny. That was really weird."

"Seen it before, kid," he growled. "Just don't do it in the door on the way out, or I'm gonna kick you in the ass."

The younger man looked around at the sunlight streaming through the shrapnel holes, and then at the blood stains on the canvas seats. Half the guys were already asleep, and he suddenly felt exhausted. As the engines warmed up and night fell, he slowly faded out.

"FIVE MINUTES!" yelled the jumpmaster, and Thorson awoke with a start. At the same time, there was a flash of light and a loud CRACK, making the engine cough and stutter. The jumpmaster put another piece of gum in his mouth and started chewing nervously, but then grinned and said, "THIS AIN'T SHIT COMPARED TO THE OTHER NIGHT! DAMN EIGHTY-EIGHT WILL KNOCK US RIGHT OUT THE SKY, THOUGH!"

The Marines helped each other stand up, while Captain Miller leaned out the door, trying to match the terrain on the ground with the map clutched in his hand, red penlight in his mouth. He put it away and motioned for Gunny McCoy, who was last in line. He waddled forward, they put their heads together to consult, and then both nodded.

Before the jumpmaster could say anything, Miller stepped out the door, and McCoy shouted over the roar of the engines, "GO! GO! GO!" The next jumper in line acted on reflex and pulled himself forward, vanishing into the night. Thorson, third in line, was shoved forward by the press of men, and fell more than stepped out. He had no time to freeze, no time to worry, just the cool night air, and then shock of the 'chute opening. He glanced up to see the chute fill, and then, despite all his training, looked down at the ground.

Below him the countryside was bathed in moonlight, and it seemed like a million fireflies were sparkling on the ground. They were tracers and explosions, muzzle blasts and burning tanks. Hundreds of thousands of men were locked in combat, and he had a bird's eye view of it all. It was beautiful, and it was Hell.

The experiences of the Army Airborne had taught them that having an equipment bag on a drop line was a sure way to lose it, and they'd been tossed in their own chutes. The ground rushed up on him and, as he always did, Thorson hit the ground like a sack of potatoes. He rolled and hit the chute release, hauled his Thompson around, and duck-walked toward the trees. Gunfire chattered in the distance, muted thumps of artillery, but around him the night insects chirped quietly. He waited for the red flashlight signal from Captain Miller, the first jumper, as he walked along the line of men, but nothing happened for what seemed like an eternity.

Thorson almost jumped out of his skin when a hand grabbed his foot, but he heard the hissed challenge, "SEMPER!" He responded with, "Fidelis," and saw that it was Lance Corporal Giuliani. The wiry Italian machine gunner held his finger to his lips and pointed to the field in front of them.

"Undead!" he said quietly, and Thorson could see two ragged figures in the moonlight, one in the field grey of the Wehrmacht, the other with a distinctive American helmet tilted on his head. They shuffled along, wandering aimlessly, backs to the Marines. Without a word, Giuliani stood up, drew his pistol, ran forward, and fired into the back of the American's skull. The dead man dropped, but the thing's companion wheeled and charged. Calmly, Giuliani waited until it was mere feet away and fired once more, the gunshot sparking before

Thorson's eyes, a brief yellow strobe light that showed the bloody hole in the walking corpse's side.

"God, but I hate the undead!" said Giuliani as he slid down next to Thorson. "Poor bastards!"

Chapter Five

D awn found them two miles from the bridge, delayed by having to wait out a German patrol for three hours. Captain Miller cursed at the lost time, but then again, fighting the Fae was always better in the daylight. Problem was, though, that they were also racing the German reinforcements.

"Move it, Marines!" said Gunny McCoy, who was at the rear of the line and physically shoving anyone who started to slacken their pace. He didn't have to; exhausted as they were, the men were starting to feel that particular adrenaline rush that came with the anticipation of combat. As they got closer, their excitement warred with the innate caution owned by veterans. Before they came around the bend that led to the bridge, Captain Miller called them to a halt, and they spread out. Two men struggled up the sides of the valley to pull flank security, and another two started moving out toward the village on the hill above. The last was a team equipped with a Boys Anti-Tank Rifle and a spotting scope, and the ten rounds they'd managed to scare up for it.

"Hey, Gunny, come with me," said Miller, and the two slowly made their way around the bend. The bridge lay quiet and still, the nighttime mist still hovering about it.

Origins

McCoy whistled and waved, and the squad came up, the security teams stopping and struggling back down the sides of the hill. Without being told to, one of the machine gun teams started setting up a Browning .30 on its tripod, facing back the way they had come.

Thorson stopped, sweat pouring off him. In addition to the weapon itself, he had twenty magazines, a half dozen grenades, and five blocks of C-3 explosive. Together with all the other gear, he carried almost eighty pounds, and the heat was beginning to rise as the sun came up.

"Hey, you," said McCoy, "yeah, you, Thorson. Go down there and see what's what."

The private sighed and started grounding his gear. He didn't need to ask why; he was the lowest ranking guy, and the newbie in a tight squad. Bodi handed him the small M-1 carbine and a bandolier of ammo almost regretfully. "Remember, it's a troll. He's big, but slow."

"And you know this how?"

"Well, I'd tell you, but then I'd have to kill you."

Thorson grimaced and said, "Thanks, buddy, I feel so much better!" then started down the hill.

Behind him Bodi hesitated, then picked up the BAR Thorson had put down. McCoy started to say something, but Captain Miller held up his hand. The corporal quickly caught up with Thorson, and together, they made their way forward across the bridge, covering each other as they moved, but swapping their weapons back out.

"Jesus Christ, this was a slaughter," said Bodi. Neither one was a stranger to combat or the dead, but what they saw now was almost more than they could take. Bones were splintered, huge bites taken out of corpses, and many had been mashed flat, the remnants of their uniforms the only thing that held them together. Brass was everywhere, and the stone bridge rails showed hundreds of pockmarks from bullets. Every weapon also looked like someone had put them in a grinder, and several had barrels bent and twisted. As they stepped through the gore, their leather boots made sticky sounds. It got worse as they reached the end of the bridge, both peering nervously over the edges, expecting something to erupt at any second and do the same thing that had befallen the others.

"OK, let's go!" said Miller, watching the two men wave at him through binoculars. Both seemed fine, and there were no disturbances to be seen. The six remaining Marines jogged forward, Miller in the front, and McCoy in the rear. They reached the part of the road where it sat directly between the first two bridge abutments, and

Miller had them kneel, waving for the two others to come back to him.

"Listen, Marines, here's the deal. The Fae are very territorial, and from what the 82nd guy said, they were trying to blow the bridge. Once we set the charges, whatever that thing is, it's going to come up at us. When it does, we're going to run our asses off, and the machine gunners and anti-tank guys are going to blow it away. Thorson, you watch the water on the right, Corporal Bodi on the left, Gunny set up an overwatch for the Germans, make sure the MGs are in place. Got it?"

They nodded pulled demo blocks from backpacks and pockets. Under the direction of Sergeant Kasnic, the combat engineer, they stacked them over the weakest part of the bridge, making a pile. As he worked, the engineer whistled a tune he'd learned from his dad, who'd served in the Great War. It helped calm his nerves as he worked with enough explosive to make him disappear into little bits. "Need something to tamp this with!" he shouted, and Miller ordered three men to go back to get some heavy rocks from the shore.

Twenty minutes passed by with nothing happening while the engineer set his charges, and a tired and bored Thorson looked idly down at the water, thinking of how the hills and river valley reminded him of back home. Every now and then he glanced over his shoulder at where Gunny McCoy was directing the other men setting up the heavier weapons, and with a chill, he realized that they were all pointed in his general direction.

Another glance at Bodi, who was across from him and maybe ten feet closer to their end of the bridge, lighting a cigarette. A glance down the bridge at where the road approached from the south—dead bodies from a German roadblock, looked like. He looked down at the water, nothing, then heard a sound behind him, a strangled, cut-off, almost slapping SPLAT.

Thorson was a combat veteran and had spent many nights in the pitch-black darkness of the jungle in Guadalcanal, surrounded by all the terrors that an active imagination could generate. What climbed over the edge of the bridge, casually popping Bodi's head into its mouth, was more than a nightmare. It was all of mankind's fears in one huge, hulking package.

The iron tailings that had soaked into the troll over the last two centuries had driven it quite mad, and that light shone in its eyes, a bright red that glared out. Still, there was intelligence there, an animal cunning, or even more. To confirm it, the troll grinned as it pulled its bulk over the edge and stood up, tearing Bodi's still quivering body in half.

"Holy, holy shi, shit!" stuttered Thorson, his mind numb, but his muscle memory didn't fail him. He raised the Browning and pulled the trigger. The bolt slid forward, stripping a thirty-caliber round forward into the breach, and the firing pin struck the primer. He felt the recoil slam into his shoulder and held the trigger, watching the barrel rise, leaning into it. Engaging a man-sized target, he would have stopped after three rounds, letting the barrel drop. The troll, though, stood almost twenty feet tall, and he emptied the magazine, letting it start at the knees and rise up to the hideous face. The only effect he could see when the bolt clicked back empty was a series of pockmarks that started to close as he dropped the expended magazine. The troll leaned forward and started to cross the twenty feet between them, huge, bloody hands extended and yellowed teeth showing in a grin. There were pieces of gristle and meat stuck in the fangs. Its hot breath washed over him in a roar, and one huge arm smashed into him, knocking the Marine down with the sickening snap of a broken arm. The BAR went flying across the stones, and Thorson collapsed, his vision drawing down into a tunnel.

He fumbled at his Colt, and the troll placed its hand on his head, emitting a huge, thunderous laugh, and started to squeeze. There was a loud BANG and a whizzing sound, and the troll dropped the man, turning to face the end of the bridge. It roared in defiance as another anti-tank round slammed into it, and turned, picking up a huge broken piece of bridge rail.

As Thorson tried to catch his breath, feeling his stomach heave, he saw the troll throw the stone in a flat trajectory, several hundred pounds of granite whipping through the air and catching Sergeant Kasnic in the back, smashing him down. A second stone flew even farther, shattering in the midst of the machine gun crew as they started to fire. The creature ran forward, tearing off more stones and hurling them with supernatural accuracy, screaming with rage as it did so. A massive volley of gunfire ripped out toward the troll, and Thorson crawled behind a solid stone pillar as the rounds zipped all around him.

At the end of the bridge, the Task Force squad faced the hell that was the oncoming troll. Captain Miller swore as he emptied his M1 Garand into the thing; normally if you put enough firepower into a supernatural creature, it went down, even if it was just because it was shot to pieces and couldn't move. This thing, though, seemed impervious to bullets, even with the extra firepower they'd brought with them. It even shrugged off his ace in the hole, the anti-tank rifle.

"Wish we had some steel-jacketed stuff!" grunted Miller as he ducked another thrown rock. The man behind him wasn't so lucky, the huge stone catching his shoulder and sending him spinning to the ground.

"Shit in one hand, wish in another. We've gotta blow this bridge!" shouted McCoy, deafened by the gunfire. Miller thought about calling for one of the snipers to hit the plastic explosive, but the troll was between them and it, and they were buried under the blocks of stone that shielded it.

Miller looked desperately around at his command, counting the men he had left. Five, including McCoy and himself. McCoy saw the look and said, "This is what you get the big bucks for, Captain!" He turned back, mind racing for some kind of plan, when the troll roared and charged, just as his sole remaining machine gun ran dry.

Chapter Six

Sven Thorson had grown up on a farm in Minnesota, spending the long winter nights listening to his grandfather tell tales in his native Norwegian, sagas going back to Viking times. He had loved listening to them, but Thorson had always been a practical person, and to him, those sagas were mere stories. He was sure more than half of them had been made up lies his grandfather had told to scare the shit out of him.

Now, long after his grandfather had passed on, one of those tales stood in front of him, a nightmare of splattered blood and scaly black- and rust-colored hide. His rational brain screamed at him that he was dreaming, knocked unconscious, dying on the beach in some godforsaken Pacific island jungle. Despite that, he felt a fierce joy well up in him, a berserker rage that wound its way through a thousand years and filled his soul.

With a shout, he ripped out the jungle machete he'd strapped to his back and ran forward, toward the back of the creature. "RASSRAGR!" he yelled at the top of his lungs, the insult his grandfather had used most often, and the troll stopped in its tracks. The Marine, unable to halt his headlong rush and slipping on the bloody flagstones, slid forward and crashed into the thing's immovable leg.

As he did, he slashed as hard as he could with the two-foot-long blade. The case-hardened Collins Machete whipped across the back of the knee with a shriek and a shower of sparks, opening up the skin and biting deep into the muscle behind it.

The giant roared and slammed down his other foot, stamping on Thorson's combat boot, crushing the bones underneath. The world turned grey, but he swung again, this time delivering a cut that spilled a loop of entrail. Then he rolled to one side as the bellowing troll turned and swung at him, getting up on one knee and holding the blade in front of him.

"WARRIOR!" bellowed the troll in Norse, and somehow Sven understood him. "I shall rip your head from your worthless carcass!"

"Rassragr," he replied calmly, insulting it again despite the screaming pain, "come take it!" He took a step back, held the machete over his shoulder like a baseball bat, and prepared to take the thing's full charge.

"Goddamn, that kid has some balls," muttered Gunny McCoy from thirty yards away.

"No shit," replied Miller, but he'd seen what the steel machete had done. A line of black blood mixed with the dark coppery red on the bridge, and he could see it favoring one leg. "Cold steel," he muttered to himself, then shouted, "FIX BAYONETS!"

At that moment, the German half-track opened up from its position on the ridge above the far side of the bridge, scattering machine gun rounds in a long burst. Miller fell, shot through the stomach as he worked to place the bayonet on the end of his Garand. McCoy fired back, uselessly, and dove behind a large stone. Seeing Miller down, he cursed and darted back out, grabbing the officer by his combat harness, and pulling him behind the outcrop. He looked around, and saw the rest of the Marines were pinned down, one lying lifelessly in the dirt. He heard the booming of the anti-tank gun firing at the half track, and the ripping, buzzsaw return of MG-42 fire.

⛨

"A thousand years ago I followed your people from the cold, icy north to this warm, soft land," said the troll, starring with luminous eyes at the Marine. "This has become my home, and you will destroy MY BRIDGE?" The last was a roar that seemed to echo, even over the gunfire.

"You know, my grandfather told me your people always talked too much," replied Thorson. As the Fae swung its massive claw at him, he wielded the machete like he was slamming for a home run on the ballfield back in Minnesota. His knife met the outstretched claw and severed it cleanly, the blade shattering into a dozen pieces, and Thorson's arm went numb.

The troll shrank back, howling and staring at its missing limb. Even as it screamed, a new hand started to bud from the stump. The man made his decision, clawing at the Colt pistol in its shoulder holster. He managed to get it out, cock the hammer, and point it at the now exposed plastic explosives.

"Leave or I blow it to hell!" he yelled in English.

The troll looked at him and stood straight up, a strange look on its ugly face. "Then I shall see you in Valhalla, warrior," it replied, also in English, and bowed its massive head. "The Germani I will fight after I have defeated you, but even I cannot beat all of their weapons. But I will have my bridge."

Thorson risked a quick glance behind him and saw three German tanks, sprockets clanking and tracks squealing, moving in a line abreast toward the bridge approach. He looked back at the troll and saw...respect. Then it leaned forward, preparing to charge and grind him into the pavement.

"'Til Valhalla then," said the Marine. "SEMPER FI!" And he pulled the trigger.

Epilogue

Gunny McCoy stood at the edge of the destroyed bridge, looking down at the waters of the river, placid, though dust still filled the air, searching to see if there were any bodies. Behind him the three surviving Task Force men were creating an improvised stretcher for the grievously wounded Captain Miller.

Fifty yards away, across the gap, a black clad figure loomed up, barely visible through the haze. "American!" yelled the Nazi commander, waving a bit of white cloth.

"What the hell do you want, shitbag?" he yelled back.

There was a pause, and then a reply. "Just to see if das Ungeheuer is todt." In the clearing smoke, McCoy saw the SS officer lean over to look at the water.

"You knew about this? And did nothing?"

"On the contrary, whenever we needed to use this road, we would sacrifice one of these stupid French villagers. A small price to pay, I assure you. And you have but delayed us for only a few hours."

McCoy said nothing to that, though he was tempted to shoot the man where he stood. Instead he gave him the finger and turned his back on him. The Nazi had to have the last word, though.

Origins

"You haven't seen the last of them, you know! The führer has taken a special interest in the occult, and we shall have more than enough help to throw your mongrel Army back into the—"

McCoy's bullet caught him in the chest, hurling the black-clad figure backward in a spray of blood. The West Virginian ran like a coal mine was collapsing around him.

"Hey, Gunny," said Giuliani as the sergeant skidded back behind the rocks around the bend in the road, "what was that all about?"

"Some people talk too much," he muttered, then said, "Let's go, Marines! We've got miles to cover to get back to the beach, and Uncle Sam ain't paying you to sit on your asses!"

Congressional Medal of Honor citation

Thorson, Sven Lars
Rank and organization: Private, U.S. Marine Corps, On Detached Duty, Task Force (CLASSIFIED) Operation Overlord.
Place: Normandy, France
Entered service at: Minnesota

Other awards: Purple Heart (posthumous)

Citation: For conspicuous heroism and courage above and beyond the call of duty while attempting to interdict German reinforcements that were maneuvering to attack the Normandy beachhead on June 7th. Private Thorson, along with a handpicked squad of Marines on detached duty to US VII Corps, parachuted behind enemy lines to attempt to destroy an enemy occupied bridge. Facing heavy opposition, Private Thorson, who had moved across the bridge as a reconnaissance element, was cut off from his fellow Marines by enemy counterattack. Despite grievous wounds and the death of his teammate, seeing his fellow Marines pinned down, Private Thorson advanced through heavy enemy machine gun and tank cannon fire and managed to set off previously emplaced explosives. His actions destroyed the bridge and prevented a counterattack by the German Panzer Lehr armor division on the allied beachhead at a critical moment. His superb fighting spirit and personal valor reflect great credit upon Private Thorson and the United States Marine Corps.

TO BE CONTINUED

Origins

Appendix A

Current Organization of Joint Task Force 13

- JTF 13 operates in a forward deployed environment, with squads rotating out to areas of operation from Joint Service Bases in Darwin, Okinawa, Stuttgart and Djibouti.
- Each platoon is on a three month on, three month off, three month training rotation. Forward deployed platoons are split between bases on Team Atlantic / Team Pacific, but may assemble as needed for larger operations, and training units are on 24/12/3 hour recall in their training cycle.
- Training Platoon, Intel and Logistics are all based out of Quantico, VA.
- The Joint Services Liaison Detachment is located in Quantico, but liaisons with all services and intelligence agencies are embedded with those agencies.
- JTF 13 falls under Joint Special Operations Command for funding and logistics but is an independent command for tasking.

Appendix B

Personnel

1)   Although JTF 13, in all of its various iterations, has been traditionally based around the United States Marine Corps, it also has a long history of admitting military personnel from other branches based on skill sets and needs. This was formalized under the Goldwater–Nichols Department of Defense Reorganization Act of 1986, and JTF members can now be recruited from all branches of service.

2)   In order to serve on the JTF, a military member must have had at least one combat encounter with the supernatural on the battlefield. Pre-requisite is an ability to keep their wits when confronted with thing outside normal human experience.

3)   JTF personnel go through a vetting process with a line platoon, often moving directly from the incident to work an operational squad. From there, they attend the following schools:

a)   JTF Basic integration course (Quantico)

b)   US Army Airborne and Air Assault Schools (if not already qualified.)

c)   Within 12 months, USMC Sniper School for selected personnel

d)   Various other specialty schools as needs and time permit.

4)   JTF Officers and NCO's attend the three month JTF 13 Leadership Level I school at Quantico, and six month the Leader II school within three years.

Origins

Joint Task Force 13 is a project of Three Ravens Publishing. We expect to follow this book up with a half dozen more in 2021, all written by experienced authors in many different timeframes.

William J. Roberts
Widowmakers

France in 1944 is a whirling maelstrom of combat and death, and a scratch team of JTF members is called on to defend forward airfields with a motley aircrew.

Look for these and many more from Three Ravens Publishing!

Follow us at www.threeravenspublishing.com